Mystery Mansion

ROSHNI RAO & MAHATI RAYADURGAM

PUBLISHED BY

 SIGMA'S BOOKSHELF

MINNETONKA, MN 55305

WWW.SIGMASBOOKSHELF.COM

Mystery Mansion

Printed in the United States of America

First Printing 2020

ISBN 978-0-9996577-7-5

Dedications

To my family, friends, and teachers who have been with us all the way. -Roshni

Dedicated to all the teachers, parents, siblings, and friends who helped us make this book what it is today. -Mahati

Intro

Lightning streaked the black sky as a plane flew overhead. As the thunder roared, the small plane tossed and turned, and barreled down into Lake San Cristobal.

A woman standing a distance away stared in shock as the plane crashed. She could feel water spraying, even though she was so far away. The air was filled with smoke, meaning there could be a fire. She strode forward cautiously. It was unlikely for there to be any survivors, but she was optimistic. The woman took her phone to call the authorities when she saw four orange dots bobbing not too far from the shore.

The woman went down to the water's edge to get a closer look. She put her hand over her eyes to block the glare from the water and saw four little girls in life jackets. They weren't too far from shore, and they were crying. She entered the water and walked out to them, helping each child back to shore.

Once they had all been rescued, she turned her attention away from the water. As a result, she didn't notice there were two more people bobbing in the dark waters. The other survivors drifted away in the distance as a silvery figure reached towards them.

Chapter 1

Seven years later...

"Took long enough! Finally, school's over." Amy bounced a soccer ball on her knees like she always did, and kicked it into the ball storage. Her red hair bounced on her shoulders, emphasizing her perky mood.

"That's great, I suppose," Skyler shrugged. "I mean, it's not going to be any different from any other summer we've had, right? Probably just more guardian trouble."

"Probably. But we'll make it fun—just like we always do!" Vic grinned. Reyna smiled at Vic's comment.

"Of course!" Amy's bouncy mood always made all four of the girls happy too. It was just how Amy was.

"Yeah, I guess. But have you ever thought about normal summers? I mean normal as in, kids who aren't orphans. Don't you sometimes wish you could feel how all those other kids feel? You know, being able to travel places—meet the world?" Reyna kicked a pebble near her foot.

"Yeah, right," Vic told her, swinging her backpack on one shoulder, catching her long, black hair under the strap. "Do you really think Mr. Mister, out of all people, is gonna take us on vacation?" Mr. Mister was their guardian, and he—well, he wasn't a good one.

Vic unzipped Reyna's bag and reached inside, pulling out

a picture of the perfect vacation. It was a beautiful beach with a silhouette of four girls that Reyna had drawn.

"I guess I wish it would happen sometime too. But at this point, I've given up any hope on that guy. I mean think about it, what type of a guardian shuts us up in a cellar, makes us cook for ourselves, do everything alone—" Vic took a breath. "Sorry, just got a little lost."

"Well," Skyler interrupted as they walked down the sidewalk, "he might have a reason to treat us like that. After all, we aren't even his children. Still, he lets us stay in his house. He isn't rich either. Oh, and technically, *I* cook the food." Skyler laughed a little. Her emerald-green eyes and blond hair sparkled in the sunlight as she picked at her jeans. The willow trees swayed in the wind as the girls walked.

"You do have a point," Reyna agreed dejectedly, fiddling around with her brown, fishtail braid. "But do you ever wonder how we ended up in *this* house anyway? And how we get to go to such a good school when—never mind." The girls' parents had died in a plane crash, along with their siblings. They remembered that, but not how they got to be where they were now.

Amy turned around. "Okay, okay. Let's not ruin our first day of summer with this kind of talk again!" Her freckles that always made her look happy were contrasting with the annoyed look in her hazel eyes. "Also, we're here," Amy added.

They looked up and saw their guardian's house. It had a grand looking exterior, but it was an average-sized house with four rooms, two bathrooms, and two small kitchens. The only thing was, the second kitchen and two of the rooms were in the cellar. The girls reluctantly walked towards the cellar door. The cellar had been their living area for as long as they remembered.

As they entered the house, the girls walked down the stairs, chatting as they reached the cellar. Mr. Mister was standing at the base of the staircase that lead to the main level. He was leaning against the wall, dialing a number on the landline. He nodded at the girls with a slight glare. The girls knew what that meant: they should not go upstairs to the main level of the house. They could almost always tell what Mr. Mister was thinking or about to say from his facial expressions.

Mr. Mister went back up the stairs, the phone ringing from his call. They went to put their stuff away in the basement when Vic suddenly froze in her tracks, and peered at the ceiling like she was looking at something that wasn't there. The rest of them sat down.

"Hey guys, I think we forgot to shut the door," Amy told the other girls. "I'll go check." Amy started towards the stairs and saw Vic.

"Hey, whatcha doing?" Amy asked. Vic didn't respond. "Earth to Vic!" Amy said, impatiently waving a hand in front of her face. "What're you looking at?"

"Shhh," Vic whispered. "Listen!" She tilted her head towards the ceiling.

Skyler and Reyna rushed towards the stairs to see what was happening. They heard someone talking. "Yes, you see, they are orphans."

"That's Mr. Mister!" Reyna exclaimed. "But, who are the orphans he's talking about? Us?" she asked. Skyler rolled her eyes; Reyna could be oblivious to things around her. Reyna smiled sheepishly after she realized that.

"Shh! Let's listen!" said Skyler.

"Their names are Victoria Harper." Vic flinched at the sound of her full name—she hated being called Victoria. "Skyler Aeroluet, Reyna Aztec, and Amy Pierre." There was a pause. "Yup, they're eleven and twelve. Mmhm. Alright, I'll send them to the orphanage tomorrow. Bye." Mr. Mister put down the phone and walked away.

The girls stood frozen in shock. Then suddenly Vic exclaimed, "I have an idea!"

"Shhh!" the girls whispered in unison as Reyna looked around at their surroundings.

"We don't want Mr. Mister to hear us!" Amy said.

"I know, I know!" Vic exclaimed, "but we have to move fast if we're going to do something about this. I think I might have a plan of how we can escape the orphanage."

"What is it?" Skyler asked defensively; she was usually the one who came up with ideas.

"W-we have to run away." Vic paused. "I mean, I haven't thought out the whole plan yet," she admitted, "but what else can we do?"

Part One:

The Hidden Jewels

Chapter 2

Reyna

Run away? Is this actually happening? Reyna couldn't stop her thoughts. Just a few minutes ago, they had been happily coming back from their last day of school, and now they were leaving? Leaving the place they'd been for over seven years?

Reyna jerked back to attention.

"Vic, are you okay? Are you sure this whole running away thing is not one of your fake pranks? Skyler looked at Vic, genuinely confused.

"Are we being sent to the orphanage as a prank?" Vic glanced at everyone. She knew that she was the one who usually came up with crazy ideas. Most of the time, the ideas were just jokes. But this time, it was real.

The four of them sat down on the ground as Amy started listing off the things they needed to do. "If we're actually going to run away, we'll need to pack some of our belongings, find some shelter, get some food. It's not an easy thing, unless you want to sprint out the door right now."

"Well, we got the food part covered," Vic said slowly.

The three girls turned to look at Skyler. " Fine! I'll cook. I always do," she muttered.

"I can pack for you if you want," Reyna told Skyler.

"Hold on. Are we sure we're going to do this? You do know

9

that it's not like the movies right? No one's going to be running across the forest in slow-motion or anything." For once, Reyna didn't know if Amy was joking or telling the truth.

"Again Amy, do you have a better idea?" Vic looked around at the other girls who stayed silent. "Okay, it's settled then."

Reyna went to her and Skyler's room. She shook her head. Running away was *not* her type of thing. But really though, whose type of thing was it? For some reason it felt like the past three hours of their lives had gone by in time-lapse. It almost seemed too coincidental that right after they talked about how they had come to live here, they would find out they're being sent to the orphanage.

Reyna shook herself out of her daze as she stacked their clothes neatly next to their sleeping bags. She then took her favorite printed pictures from the neatly stacked pile in the corner, including the picture of the place she wanted to travel to. She smiled, thinking about just the four of them together. Reyna sighed and strode over to her sleeping bag. She took out a slim parcel and opened the cover. Inside were a few colored pencils, some paper, and a picture.

Even when Reyna was a little girl, she had always remembered her big sister. Their last picture was oddly charred, but Reyna had always loved the picture of her big sister. Nina was eleven at the time, holding two year old Reyna in her arms as she chewed on her sister's long, fishtail braid and staring lovingly with big, gray eyes. Their parents were standing by them, laughing at the sight.

Reyna never wanted to mention anything about her sister to any of the others; well, except Vic. She was the only other one who had a sibling. But Reyna was just too shy to talk about it with her. It would seem odd to others that Reyna could be shy around people she had been best friends with and known for practically her entire life. Even Reyna didn't know why, but sometimes it seemed to just be how her brain worked. She wondered if her sister was just as shy as her since they had so many similarities already—their brown hair, gray eyes, oval face, and thin figure. Nina was also a really good artist from what Reyna could remember. Reyna had always wanted to be just like her.

Reyna and Vic were the only ones who knew about their past and some of the other girls' pasts too. She even remembered Skyler, Amy, and her parents crowding around a baby boy who was being carried by Vic's parents. Reyna knew the baby boy was Vic's little brother since he looked just like Vic. He had jet-black hair and big, bright, blue eyes. Reyna had always kept those secrets to herself, talking less because she was afraid she might blurt the secrets out, and inside she feared her only friends would turn on her for even mentioning their painful past.

Suddenly, Reyna realized it was already 4:56. She had spent twenty-five minutes just thinking about her family. Reyna put the picture back in its parcel and started packing up their bags.

Once she was done, she walked to the small kitchen where Skyler was cooking on the stove that was in a run-down state. At least Mr. Mister had come down to check if the oven was safe. Granted, that was three years ago when they started cooking by themselves and Mr. Mister wasn't just sliding them cold food under the door.

"Hey, Skyler, I finished packing our stuff. You need any help?" Reyna asked.

"Thanks Reyna. Can you put the food in plastic containers? Apparently, I have to 'make a lot of food for this journey.' Sometimes, I don't know where Amy gets her phrases."

They worked silently until Amy and Vic burst into the room.

"We finished packing," Vic told them. "Amy and I can get the sleeping bags ready."

"Okay," Skyler said. "Meet up here in the kitchen once you're ready."

Amy and Vic turned back and rushed off to finish packing. Reyna thought to herself quietly: *How did we get here?*

Chapter 3

Vic

Vic and Amy split up to get their sleeping bags, which they regularly slept in. Vic went to their room and Amy crossed over to Skyler and Reyna's room.

As Vic entered her and Amy's room, old memories came back to her. Pillow fights, kicking soccer balls, and music. She realized she would miss this room, not the room itself, but all the memories that happened in there.

Suddenly, Vic realized that she had forgotten to pack her most prized possession, the one thing that made her special: her harmonica. She never quite knew why she had it, but it was always with her. She quietly slipped her harmonica in her pocket and picked up the sleeping bags. She hurried to join the other girls in the kitchen.

She started thinking about their escape. Where would they go? What would they do there? In the fall, would they still go to school? More questions piled up in her head.

She felt scared and nervous, but remembered she was the one who had come up with the idea of running away, and that there was no other option. What else could she do? Wait there for Mr. Mister to take them to the orphanage and live the rest of their lives in a dorm with nothing close to homemade food and a proper home? Not that she had one here, but that was beside the point. She took a deep breath and readied herself as she entered the room.

"Finally!" Amy exclaimed. "What took you so long?"

"Nothing," Vic casually said. Amy looked at her curiously. After all, Vic never acted like that.

"Well, doesn't matter," Amy said. "We wanted to tell you, we're going to leave the house at four in the morning.

"Fine with me," Vic said. "We should probably get some sleep so we aren't tired."

"Yeah, we should," Skyler agreed.

"Okay, but one thing," Reyna said with a slight shakiness in her voice, "do you think Mr. Mister will come looking for us? Or send the police or something?"

The other girls looked at each other. They hadn't thought much about those circumstances. Reyna continued ranting, "And if he does, what do we do?" It was obvious that Reyna was worried about running away.

"You have a point, but if Mr. Mister cared that much about us, why are we stuck down in this cramped, rundown basement?" Vic answered.

"Okay, enough talking. Like Vic said, we should get some sleep," Skyler reminded them.

They all agreed and headed to their rooms. "Remember to set an alarm for 3:00," Skyler added, walking up to the other girls. "And make sure it's muffled so we don't wake Mr. Mister.

The girls went to their rooms. Amy and Vic soon heard Skyler and Reyna's snores while they were talking.

"I guess we'd better go to sleep too," Amy yawned, and laid on the floor.

Vic went to set her alarm when she saw her harmonica sticking out of her bag. She took out the harmonica and started to play something soft. She didn't have a music book or know which notes to play but her fingers seemed to know exactly what to do. It was like they had a mind of their own. It reminded her of her younger brother, Aaron, who had just been born when they left their home. He would always laugh and smile at the music she played.

The next morning, Vic got up before the alarm and turned it off. She started to get ready, taking clothes out of her bag. After she got dressed, she went to Skyler and Reyna's room to wake them up. She found Skyler and Reyna awake picking up their bags. "Looks like someone's an early bird!" Skyler teased her jokingly. Vic was usually not the first one to wake up.

"Yeah," Vic laughed, "Amy's still sleeping. Like usual," she added.

"You better go wake her up," Skyler told her.

"Yeah, we plan to leave in thirty minutes," Reyna agreed, looking at the alarm clock.

"I'll go wake her." Vic went back to their room. She shook Amy until she opened her eyes. "Do we have to wake up this early?" she whined groggily as she sat up.

"Yeah! Unless you want to go to the orphanage!" Vic said.

"Fine, what time is it?" Amy questioned.

"3:34," Vic said as she glanced at the alarm clock.

"Already?" Amy got up, suddenly awake as she patted down her tousled hair.

Vic laughed and headed back to check on the others. Skyler was talking to Reyna who was looking a little nervous now that she was really going to run away. Vic joined them, feeling more steady than she had been last night.

As soon as Amy joined them, they left. Vic led them silently since she was good at sneaking around. They tiptoed up the stairs, leaving the cellar. Whenever they paused from the creaking noise of the stairs or the sound of containers hitting each other from their backpacks, the girls felt a little more nervous.

Suddenly Vic heard a snore then the words, "No, stop!" It occurred to Vic that Mr. Mister must have fallen asleep on the couch, probably having nightmares after watching a late night horror movie.

"Oh this is just great," Vic whispered to the other girls. "Mr. Mister is sleeping in the living room."

Reyna, Skyler, and Amy were silent, but judging from their expressions, Vic could tell the news made them nervous. Moving from the stairs, they silently opened the door, careful not to make a sound, and stepped out.

The morning air was crisp and clear, but there was an eeriness in the air that made the girls shiver. They went and hid behind a huge oak tree to make sure nobody had seen them.

"Okay," Vic took a deep breath. "We should start heading—"

"Wait, where's Reyna?" Amy asked curiously.

They all looked around and saw Reyna crouching on the sidewalk, bent over her backpack. They gathered around her.

"Hey Reyna, what are you doing?" Skyler asked her.

"Oh, uh, I just went to take out this map of the city I found at school."

"Wow. Great timing! This is going to help us a *lot* for our trip," Vic said.

And with that, she put down her bag and started examining the map, making plans for their journey ahead as a dark shadow floated overhead.

Chapter 4

Amy

Amy felt a chill run down her spine. She looked around, and up, but didn't see anything. She shrugged it off and turned her attention back to Vic.

"Okay then," Vic said, putting down the pen Skyler had given her. "I've mapped out the place where we should go."

She pointed to a line leading from near Lake San Cristobal to a small forest not so far away from their school. Amy smiled and rolled her eyes. She knew Reyna would freak out if she realized that they would stop in a forest. But honestly, who wouldn't?

"So," Vic continued with the others listening and Reyna looking wide eyed, "since the forest is near the school we can still go there when the school year starts again." Vic noticed that Reyna still looked scared. "Reyna, we won't be staying in the forest. Beyond it, there is an area with a couple of houses and lots of places with shelter."

"Oh," Reyna said, relieved. Amy felt the same. Even though she wasn't so worried herself, she was happy Reyna was relieved. Even though she might tease Reyna for always being scared, Amy really did care for her; same as the others.

"Okay," Skyler said, "I get your plan, but we should get moving. The sun is almost rising." They turned to the east where a glimpse of sun peeked out. The girls looked at each other. They started heading away from Lake San Cristobal, near where they had lived.

Amy looked back to see if they'd forgotten anything and gasped. "Guys, look!" she exclaimed, making the others jump out of their skins.

"What happened?" Reyna asked, looking frightened.

"We almost forgot the map!" Amy said, pointing. "Mr. Mister could figure out where we're going."

Vic hurried over to the map lying on the ground and picked it up. "Thanks. That would have been really bad."

Amy laughed. She felt a little sad that she was leaving the place she grew up in. She put it out of her mind though and turned around. Just when she did, she froze up. Her mind couldn't comprehend what was right in front of her—a transparent lady.

The woman had a friendly look to her. She was wearing a flowing dress, had a round face and huge eyes, and was pretty for being transparent. The others had noticed her too. They were staring at it— er, her—with their mouths hanging open. It took Amy a while to realize that standing in front of them was a ghost.

"Um, Amy are you seeing what I'm seeing?" Vic questioned, taken aback.

The ghost just smiled and said warmly, " Girls, I came to talk to you."

"To us?" Reyna asked, her voice strong.

"Wait, who are you?" Vic asked suspiciously.

"I'm a ghost, but no time for questions now. Just follow me."

The four of them didn't know what to do. They all glanced at Skyler. She was often the one to make decisions.

"Come on," said Reyna, as she beckoned to them to follow the ghost.

Amy and Vic followed her. Skyler was the last to move. Amy was worrying about Skyler. Usually she would be the one to worry about one of them, but Skyler looked scared and hadn't said a word for an awfully long time. Still, Amy had to admit she was scared too. Since when do ghosts exist?

The ghost lead them to a path that looked like it shouldn't even belong in Colorado. It was rocky with twisted vines and trees with thick moss. Their bags snagged on tree branches, and all of them set their things down, planning to go back for them later. The girls started climbing higher, and higher, and higher up a rocky cliff. Amy took a deep breath. She made sure not to look down.

They traveled in a line. The ghost went first, followed by Reyna, Vic, and Amy running to catch up.

"Wait a second, where's Skyler?" Amy looked around, mad at herself for not realizing she was missing earlier. They skidded to a halt when they realized that Skyler wasn't behind them.

"She was there just a few seconds ago," Vic said. Amy could tell that she was also worried about Skyler, maybe even more than she had realized. Reyna looked around suspiciously. She glanced at the ghost, but the ghost just shook her head.

Amy started to feel a bit panicky. "How could this—"

"Amy!" Vic hissed. She pressed a finger to her lips as she crouched down behind a big rock. "Do you—" But Amy and Reyna never heard the rest of the sentence as Vic was interrupted by a loud rumbling noise and a scream.

Chapter 5

Skyler

Skyler backed away. What she was seeing was *not* a pleasant sight. Walking, no, *slithering* towards her about ten feet away was something she had never seen or imagined before.

It was green with speckled brown spots. It was bigger than her, though it was less wide, only about six inches. It looked kinda like a *huge* cobra except its eyes were so bright they seemed to glow. Skyler didn't even look at its eyes and she could still see a mild glow.

What? This can't be possible! Skyler knew what it was. Her mom used to read to her, and this creature was in one of the stories she had heard. *A basilisk.* It was extremely dangerous and could kill her by just looking at her, or if its venom touched her.

The basilisk was coming closer. Skyler could see its forked tongue flicking as if it was licking its lips. *If I die, I might as well go down fighting,* she thought. Skyler grabbed a branch that looked like a stake and charged towards the basilisk right as it lunged to kill her.

She foolishly went straight at the basilisk, making sure not to look at its eyes, and jabbed the branch at it. Miraculously, she hit the basilisk, causing it to suffer a gash to its side. It hissed in pain as Skyler crept away. She felt something fall on her shoulder, but she didn't pay attention to it since she suddenly heard voices.

"Skyler!" somebody whispered. She turned around. Vic was crouched down behind a clump of vines. Skyler ran towards her.

"What happened?" Vic asked, still whispering.

"Vic!" Skyler exclaimed. Vic glared at her as the basilisk swirled its head around, looking at the clump of vines.

"Sorry Vic, but that snake is a basilisk and we need to get away, *right now.*"

"A what?" Vic asked, confused.

"A *basilisk,* a giant snake that can kill if it looks at you. Hey wait, where are the others?" she added quickly.

"They are waiting behind the rocks," Vic said. She was not as frightened as Skyler expected her to be. Skyler assumed that was probably because Vic didn't believe her.

"But are you sure it is a basilisk or whatever? I don't even think those exist, and you know it's going to freak Reyna out, right?"

Skyler rolled her eyes in response to Vic's comment and said, "Yes, I'm *sure* it's a basilisk. And if ghosts are real, why can't this creature be? And—"

"*Sssssssssssssssssss!*" The sound of a snake hissing filled the air.

"You might be right. It *definitely* sounds like a giant snake," Vic agreed, a look of fear crossing her face. At least she knew the situation was bad now. They dashed towards the boulder that the others were hiding behind.

" Umm, what happened?" Reyna asked.

"No time to talk now!" Vic led the others into an enclosed area full of shrubs and vines wrapped around branches like snakes.

"What happened? Come on, tell us!" Amy said impatiently after Skyler didn't answer.

" Okay listen, Skyler thinks she saw a—"

"I *know* I saw a basilisk!" Skyler was watching Reyna's face, waiting for her to freak out. *Come on, any moment now.*

But instead she just took a deep breath, stood up straight and tall and said, "Then we'll just have to face it."

Chapter 6

Reyna

The girls stared at Reyna in shock. Reyna was surprised too; *when have I ever said anything like that?* She felt her confidence wavering, but she pushed herself to keep staying strong. She suddenly wondered why she put herself in this position.

She had to say something, but what could she say?

"So, umm—Skyler, where did you see the basilisk?" Just saying the word *basilisk* made her shiver.

"Remember the place we stopped and heard something weird? When the rest of you left, I stayed and—and—"

Skyler couldn't say anymore. Reyna didn't know what to say either.

Vic gave Reyna an "I can take it from here" look. Reyna nodded and Vic started to talk. "Okay listen. I have a feeling that if we don't get rid of the basilisk sooner or later, well, let's not find out." Vic looked worried. But then, suddenly, almost as if the forest could hear Vic, the trees and vines started to close in on them, creating a small den. The only path leading out was the path the basilisk was in.

"Oh no. This is bad! This is *very bad!*" Skyler started panicking. Reyna did too, but she didn't let everyone see it. *I stayed bold for ten whole minutes! If I can just stay strong a bit longer—*

"Sssssssssss!"

"It's the basilisk! I told you. We have to get out of here!"

"Calm down, Skyler. We have no other choice. We have to pass the basilisk." Vic tried to comfort Skyler. "Guys, we need a plan. Think fast."

"I have an idea. Let's just collect a bunch of twigs that seem heavy enough to throw at the basilisk and distract it," Reyna said. For once, she was the one coming up with the plan.

"And then?" Amy looked down the path, worried.

Reyna took a deep breath. "We hope for the best."

The girls started collecting as many big sticks as they could find. They even started taking the really big ones that looked like they could hike with them. After a while, they had built a pile right outside the small den.

"I think that's enough." Reyna said, a little hesitantly. She wasn't used to giving anyone directions.

"Are you guys ready?" Vic asked.

"No."

"Well whatever. We have to do it," said Amy, responding to Skyler's comment.

"Wait, but don't we need a more detailed plan?" Skyler clearly wasn't going to back down.

"No, let's not overthink this."

"Well—" The girls continued contemplating for another two minutes before Vic finally said, "Okay, no more think-ing! Let's just do it." Vic was right. The longer they waited, the harder it was going to be for them to get moving.

"Okay. We got this." Skyler readied herself. While they had been collecting sticks, Skyler had told them about how her mom had read her stories about these creatures. Reyna realized how hard it would be for her to fight something she had always believed never existed. But then she real-ized something. Whoever promised them that these things didn't exist?

Chapter 7

Vic

"Ssssssssss!"

"Ready? Vic asked. Everyone nodded. "Go!"

The girls ran into the clearing with the basilisk. Amy started to try to distract it. Skyler ran around the side, thinking that Amy was doing okay. Then suddenly, the basilisk hissed and whipped its tail in Amy's direction. Thankfully it missed and Amy just fell into a tree, her shirt snagging on a branch.

"Amy!" Vic yelled, checking that she was okay. Vic saw Skyler sneak around behind the basilisk to the spot on its tail where there was a gash. Skyler took a stick and stabbed the gash once again. The basilisk turned around, furious in pain. Skyler ran in the opposite direction. Vic took this opportunity to go and run around to the other side of the path. Suddenly, right after she ran, instead of the path continuing into the forest, Vic was now on the edge of a cliff. If Vic had run any further, she wouldn't have survived.

Vic had no idea what to do. There was almost no way to get out now. Either they had to find a way out of the den, but there didn't appear to be one, or find a way down the cliff to safety. Vic realized they had no option but to climb down the cliff. There was no other possible way to escape.

Vic shook her head and decided to focus on defeating the

basilisk. The basilisk was now swarming around the frozen Reyna, who was trying to stand still so it wouldn't harm her. Amy, meantime, was trying to get the basilisk to turn around. Then, out of nowhere, Amy decided to turn around and back up into what she thought was the path. What she didn't realize though was that they were on the edge of the cliff. Amy was still backing up. Amy was afraid of heights.

"Amy! WATCH OUT!"

Chapter 8

Amy

Amy turned around, right before she fell. If it hadn't been for Vic screaming, she would have fallen to her doom. When Amy saw where she was, her stomach flipped upside down. She was standing right at the edge of a cliff, which was probably over fifty feet in the air.

Don't look down, don't look down. Amy closed her eyes, trying to imagine that she was still in the forest surrounded by big, tall trees instead of being on the edge of a cliff. Then she realized that the cliff might be the only way to escape.

"Amy," Vic whispered from a nearby bush, "are you thinking what I'm thinking?"

"Yeah," she replied, quietly.

"Reyna! Skyler! You have to come here!" Vic yelled, hoping to get their attention. Thankfully, Skyler noticed and made it to the other side. Reyna, meanwhile, was still stuck in the middle of the circle made by the basilisk's tail. Amy had no idea how to help her.

Suddenly, after a few minutes, Reyna jumped over the tail onto a huge rock wall. But the wall was much steeper than Reyna had anticipated. She started to fall, catching herself at the last possible second, right before she crashed. Soon enough, Reyna made it to the other side too.

Vic turned around, then turned back and came out of

the bushes. The others were with her. She jumped onto a boulder and started to slowly climb down the cliff. The others followed, but Amy waited until she was the last one who wasn't climbing. She waited so long she heard Skyler shouting, " C'mon Amy! The basilisk's right behind you!"

"Okay! I'm coming!" Amy shouted back. Amy suddenly saw the shadow of the basilisk behind her. She panicked and started to climb. *What have I gotten myself into?*

She jumped on the boulder like the others had done and slowly made her way down. *I'm almost there, I'm almost there.* She looked down for a quick second to check where her friends were, and they weren't there. She turned her head to look down again, and when she did her hand slipped off the rock and she fell.

She was so shocked she didn't even scream as she was falling. She just kept thinking, *I'm going to die, I'm going to die!* Then, out of nowhere, a blinding flash of deep indigo swirled around her, and she landed on her back on hard ground.

"Finally!" Vic's voice came from behind her. Amy turned around and got up. She winced and rubbed the side she had fallen on.

"Where are we?" she asked.

"I have no idea," Reyna answered.

Amy turned around. She must not have been paying attention before because standing about twenty feet away from her was an enormous mansion. It looked dark and mysterious thanks to the shade created by the black clouds above it. Amy spotted a sign that said *Mystery Mansion* on it.

Vic saw what she was looking at. "They must have been really rich people."

"What do you mean, *have* been really rich? Don't you think there is someone in there?" Skyler questioned.

Before anyone could answer, they turned around and

standing there was the same ghost they had met before. Skyler almost jumped out of her skin.

"Follow me." The ghost motioned to them.

"Where are we going?" Amy asked the ghost. She realized she was the first one who actually talked to the ghost.

"Inside of course," the ghost answered.

Amy shivered. Standing in front of the mansion was one thing, but going inside was another. She followed the ghost while the others took time to realize what was going on.

The grand black gates creaked as they slowly opened. Amy looked around the garden. It looked as if nobody had cared for it in years. Plants and bushes were withered and trees were leafless, even though it was the middle of summer. Suddenly, it started raining. The ghost walked, no actually *floated*, faster and faster.

"Girls, I'm sorry but we need to hurry. Good ghosts dissolve in rain," the ghost explained.

"There are, uh, bad ghosts?" Vic asked.

"I thought all ghosts were bad," Skyler said. "Oh, don't take me wrong," she added hurriedly, "I meant, I thought all ghosts were bad till I met you."

"Oh yes there are bad ghosts, and they can only be dissolved by basilisk blood—" The ghost said, but stopped. "Well come on now, that's a story for another time."

After walking for a while, they finally reached the entrance. It had big, French doors made of tarnished, stained glass. The door opened just as roughly as the gate. The ghost entered first, beckoning them to come forward. Amy crept behind Vic. She expected the inside to be filled with cobwebs and dust, but it wasn't.

It was rather clean for an old, empty mansion. It was also dark and spooky. Suddenly, she saw a light. The ghost was holding a lantern. *How did she just do that?* Amy usually spoke her mind, but she was short on words at that moment.

She didn't say anything at all as she followed the ghost into a small lounge.

"Girls, I think it's time for you to learn more about your past." Skyler, Amy, Vic and Reyna smiled at each other excitedly, then turned to follow the ghost, which had beckoned them to sit down on the velvety sofa. "But first, tell me what you know."

Chapter 9

Skyler

"Well, we know our families were on a plane heading to Colorado: here. Then we ran into a storm over Lake San Cristobal. The plane crashed and—" Skyler stopped herself from saying any more.

"This is where Patricia Mister comes in," the ghost finished off.

"Who is Patricia—wait, did you say *Mister?*" The others gasped.

"Yes, John Mister's wife." Skyler could see a sparkle in her eyes. "Now let me tell you what happened. So, Patricia saw all this on her normal evening walk she would take. She had seen four toddlers in life jackets who were crying. They were the only survivors."

"Us," Vic murmured, her eyes wide. Skyler saw a tear roll down Reyna's cheek. For some reason that made her angry.

"Patricia picked them up and brought them to her house. She never had any children of her own so she promised to keep them safe. But a few months later, she became ill and died an early death. A few days before in the hospital, she made her husband promise to send them to Cristobal Academy, the best private school in the town. After her early death, her husband became bitter and he took out his emotions on the children, but he still kept his promise. And that is how your story starts."

Reyna was quietly crying. Skyler felt like crying too, but she tried not to since she didn't want Reyna thinking she was crying because Reyna was.

"I can't believe we never got to know Mrs. Mister," Reyna said, saying the first thing she had said in ages.

"Well now you have."

"What?" Amy exclaimed, looking astonished.

"Girls, it is time to reveal the truth. *I* am the ghost of Patricia Mister."

Chapter 10

Reyna

Reyna was shocked, and terribly confused. "You're Mrs—?" Reyna exclaimed incredulously, but was cut off.

"Yes, I am Patricia *Mister.*" She pronounced it like Micestir, "But you can call me Patricia," Mrs. Mister said. The girls just stared in shock, no one breaking the silence.

"Wait you're good right? We can trust you?" Amy asked quickly, as if to get on good terms.

"Yes, but it's up to you to decide. Well, girls," Patricia said finally, "let me tell you something about this mansion. This Mansion was built about fifty years ago. No one had lived in it for many years until someone came and bought the Mansion. But the owner died a little more than a decade after moving in for reasons I don't know about. He was an evil ghost and with his death came a curse that causes all the ghosts that are in Colorado to be imprisoned here. And that is how I wound up here. There are good ghosts and bad ghosts, depending on if they died good or bad. The ghosts—"

As Patricia spoke, Reyna's shock went away and she started thinking about her sister. It was bad enough that all the girls' parents had died, but it was even more sad that her sister had died along with them too. She just wished that the plane crash had never happened, and their families were alive.

"Now that brings me to your quest." Patricia almost looked scared. "But I—"

"What? A quest?" Vic seemed to have been thinking about something else just like her.

"Four children are picked to take on a quest, but only if they are chosen."

"But, how could *we* be chosen?" Skyler asked. "We're just random people!"

"Because *I* choose all of you," Patricia answered. "That's how you found the portal to Mystery Mansion."

The girls looked at each other. Just hours ago they had been running away from Mr. Mister, and now they were sitting next to his wife—a ghost—who was telling them they had been chosen for a quest?

"Now, let me explain this again since this must be very confusing. This mansion is under a curse. A curse caused by the old owner who died here. No one knows why he caused this curse in the mansion But it's the one that caused our unfortunate predicament. Every ghost in Colorado is trapped in the mansion by the owner."

"So our parents might be here?" Amy asked.

"I can't answer that, or rather, I don't know. Your quest is to undo the curse."

"Wait, how did *you* get out?" Vic asked.

Patricia sighed. "I escaped the hold of the owner because of some powerful people that helped me find you for the quest." That answer seemed to satisfy the girls.

"Wait, you'll help us on our quest, right?" Skyler asked.

"I'm sorry girls," Patricia answered apologetically. "The only other thing I can tell you is that weapons can slice ghosts, but won't harm them. A weapon will only be useful against a ghost if it has water or basilisk blood on it."

"But—" Amy started then stopped abruptly, for Patricia had disappeared, leaving behind a small green bag.

Reyna reached out for the bag. This day had been a complete shock for all the girls, but Reyna seemed to be the only one who wasn't just staring blankly at the spot where the ghost had been. Reyna opened the bag to see a scroll inside, along with an emerald.

"Hey guys," Reyna said, making the girls draw their gaze from where the ghost had sat. "I think this is the first clue, for our quest."

"Of course! *Everybody* knows that," Skyler scoffed and rolled her eyes.

Reyna ignored Skyler's rude comment and cleared her throat. "Inside but outside, green not anymore. Hidden to the naked eye."

Inside but outside
Green not anymore
Hidden to the naked eye

Reyna furrowed her brows in confusion. She had no idea what the riddle was supposed to mean, and now the other girls were looking at her like they expected her to solve it. They all sat there, silent. Reyna felt like time was slowing down just to make fun of her. As every second passed, she could feel her face getting red.

Skyler scoffed, "I know what it means when it says 'hidden to the naked eye'. It's definitely hidden or blends in with the surroundings."

Reyna sighed and felt more embarrassed. Thankfully none of the girls were looking at her, expect for Amy, who was looking back and forth between Skyler and Reyna. Reyna decided not to pay any attention to it.

"What the heck would 'inside but outside' mean?" Amy asked, groaning. She paused. "I think it connects to the second line too."

Vic furrowed her brows. "So what's green and inside but also outside? Oh, and not green anymore?"

Skyler twisted her thumbs. "So, it needs to be something that was green and can be inside, but looks like it was outside."

Reyna thought for a second and then the answer came to her. "Plants! Plants can be inside but outside, and they can make it look like you're outside. And when it's 'green not anymore'—"

"Dead plants," Amy looked around and shivered. "You're right Reyna. So where are we supposed to go then?"

Again, the girls looked at Reyna for the answers. Her confidence was withering away as she racked her brain for an answer. She could feel her eyes watering.

"A greenhouse!" Skyler announced, breaking the silence. "Plants grow in a greenhouse and it's almost like you're outside in a greenhouse. That's where we need to go!"

Reyna was glad that Skyler had saved her from

embarrassment, but unlike all the other times Skyler had saved Reyna, she didn't smile at her or wink. She wasn't even looking at Reyna. Instead, she had fixed her gaze on the other girls. Vic must have noticed that because she gave Reyna a shrug. Amy agreed excitedly.

"What do you think we'll find? It doesn't mention anything about that," Skyler added.

"I don't know," Vic said, giving Reyna a look again. Skyler didn't say anything.

Vic got up from the velvet couch and gave Reyna another smile while the others followed Amy out of the den. The start of their quest awaited them.

Chapter 11

Vic

Vic and the others soon realized they had no idea where the greenhouse was! *How are we supposed to finish a quest if we can't even go one step in this huge mansion without getting lost?*

They walked along the side of a long hallway. Vic studied the walls that had lanterns hung on them. The place was like a maze, every part led to another! They crossed a section with an old, crystal chandelier that was covered in dust and had a bluish glow to it. The girls turned corners, sometimes that led to dead ends, or even more corridors. Then they turned down a narrow hallway that was pitch black and found a door covered with vines and branches—it reminded her of the forest.

The girls looked at each other. This was definitely the right place. Skyler tentatively reached out for the blackened brass handle, and opened the door. A gust of wind came at them, and Skyler cautiously stepped inside.

Vic thought Skyler was crazy just going in there before she even looked inside, but as she followed her, she saw that Skyler was right. It felt like they were standing outside instead of in a greenhouse since you could see the sun and feel a cool breeze. It was already daytime.

The only thing that was not so amazing about this

greenhouse was that all the plants were drooping and dead. Branches were broken, leaves were withered, and bark was peeling off the tree trunks. The other girls were just looking around silently, so that gave Vic a chance to think about what was going on between Reyna and Skyler. Ever since Reyna had taken charge when they were planning to fight the basilisk, they hadn't talked to each other at all.

"Where do you think the next clue will be?" Amy broke the silence when she saw Skyler looking at Reyna as if Reyna had done something wrong.

"I have no idea," Vic said, realizing that Amy also realized that Skyler and Reyna were mad at each other. They exchanged looks, but knowing that they had to move on, they started searching the greenhouse. Reyna and Skyler followed, but went in opposite directions. They searched for over ten minutes.

Suddenly, Vic tripped over something sharp and gasped. "You guys, I found a blue bag!" Vic bent down. Her long, black hair brushed the blue bag as she pulled out another scroll and a bright blue sapphire that was the same color as Vic's eyes.

"The next clue! And a sapphire!" Reyna exclaimed.

The others gathered around Vic to read the next clue. "Long corridors hold secrets. Find it before the time runs out—"

Long corridors hold secrets
Find it before the time runs out

"Long corridors—" Skyler gave a questioning look.

"That can't be right!" Reyna exclaimed. "Do you know how many long corridors we walked through? This doesn't help us at all."

Amy closed her eyes and shook her head. "What about the second line, 'Find it before the time runs out'? I thought there wasn't a time limit!"

"Well, there isn't," Vic sighed. "Maybe instead of a time limit it's talking about the time we have in this day— I don't know, it's probably stupid."

"No wait, I think you're right!" Skyler exclaimed. "It's not like time will stop so the day is probably going by fast."

That made Vic feel just a little more stressed. She knew they couldn't be in this mansion forever doing the quest, and this riddle made her more anxious.

Suddenly, an idea struck her. "Wait a minute, you know that hallway with the grandfather clock? Since the riddle talks about time, maybe we need to be near something that *shows* time!" Vic exclaimed. They all started to rush out of the greenhouse, but Vic stopped them as she stuffed the bag in her pocket.

"Wait, how are we supposed to find that hallway again? We walked through so many of them!"

"We'll find it all right!" Skyler rushed them out. They stopped by the greenhouse door.

"There's no way to be sure we will find the hall with the grandfather clock—" Reyna trailed off. "What if we don't?"

"Well, we don't have a choice." Amy rolled her eyes. "Don't worry though, we'll find it."

Reyna took a breath and nodded. Vic smiled at Amy. They headed through the winding paths, taking lefts, rights, and just wandering through hallways until finally they found the grandfather clock. It took a while, but then the girls had started to recognize some areas when they stumbled across the clock. It was grand, but old and dusty. The dust coated it like a carpet. Just looking at it made Vic want to sneeze.

"Where do you think the next bag will be?" Skyler asked. The other girls shrugged and headed closer to grandfather clock. They took one step, and suddenly the lights started to dim.

Chapter 12

Amy

That's odd. The others noticed too but they kept looking. "What if we open the glass case door? It might be inside," Vic said.

"Good thinking, Vic." Amy unlatched the door. She looked around. All she saw were dark corners. The pendulum swung from side to side. Amy's eyes followed it and she thought she saw a glimmer of red. She caught the pendulum and saw there was a hinge along the side. She dug her fingernails into the opening and pulled it open. It popped open with a loud noise and sure enough, the next bag was there. It had a soft, velvety texture. Amy opened it and found the next clue, and a red ruby.

"Nice," Skyler grinned at Amy.

"What does it say?" Reyna asked as Amy stood back up.

"Mix and match, stir and spy, find it hidden while you can *fry.*"

Mix and match
Stir and spy
Find it hidden while you can fry

Before they could say anything else, a door flew open and floating there was a ghost, but not the one of Patricia Mister. Amy gasped. The ghost flickered in front of them, staring at them with his blood-red eyes.

"Quick! Follow me!" said a voice behind them. They turned around to see that Patricia was calling them over. The girls followed her, running to keep up. Patricia brought them to a hidden spot, a corridor of some sort.

"Are you girls okay?" They all nodded, too breathless to answer. "I forgot to warn you. Evil ghosts roam the halls at daytime and at night—*especially* at night."

"So, they could attack us at any given time?" Amy asked.

"Yes, you girls should be very—"

Patricia flickered and disappeared before she could finish her sentence, but they knew she was going to say careful.

"I hate it when they just appear and disappear randomly!" Skyler complained.

"Let's figure this clue out," Vic urged them. Amy pulled out the clue.

"Mix and match, stir and spy, find it hidden where you can *fry*," Amy read it exactly like before.

"Fry? What is that supposed to mean?" Reyna asked.

"Fry—fry—fry—I think I got it!" Amy looked pleased with herself. "This is a mansion right? The kitchen! Every house has one."

"You're right Amy!" Skyler agreed. "But how do we know where it is?"

"If only we had a map—"

The girls couldn't risk wandering and getting even more confused than they already were, but they also had no other way to get to the kitchen! As the other girls huddled together around the riddle, Amy took a breath and walked a couple feet away. She needed a break from all this drama.

She suddenly froze up. Out of the corner of her eye,

Amy saw two figures walking not too far away from them. *Wasn't this corridor a hidden spot?* Amy watched carefully as the two figures emerged from the darkness. One seemed like an older, teenage girl. The other one seemed to be a little boy holding her hand. For some reason, their faces looked familiar, but Amy was positive that she hadn't seen them before.

The older girl seemed to notice them first. Her face first turned to fear, anger, then a mixture of shock and sadness. "Wait, R-Reyna?" For some reason, she had tears in her eyes.

"Yeah Amy?" Reyna said without even turning around. Then realization hit her. She turned around, quick enough to knock someone down. Her eyes widened at the figure. "Wait, N-Nina? I-Is it really you?" A couple of tears fell down her face as she turned to look at the younger boy with jet-black hair and electric blue eyes. "And you—are you—Vic's brother?"

That seemed to get Vic's attention. What happened next was like a movie scene. Vic turned around, shocked. She took a couple of slow steps before running at full speed and kneeling down to hug her little brother. Aaron hugged her back. "I always wished I remembered you! Nina told me so many stories, but meeting you here is even better."

"I—I can't believe I actually have the chance to see you again! Aaron! I thought I lost you." Vic's eyes were glassy. "I've missed you so much."

Aaron gave a tooth-gapped smile. "Me too."

As Vic and Aaron were having their moment, Nina and Reyna were too.

Nina sniffed. *"Hermanita*—I can't believe how much you grew up. I—I can't believe we were lucky enough to find each other again.

A tear streaked Reyna's face. "I've missed you Nina." They both hugged again. Amy smiled at the sweet moment. Even though she felt a little left out, it was nice to see her best friends meeting people they thought they had lost forever.

Meanwhile, Skyler—well, she just seemed weird. They all knew something was up with Skyler, but it didn't make any sense. Skyler smiled when she looked at Vic, but at Reyna she glared. Amy knew Reyna and Skyler were inseparable before, and nothing would change that. So, what changed?

Amy went over to Vic and talked with her and Aaron. It felt a little awkward at first, but Aaron slowly became more comfortable. Amy's mind was still on Skyler and Reyna's fight. *Why should I even care about some stupid fight?* But she knew why she cared. She didn't want anyone arguing so everyone would get along.

"C'mon Vic," Amy said, " let's go join the others."

"I'm sorry about Mr. Mister. But I promise you, there's much more to the story than you know right now." Nina looked sympathetic

"Wait, how did you know that?" Vic asked

"Patricia told us, Vic," she explained.

"And now it's *your* turn to explain your story," Reyna told Nina playfully.

Amy caught herself staring at Reyna. Somehow she looked different now. The air of shyness that usually surrounded her was gone. Her eyes weren't fixed on the ground. Instead, she was looking back at them with a kind of boldness Amy never expected Reyna to have. Nina and Aaron weren't shocked since they had thought it was normal for Reyna to act like this, but Vic had noticed it too.

"Well, when you were taken away, we were brought here by an evil ghost. The ghost wasn't allowed to kill children because of a spell he had been put under, so he—"

"Petrified you!" Aaron interrupted.

"Exactly. So I was petrified for four years, and Aaron was taken in by Patricia, 'till she freed me and Aaron and

I have lived here ever since. That's why I am only sixteen, not twenty."

"That's pretty scary," Amy said.

"I know. We know your story because Patricia always told us about you after she, um—became a ghost.

Chapter 13

Skyler

Skyler was surprised at what Nina said. In fact, all of the girls looked like they were too. Skyler was so mad at Reyna for becoming more independent at the time when she was the scared one. Skyler was also jealous of Reyna not being afraid of ghosts, but that wasn't the real reason she was mad at Reyna.

It was something that Skyler couldn't figure out herself. Some reason that laid deep inside her. Something that weighed her down with darkness and anger. If Skyler had been a person who showed her anger every time she got mad, she would have probably killed Reyna by now. But Skyler didn't like to show her anger, and she was already saying rude comments to Reyna. Skyler wasn't sure how much more anger she could keep hidden.

"Hey Skyler, shouldn't we keep moving?" Reyna asked.

"Go ahead," Skyler answered. "After all, you're the *leader.*"

"So, let's go!" Reyna said, a bit impatiently. "We need to go find the next clue, remember? I already told Aaron and Nina about our clues and we were talking about leaving while you were just *staring* at us." Reyna rolled her eyes.

"Sorry," Skyler apologized, even though she wasn't at all remorseful.

Reyna rubbed her forehead and sighed, "Let's go."

Reyna turned around and started walking, her braid swinging like a pendulum. Nina and Aaron looked at each other, clearly discussing in their heads. Vic and Amy followed Reyna. Skyler scoffed and went to catch up with the others.

"Hey Reyna," Nina called out. They turned to see Nina still standing behind with a hand on Aaron's shoulder, checking her watch. "Sorry, we don't think we can come with you. Aaron and I have to head out."

"What? You just got here! And why do you have to 'head out'?" Vic asked disappointedly. It didn't seem surprising to Skyler. After all, Vic would want to spend as much time as she could with her brother after not seeing him for so long.

"We have a little mission of our own. You see, there are a lot of people trapped here. We rescued a few people and are taking care of them. You know, like giving them food," Nina answered.

"We're on our way to the kitchen," Aaron said.

"Oh, that's great! That's where we're going too. You can lead the way!" Amy exclaimed. The group headed out, but this time with two extra people. Skyler started to realize that she was the last one in the crowd. She hurried forward, past Reyna. She found herself standing next to Amy and Vic. Reyna caught up and started to chat with them.

"Where do you guys think we'll find the next clue?" Vic asked.

"I have no *clue*, get it?" Reyna's puns weren't heard very often and kind of cheesy, but everyone laughed—everyone except Skyler.

"Here we are!" Nina announced after walking a long while. She pushed open grand French doors.

"Wow!" Amy looked around. This was the biggest kitchen she had ever seen in her life. It had seven stoves lined up, big stained-glass cabinets, and everything that Skyler could ever imagine cooking with. Skyler walked around, looking for the clue. She searched in cabinets, in pots, but she couldn't find it anywhere.

"You know, there might be a pattern to where the jewels and clues are hidden," Reyna said.

"Well, we found the first clue with the help of a ghost," Amy said thoughtfully.

"Then we found one on the ground. No pattern to that," Skyler said irritatedly.

"Then the clock," Vic finished.

They all stood there thinking, while Skyler searched around the kitchen.

"Wait!" Reyna exclaimed.

"What is it?" Vic asked.

"Where you can *fry!* Remember the clue?" Reyna realized as Vic pulled out the clue from her pocket.

"Hey Nina? Where are the pans?"

"The pans? Oh, they're on the shelf over there." She pointed to a tall shelf with a glass door.

Reyna ran over. The others followed after her, and opened the door. Skyler found a stool and climbed onto it. But one of the legs crumbled under her weight and she fell to the ground. Luckily she landed on a soft rug.

"Are you okay?" Amy asked, concerned.

"Oh, sorry, I should have warned you about that," Nina apologized. "You—"

"—Look!" Reyna jumped in, cutting off Nina.

"What is it, Reyna?" Vic asked.

"The next clue! Look!"

Skyler reached for the yellow satin bag and pulled out a diamond-shaped topaz and the next clue.

This will last brighter than the rest
And finish off your quest
But only one
Sleep tight underneath
For this might be

"This will last brighter than the rest, and finish off your quest, but only one. Sleep tight underneath, for this might be," Skyler read aloud.

"What? That doesn't make any sense!" Reyna asked.

"Oh no, look at the time! We have to get to sleep!" Nina exclaimed. "Let's get to our room."

The girls looked at each other, confused. "What do you mean?"

"But—we still have more work to do. And why do we need a bedtime?" Reyna asked.

"We can't be in the corridors at night, otherwise we're basically giving ourselves away. Aaron and I know a safe spot to spend the night, so follow us."

The girls followed Nina and Aaron through winding paths. Skyler had no idea how they managed not to get lost in this huge mansion, even after living here for seven years.

"Clank."

"We're here," Nina announced, as she knocked on the oak door again.

The door creaked open, and everyone crept inside. There were six twin beds inside that had been pushed together in pairs of two so it was more like three queen beds than six. There was also a pair of pajamas on each one. There were also six doors leading to what Skyler assumed were bathrooms. Though Skyler expected the room to look like a basement after living in one for so long, it was surprisingly comfy. The beds had thick mattresses, soft, light-blue blankets that were just the right thickness, and fluffy pillows. The doors were a warm mahogany with golden handles. The room itself had soft, patterned wallpaper. There was a clock right above the beds, and lamps all over, creating an inviting atmosphere. The carpets were a dark brown color and much nicer than the cheap carpets Mr. Mister had. On one side, there were tall bookshelves reaching the ceiling that were filled with books. *Whoa.*

"Patricia was the one who showed us this room. This room came with six beds and six bathrooms, but we never expected to use all of them." Aaron explained to the group. "Nina and I just thought the two of us would be using it as a place to sleep."

"But now," Nina interrupted, "we have to get to sleep before all the evil ghosts come out." She quickly strode over to the door and locked it. Nobody uttered a word as they all got ready for bed.

"Good night," Nina whispered. "Try not to make a lot of noise now. The evil ghosts should start coming anytime." The others smiled back in return.

"Since there are three beds made of two beds pushed together, we can sleep the normal way," Amy whispered. "You know, Vic and I, Reyna and Skyler."

"No!" Skyler yelped.

"Shh!" The rest of them hissed, looking alarmed.

"Sorry, I meant, how about we switch it up. Amy and I, Vic and Reyna," Skyler said. "That wo—"

"Actually, if you don't mind, Skyler," Nina interrupted, "I'd like to be with my sister and if you want Vic, you can be with your brother."

"Sure," Vic agreed. "C'mon Aaron." They all split up to their different beds while Skyler let out a sigh of relief.

"Hey," Amy whispered to Skyler as they were getting into their bed, or *beds.* "Why did you scream back there?"

"I'd rather not talk about it," Skyler replied, rolling away from Amy.

Skyler was glad Amy didn't pester her for more information because Skyler didn't know how to explain why she was mad at Reyna. She knew the others would *never* understand why she was mad. In fact, Skyler barely understood it herself.

Chapter 14

Reyna

Reyna woke up the next day, thinking about why Skyler was mad at her. Was it her fault? She realized that maybe it could have been her fault since she started becoming less shy. *But why would Skyler be so mad at me just for becoming more independent?* She shrugged off the thought and opened her bag; she nearly forgot she had one.

She pulled out her toothbrush and headed for the bathroom. *That's weird, one bathroom for each person. Why can't we just take turns using it?* At the next moment, she found herself walking into the third bathroom without even thinking. When she entered, she didn't know what to think. It was spotless. She could actually see herself in the sink countertop. It was fully set up. There were neatly folded towels, curtains, and even hair brushes and clothes, all in her favorite color, purple. *This just got ten times weirder.*

She poked her head out the door and saw Vic doing the same thing.

"Reyna, come here. My bathroom is so weird. It's all set up and everything is my favorite color. Is that the same with you?" Vic whispered.

"Yeah it is, I'll come and see yours."

Reyna went to Vic's bathroom. It was the same as hers, except everything was electric blue. She peered inside the others. One was all red, probably Amy's. The next was bright green. She guessed it was Aaron, and her sister's was orange. The last one was pink and yellow, definitely Skyler's.

"Hey Nina, what's up with the colored bathrooms? It's kind of weird," Reyna asked Nina as she walked towards the first bathroom.

"Yeah I know, Aaron and I have been trying to figure out how this mansion does stuff like this," Nina answered.

Skyler and Amy got up and started walking towards their assigned bathrooms. They seemed to be in some sort of trance.

"What's wrong with them?" Vic whispered.

"Oh don't worry!" Nina exclaimed. "That just happens the first time you find the 'matching' bathroom."

"But weird right? Bathrooms of all things? Why couldn't it be the beds or something?"

"I don't know, but go and take a shower and try on the clothes. They'll fit you perfectly."

Vic and Reyna did as they were told while Nina filled the others in.

The water was surprisingly warmer than she expected it to be. Reyna tried on the clothes she found and Nina was right. They fit perfectly.

When she came out, she explored the room a little bit. The beds were in their usual spots and the shelves lining the walls were still filled with books. She walked over to the bookshelf and saw that the books were actually really old and dusty. Reyna took another step and stopped abruptly. She peered closer at the wall and saw something carved into it.

"Guys come here!" Reyna called the others to the spot.

"What is that?" Amy asked once they had reached the carving. Amy traced it with her finger.

"What is it?" Skyler asked. "Do we even know if it's important?"

Vic pursed her lips. "It looks familiar—and why is it here of all places."

Reyna rolled her eyes. "Remember when we were researching Egyptian Hieroglyphs in school? When we were doing that, I came across a bunch of Greek letters or symbols. This one is Omega!"

"What does that mean?" Skyler asked, crossing her arms. "Not all of us research this stuff for *fun. Nerd.*"

Reyna was hurt and thrown off by Skyler's surly attitude, but she blinked away the tears. She had more important things to think about.

"Omega is the last letter in the Greek alphabet," Nina explained. "Aaron and I learned a lot of random information while Patricia taught us school lessons."

Reyna ran her finger over the carving; it was rough and sandy.

"Actually, I found that before, but I left it because I didn't think it was important," Aaron added quietly.

They stood near the carving for a few minutes in silence. Then Nina spoke up.

"Sorry, but we'll be late for the kitchens! We'll see you at breakfast!" Both Nina and Aaron left quickly.

"Wait! We almost forgot the clue!" Skyler reminded them. She pulled it out of her pocket and read it out loud again. "This will last brighter than the rest, and finish off your quest, but only one. Sleep tight underneath, for this might be."

"Wait a second—you don't think that this symbol could be the end of the clue, do you?" Vic said excitedly.

"Sleep tight underneath—"

"The beds!" Amy turned to see the beds.

They scurried to the cluster of beds and looked around each of them. Finally, Skyler found a big bag underneath her bed.

"I found it! Come here, hold on," Skyler tugged the bag open. Inside the bag were some jumbled items. There was a small flashlight.

"Brighter than the rest!" Reyna realized.

Also inside was an ancient case. Skyler wiped off some dust and then slowly opened it. Inside were empty compartments.

"I think the four jewels fit into the small circles, and the clues fit into the compartment underneath it," Vic said.

Skyler grabbed the clues and placed them in the box. The girls took their jewels and placed them in the four circles, but there were still three empty compartments. One looked like it was meant to hold a bottle, one was square-shaped, and the other one looked like it was meant to hold some kind of key.

Vic grabbed the bag from Skyler's hands and looked inside. "Hey guys, there's another clue!"

Part two:

The Ghostly Maze

Find a ghost
Beware the bad
Find a maze
Beware, the quest has only begun

Chapter 15

Vic

"Find a ghost. Beware the bad. Find a maze. Beware, the quest has only begun," Vic read.

"Only begun? But the last clue said that we would *finish* the quest!" Skyler said exasperatedly.

"But only one," Reyna muttered quietly.

"What do you mean, Reyna?" Amy asked.

"We have more to do than we thought," Vic answered instead of Reyna. "That was only part one of the *entire* quest. Who knows how many more parts we have!"

"Vic is right. I don't think we know what's really in store for us," Reyna said, backing her up.

"Well, let's face it then!" Amy exclaimed. "But first, let's figure out the Omega symbol."

"What do you mean?" Vic questioned. "There's nothing to figure out."

"Oh yeah? I was thinking about this and found something. The carving has a box around it. We didn't try to push it or something yet, did we?"

"No we didn't," Vic answered Amy. "I doubt the square is an actual opening, but let's give it a try anyway."

Skyler placed the box under the bed where they had found it. The girls walked over to the carving and studied it again. Amy was right. There was a carving of a box around it. But before they decided to try to push it, Vic realized something. It was dusty and old for sure, but it didn't seem rusty or tarnished in any way.

"You know, for such an old carving, it's not spoiled in any shape or form. That might mean something." Vic finally poured out her thoughts.

"You're right, and it's not like somebody cleans it. I mean, it's an old carving!" Skyler started to say something, but then stopped to see a bright light behind the carving. The others noticed it too. Then suddenly the carving flew out of its spot and landed before them.

"I think this goes in the square compartment!" Reyna exclaimed.

"You guys! Look what's behind it," Amy said.

There was a small crumpled clue. Well not really, just a scrap of paper with a message. It read:

Regal Seville
Bad ghost

"What is this?" Skyler asked.

"I think I know what this means. This is the bad ghost we're supposed to find," Vic whispered. *"Beware of the bad!"*

"Well girls! Long time no see. How's everything going?" Patricia appeared out of nowhere.

"Patricia!" Skyler jumped.

"Settle down now, it's time for lunch. You all worked on the quest right through breakfast!"

The girls looked at each other. *Has it already been that long since we woke up?* Vic looked alarmed. If they had spent so much time on a small part of the quest already, how long would it take to finish the quest?

"Will you show us where to go?" Vic asked her.

"Oh yes, not to worry. I'll be there all through lunch. I believe there is a lot for us to discuss." And with that, Patricia led the way to the dining hall.

When they finally reached the dining hall they took a seat, even Patricia. *Wow, this place is grand. Twelve chairs! They must have been a big family.* Vic and the others looked around. There was a high ceiling and a grand table with a crystal chandelier hanging down low.

"Hello!" Aaron greeted them with a wave. "Nina is bringing the food!" He bowed, imitating a king's waiter, and slipped out of the room. Vic laughed to herself. She still remembered how much her brother laughed when he was a baby. It made her a little sad.

"Sit down girls!" Patricia beckoned them to sit down. After they did she started to talk again. "I wanted to see if your quest is off to a good start, but before we talk about that, I need to say something else."

"What is it?"

"It looks like somebody here has touched a drop of basilisk blood."

"So?" Reyna looked at Patricia questioningly, as her sister walked in holding bowls of steaming hot soup on a platter.

"Bon Appétit!" Nina winked and walked out with two bowls for Aaron and her.

"Well," Patricia continued, "basilisk blood isn't harmful to your body, but only harmful to your soul. Of course that is only for humans. Bad ghosts can be dissolved by basilisk blood."

"I still don't get it," Amy answered.

"To get to the point, at the touch of basilisk blood, the person gets reversed. In other words, it turns the person against the person they are closest to."

Vic didn't have to think about who it was. All eyes shot towards Skyler. She just shrugged.

"Aha! It looks like we have found the one." Patricia's eyes twinkled.

"Me? But who was I turned against?" Skyler looked embarrassed.

"Here, take this."

Patricia handed Skyler a bottle of some kind of potion. She hesitated for a second or two, but then finally drank it. For a second she looked dizzy, but then she steadied herself and turned directly to Reyna.

"Reyna? But-t-t, I don't know what came over me. I'm so s-sorry, I—" Skyler stammered. Vic almost felt bad for her.

"It's okay Skyler, I know you didn't mean it. I'm just glad you're back to normal." Reyna looked like crying again but stopped herself.

"I am too," Skyler agreed.

Vic was glad that Reyna and Skyler had made up, but they really needed to get back to their quest.

"So, Patricia," Vic started, "what were you going to say about our quest?"

"I will tell you," Patricia said, "but first you must take this potion for an emergency." She handed a silvery potion to Vic, identical to the one she gave to Skyler.

"This potion heals basilisk blood," Patricia announced. "It also heals anything that could be harmful to you. Even small cuts, but you should only take it in times of desperate need, for there is sometimes only enough for one use."

Vic eyed the potion. She didn't like how it felt, all heavy and thick. It swirled around, making her nauseous. She gave the potion to Amy, who slipped it in her pocket, then turned her attention back to Patricia.

"Now, about your quest, as I already told you, I can't help much but I will tell you one thing. Regal Seville is a bad ghost, like you already know, but really, he is an evil ghost. He is the old owner who is the cause of it all, the bad ghosts' leader, and he is the evilest of them all. He—oh, thank you Nina." Nina entered with a plate full of sandwiches followed by a French dessert that she called créme brûlée. The others looked at her like she was crazy. They had never had that much food in one meal before.

Nina started to leave the room when Skyler called out, "Hey Nina, why don't you and Aaron sit with us and eat?"

"Sorry," Nina replied, "we can't sit with you right now. Patricia told us that humans cannot help with your quest; only ghosts."

The rule didn't make much sense to Vic, but she shrugged it off. After all, this quest didn't make much sense! She decided she just needed to accept whatever happened in this weird mansion.

Amy furrowed her brow. "But— you were with us when we were looking for a clue, and the Omega symbol—"

Patricia smiled and leaned closer to the girls. "While Nina and Aaron might have been with you, they didn't help you solve anything or help you understand why it contributed to the quest. Either way, if it was classified as helping, you definitely wouldn't see Nina and Aaron until your quest was finished." Nina nodded along and walked over to the table.

Vic felt a pang of worry. If they put Aaron or Nina in a situation where they were helping the quest, what would happen to them? No matter what, Vic couldn't let that happen.

"So wait—" Skyler said. "Does this mean we *can* get help for our quest? You know, from another good ghost?"

Nina pursed her lips. "Well, yes. The problem is, it's very hard to find a good ghost free in the mansion, let alone one that would want to help. After all they've been through, most wouldn't want to risk going against Regal Seville. But don't worry. I know you girls can accomplish anything; but the ghost you're looking for help from may not be a good one.

It warmed Vic's heart to know there were people who had faith in them. Looking over at the girls, it was clear they felt the same—especially Reyna. They thanked Nina and she left the dining room, leaving the girls alone with Patricia.

Patricia tucked a strand of hair behind her ear and continued talking. "Anyway, Regal Seville is somewhere in this mansion and it is crucial to find him for your quest. The only way to find him is to ask the boss of the servants, Midnight Wolfhart for help."

Patricia took a deep breath. "Midnight Wolfhart is a very bad ghost too, and the one way to get past her is to lie and say that you are a servant. She will most likely not believe you and will ask you to do something that will prove you are trustworthy. But I have faith in you girls. If you try hard enough you will gain her trust."

Vic looked at everyone at the table. " First of all, what kind of name is Midnight Wolfhart? And where do we find her?"

"Bad ghosts sometimes have names unlike the ones living beings would have," Patricia explained. " Midnight Wolfhart is on the very top floor, in the first room on the first left," Patricia answered. "The stair—well rather than explaining all of it to you, Nina and Aaron can show you."

"We're ready when you are!" Nina called out to them.

They started eating the food, at first half-heartedly, then just like normal. The food was better than anything they had ever had, especially the crème brûlée. But it was hard to enjoy the food when an uneasy silence had settled over the table. It felt like it was consuming all the happy thoughts.

After they finished eating, the girls followed Nina to the staircase, a huge one. Vic felt like falling over when she looked up. The staircase was wide and twisted. It even spiraled around in few places. Nina looked at them and chuckled.

"I know how you feel. It takes some getting used to—walking up and down the long staircases."

"You know," Reyna said, "I thought this mansion was big before I realized there was a top floor!"

"Top floor? There are at least four or five levels! Good luck, we better be off!" Aaron said, hugging Vic. Then Nina and Aaron left.

"What? Five of those tall levels?" Amy said, looking worried.

"Oh, don't worry! Just don't look down," Skyler winked and led the way. Reyna followed as Vic dragged Amy along.

They walked up the stairs slowly, trying to ignore the echoes of their footsteps. They walked, ran, jogged, anything to make it up three flights of stairs. Vic looked up and saw there was one more flight. She groaned. Amy was panting when she reached where Vic was standing and went first, surprisingly. When they all finally reached the top, Vic asked, "Does anyone remember the directions that Patricia gave us?"

Skyler pulled out a piece of paper from the notebook that she always carried, panting, and handed it to Vic. "Here, I wrote down some notes."

> *Top floor*
> *First left*
> *First room*

Vic studied Skyler's neat cursive handwriting and announced, "This way." She led them into a wide, dimly lit corridor.

Chapter 16

Amy

Amy thought she was going crazy. The girls' biggest troubles used to just be Mr. Mister and his shenanigans. Now they had ghosts to find, quests to solve, and most importantly, not to die. So far the only life threatening thing the girls had faced was the basilisk. But even then, Amy knew that wasn't the end. After all, it was lucky they made it out alive, considering that because of the first danger they faced, Skyler had gotten poisoned against Reyna.

Amy knew for sure they would be meeting real trouble now, just after that one long staircase. She hated that she had a fear of heights, but there was nothing she could do about it. Patricia made it seem like their quest would be as safe as playing a board game, but Amy knew it wouldn't. It was like soccer. First, it's just a game and then all of a sudden, there are injuries, anger, yelling. Amy could just keep going on and on. Soccer had always been Amy's life passion. She grew up around it, the anger, screaming, injuries, everything. But this quest made all of that seem like child's play.

Amy knew the others were probably thinking, *What's the worst a ghost can do?* And Amy had thought, and thought about it, and so far the only answer she could come up with was *you'll find out soon enough.*

Amy didn't want to admit it, but she was scared. She

70

tried to keep the jarring thought out of her mind that she felt safer at Mr. Misters house.

"I really hate this stupid quest," she muttered.

"I hate it too!" Vic appeared next to Amy. "But we've got to get it done so we can go back— home."

Amy didn't reply. She knew Vic was right. The sooner they finished their quest, the sooner they could get out. But where would they go? They had no home to go back to thanks to Mr. Mister, and she knew they wouldn't go back to their former plan. Now that they also had Aaron and Nina, there would be no turning back, no going back to their old life. She didn't want to admit it, but she actually missed her old life, her old innocent life.

Actually, scratch that, there was no old life for her. After all, Amy was always up for an adventure, but she preferred the small ones that don't get your heads sliced off by a ghost's giant toothpick of a sword.

They had walked a lot and now Amy felt a little panicked. *What is she going to ask us to do? This Midnight Wolfhart?* All of a sudden she found herself thinking about the old lady across the street from Mr. Mister's house, who gave out the best candy during Halloween.

Vic nudged her out of her thoughts and whispered, "We're almost here Amy. Remember, we're going to pretend to be servants and we can't talk about things the ghost might find suspicious." Vic seemed like she was readying herself, not Amy.

Amy nodded. She didn't want to think about all that now. She just wanted to distract herself, but Amy was snapped out of her thinking once again as they stopped in the part of the corridor which was especially dark, and Skyler pushed the intricately carved door open.

"*Creak.*"

Skyler had barely pushed the door open when a shadowy figure stepped out.

"Well, well," said a hoarse voice with a southern accent. "Who are y'all, and what'd y'all want?"

The girls remained silent. They were trying to see who was talking, but the figure was hidden in the darkness of the corridor.

"Answer me!" the voice demanded.

None of them made a single sound. The girls were too shocked. What if their quest was already ruined?

"How *dare* you not answer me, Midnight Wolfhart!"

The girls looked at each other. They couldn't say anything that would make the ghost suspicious, but they all knew what the others were thinking.

"We're sorry," Amy finally stammered out. "We are the new servants, Skyler, Victoria known as Vic, Reyna, and I'm Amy." Amy pointed to the girls in the order she said their names.

"New servants? I didn't hear of any new servants!" Amy held her breath. This ghost was not going to be easy to convince.

"Oh, um, that's strange. It must be because, um, because, we just arrived a couple of minutes ago and we were told to come directly here."

"Oh."

"We were told it would be better to show up directly to your, um, great self, because your pleasure is, um, very much sought." Amy felt like she was going to faint. *Did I just say that?*

"Well, of course. Who would dare to disobey me!"

"So, now what are we here to do?" Skyler finally spoke up beside Amy.

Midnight Wolfhart was silent. Suddenly, Amy heard a snap. The lights had slowly became brighter and they could see clearly.

Oh, that's how the lights had dimmed in the clock room.

"So what's your question?" Amy froze. How did she know they had to ask her a question? Could she read their minds? Did she know who they really were?

Midnight Wolfhart was an evil ghost, as Patricia had told them, and they could tell. She was the literal opposite of Patricia. In fact, instead of Patricia's friendly, brown eyes, her eyes were like black ice. And instead of a round, warm face, she had a cold stare, and sharp bones that structured her face. On top of all that, Midnight Wolfhart was wearing a Medieval gown, and her height suited the malicious glint in her eye.

"Ask the question and stop standin' there like a bunch of old turtles!" Midnight Wolfhart commanded. "I haven't got all day!"

Amy tried to hold back a laugh. Even though they were in front of an evil presence, she couldn't help but laugh. A bunch *of old turtles!* Her accent was like those in the old Western movies that Mr. Mister used to watch.

"What're you laughin' at?" demanded Midnight Wolfhart.

"N-nothing," Amy stuttered.

Midnight Wolfhart looked suspicious but Vic intervened.

"We wanted to ask, where is Regal Seville?" Vic questioned.

Midnight Wolfhart smirked. "Regal Seville, eh?" She reached in her pocket and pulled out what looked like a dagger, except its blade was two feet long. "You want to be the master's servant it seems.

She twirled the dagger around in her fingers. The girls seemed to be paralyzed with fear. The blade wouldn't do anything to Midnight Wolfhart, but it could definitely chop the girls into pieces.

"Well then," Midnight came closer, still twirling her dagger, "I hope you won't mind a test." She snapped her fingers, smirking, and suddenly the girls were alone in the darkness.

Chapter 17

Skyler

"Reyna, Amy, Vic!" Skyler called out. She couldn't see anything so she couldn't pinpoint the girls' location before moving. It was all so odd and quick. What could Midnight Wolfhart be planning?

Suddenly the lights flickered. Skyler was surrounded by ghosts. Skyler froze. She had just mastered her fear of being next to one ghost, but a whole room full of them? She was terrified of ghosts. She had no idea what to do at this moment. *Take a deep breath*, she thought, but nothing could make her calm down when she was facing her greatest fear. Then it flashed in her brain. This was the test, a test for her to face her greatest fear, the fear of things considered fake actually existing.

Reyna

S nake, monster, knife, being alone. Her fears were as vivid as they would ever be. She wondered what the others would do in this situation. Suddenly, she thought about what the other girls might be going through—it could be worse than what she was facing.

She steadied herself and looked around. What she was looking at appeared to be a scene from a horror movie. A dark room with no windows, no doors. She decided that if she was going to get through this, she was going to have to fight—somehow. Reyna slowly picked up the dagger lying on the ground, shaking as the snake slithered towards her.

Vic

Vic was scared. Not that it happened that often. She looked around the scattered room. There was nothing to threaten her, no monster, no ghost, nothing. She sensed what the rest were going through. What was happening here was nothing compared to that. It was just much, much worse.

There were secret entrances through this room that led to others, and more, till she reached where the others were. How did she know this? She had no idea. She picked up a shield, a spear, and her courage. She knew there would be unexpected surprises waiting to take her into her only fear: not knowing what awaits.

Amy

Amy felt like she had woken up from a long, dreadful sleep full of nightmares. She didn't know where she was. It was almost like she was in four memories all at once. She was on a tall hill in kindergarten where she didn't want to go sliding down like the others. She was getting harnessed to the zip-line of her field trip in fourth grade, on a tall pole. She was crossing a bridge that was thirty feet over a big gorge. And finally, she was at the edge of the cliff, fighting the basilisk.

Every direction she turned was at the edge of a different story, a different place, a different height. The one thing that wasn't the same was that she wasn't with her best friends she'd always known. She felt every location as if it were real. Where was she? How did she get here? She found some extra rope that she used to tie herself to the zip-line pole, and she hesitated before she had to jump down into what looked like a pit full of lava that was the same color as her hair, knowing she couldn't waste time.

Then, she knew that this wasn't normal, it was all Midnight Wolfhart. She had no other option but to jump into that pit to find the friends she'd always known. The friends who she depended on. The friends who were her only chance of survival in this mysterious mansion.

Chapter 18

Skyler

Skyler immediately referred back to what Patricia had said about ghosts, how good ghosts can be dissolved by water, and bad ghosts by something harder to obtain—basilisk blood. Where would she ever find that? A knot twisted in her stomach as a ghost floated towards her. Then suddenly, out of thin air, an entrance to what looked like a long tunnel appeared. She realized this might be her only chance.

She ran for the tunnel, dodging the ghosts and ran through the tunnel. Skyler found herself transported back to the edge of the cliff, where she and her friends had been fighting the basilisk. The basilisk was there again, but instead of being alone with the basilisk like Skyler expected, once she realized she was there, Reyna, Vic, and Amy were there too, along with her past self.

Skyler realized that she must have gone back in time, and this was her opportunity to get the basilisk blood. I guess *Midnight Wolfhart is giving us a fair chance in her test.*

Suddenly, she saw Vic coming her way. Vic turned around and looked straight through Skyler like she wasn't even there! *Nobody can see me,* Skyler realized. *Maybe the basilisk can't either!*

Skyler headed straight for the basilisk. Like she had thought, the basilisk couldn't see her, but she made sure not to look at the basilisk, just in case it could still kill her with its eyes.

As she crept towards the basilisk, Skyler suddenly stopped. She didn't even know how she would get the blood! She looked in her pockets for something, *anything*, that would help her get the blood. She found one thing that definitely hadn't been there before. A syringe with a sharp needle like tube. Skyler knew immediately what she had to do, but the problem was *how?*

She was going to have to draw blood from the basilisk and store it in something. The only thing that confused Skyler was why hadn't Midnight Wolfhart made it harder to find out how to get the basilisk blood?

There has to be some kind of catch. Midnight Wolfhart, if you can hear me, you will pay! Skyler shook that thought out of her mind as she started running towards the basilisk. She stopped again. She remembered when she felt that small drop on her shoulder, the drop of basilisk blood. Creepy.

Reyna

Creepy. Skyler would say that if she was here. Vic would know how to get away. Amy would just take all the pressure on her shoulders.

As the snake slithered around her ankle, Reyna flinched, trying not to move, fearing the snake would bite her. It slithered away and opened its mouth, letting out green, poisoned gas. Reyna watched as the snake began to change, slowly rising till it was coiled into a huge pile with its head poked out.

"Stay calm, stay calm," Reyna muttered to herself.

The dagger slid out of her hand and fell with a, *"clank".* Suddenly, the floor began to shake. The dagger had made the mark of an omega symbol Ω, the same as the one on the bookshelf. The floor cracked in half, opening a chasm and separating Reyna and the snake. Reyna picked up the dagger and studied it. She noticed that the dagger itself had the symbol. *That's odd,* she thought. *It's almost like the omega symbol is trying to help me!*

But Reyna didn't have any more time to spend. Before she knew it, she realized that the snake was unfolding to its full body length, and had revealed at least seven more meters of its body. Now, the snake was *crossing the chasm* to get to Reyna!

Reyna spun around and ran as fast as she could away from the snake. She didn't dare look back, but she could hear the snake getting closer. The only thing that she wanted right now was to escape from that creature, that snake chasing her.

Wait, she thought. *I have a dagger. There are so many things that you can do with a dagger, other than killing something!* She tried thinking of ways to put off the snake until she could get to a safe place since, well, she didn't like the thought of killing people or creatures.

But when Reyna looked at the dagger, all she could think of was killing the snake. But she couldn't just get away from the snake and hide. Midnight Wolfhart would never make the test so easy. She had to defeat the snake someway. But how?

Vic

Vic slowly clasped the first door knob, daring herself to turn it. *Well what do you know?* She turned it. The door made a clicking noise, as the lock magically unlocked. Vic took a deep breath and walked in.

Looking around the dark space, she saw a cobblestone room. It was lined with mosaic patterns from floor to ceiling. Then she heard a raspy voice. As she spun back towards the door, it locked her in and a faint glow of white shimmered into view. An old lady sitting in a rocking chair stitching looked at her. Wait, not an old lady, a ghost of one.

"I've been waiting for you dear." The old lady waved her hand and a chair appeared opposite from her. "You must be wondering why."

Vic hesitated, but gripping her spear and shield, she slowly took a seat. She sat on the edge, ready to get up whenever she needed to defend herself.

"Calm down child, I don't bite." Then Vic felt herself being pulled into the chair, as if it had listened to the old lady.

"There, there. Now, you are probably wondering who I am. Well, I am Ūnus, also known as number One in English. Ūnus is actually Latin. You are going to meet four more like me. So don't be afraid. They are all my sisters and brothers. Duo, Trēs, Quattuor, Quinque. Yes I know, they

are two through five. Duo is the second child, my younger
sister, then Trēs, oh he will be pleased to have a visitor. And
of course Quattuor and Quinque, the twins, can never be
forgotten. Quattuor though, couldn't go on without his
sister Quinque. Oh my, you look confused." The old lady/
ghost looked at her sympathetically.

What a weird lady, Vic thought. *Who goes on about siblings
who are named after numbers in Latin? Well first of all, what
family is named after numbers? And where am I? And why did
I run into this lady? Is she important? Well, she makes herself
seem pretty important.* Questions buzzed through Vic's head
as the lady continued.

"Well, the reason I'm here is to talk to you is—well let
us start with this. You probably realized what this test with
Midnight Wolfhart is about. Facing fears. Yours is not knowing what beholds. What do you think, dear? What do you
think is behind all these doors?"

"I—um— don't know," Vic stammered. She felt herself
tense even more.

"Exactly! That is what this test is all about! You see, all
I am here for is to make you realize that it is okay to be
scared. You of all people should know that."

"I—um—thank you. For everything, but I really must
be on my way," Vic said.

"Of course, but let me tell you one last thing. My brothers
and sisters will be very different from me. Except the one
thing similar is that they will all give you a different piece of
help. Now see this." Ūnus waved her hand and a ball with
a milky potion inside appeared. "In this mansion, as you
have probably realized, there are many secrets to be found.
And I am to reveal one of them to you." As she waved her
hand, an image appeared in the ball. A dark room that
looked like a prison came into view. Inside, there was a
woman with long, black hair and faint, blue eyes, much

like Vic's, and a tall man, who had spiky black hair and teal eyes, like Aaron.

"Mom—Dad—they're here? In this mansion?" Vic's voice was now nearly a whisper.

"Yes, Victor and Aaronia Harper," Ūnus replied, her hands skimming the crystal ball. "They are here, and so are the other's parents. But they are *bonum manes* now. Good ghosts, like me." She paused. "You better hurry on. Your adventure awaits."

Amy

Amy jumped off the pole and zip-lined down towards the bubbling lava. Just when it seemed like she was about to be burned alive, the tip of her shoe touched the lava and as quickly as she had gone down, she rose up.

The tip of her shoe was now gone! And if that wasn't bad enough, the lava was magic and was starting to eat away at her shoe! Amy knew it was only a matter of time until it reached her skin.

"Seriously, Wolfhart!" Amy screamed out of frustration. "Haven't I already proved myself by getting on the zip-line? How much more do I have to do?"

Like Amy expected, Midnight Wolfhart didn't reply. Or maybe this was her way of answering. Suddenly the air shimmered and now Amy found herself on a rickety bridge over a gorge.

The lava was still eating away at her shoe and now only half of it was left. Amy, eyes widened in terror, took off the shoe with one finger and threw it as far as she could. Luckily, her shoe landed on the bridge. Unfortunately, when the shoe landed on the bridge, it quickly became consumed by lava and disappeared.

"Are you kidding me?" Amy said in anger. She took off her other shoe and flung it like the other one, but this one didn't go that far. It quickly sank into the lava river.

A split second later, a portal appeared in front of Amy, showing a spooky looking island with bare trees. Amy saw a hole in the bridge from the lava and felt the bridge getting unstable. She lunged into the portal just as the bridge collapsed from under her feet.

Amy felt like how she had when she fell through the portal to Mystery Mansion, and how it felt like she couldn't breathe, as if her lungs had been expelled of all air. She landed hard on the ground as a pain shot through her arm. Amy closed her eyes from the unbearable pain, and could feel tears pushing their way through the corner of her eyes.

She looked at her right arm and saw that it was twisted at an angle that it *definitely* shouldn't have been at. *Ugh, I must have broken it.* She winced as she got up, holding a tree branch with her good arm. Steadying herself, Amy tried to make a cast. She used a stick she found on the ground, and put together a bunch of leaves, then tied it all together with a piece of twine. When she was done, she finally took a look around at where she was. It was a big area full of trees, like a spooky forest. Mist was swirling around, making Amy shiver. She turned to hear a sudden sound coming her way.

Chapter 19

Skyler

Skyler took a step forward. She remembered hitting the basilisk. *If only I could take the blood from where I had hit it.* She ran to the basilisk, trying not to get hit by the tail that was moving around when the past Amy came and started to distract the basilisk. She took this chance to kneel at the tail and poke the tail with the syringe, careful not to touch the blood, so that she wouldn't be turned against Reyna again.

Once Skyler had the syringe filled, she ran to a nearby hiding spot and looked for something to put the blood in. But instead of finding a container, Skyler found herself back where she'd started, surrounded by ghosts. This time they had swords. *I knew Midnight Wolfhart would find a way to make it harder.*

"We fight fair," hissed one of the ghosts, as it tossed her a sword. When she looked closer, the sword had a compartment in the hilt with *a container perfect for the blood to go in.* Skyler put in the blood, closed the hilt, and got ready for a fight that she hoped to live through.

Wait a second, the sword can't hurt the ghosts! Skyler saw that they were smirking. "We fight fair." The words rang in her ears. "Yeah right!" Skyler yelled aloud. Skyler took out the basilisk blood's container, and poured some on the blade of the sword, careful not to touch it.

"Foolish girl," hissed a ghost. "You don't know what's coming."

"Or maybe you're the one who doesn't know what's coming," Skyler countered.

Skyler readied her sword as she got ready to fight a battle she hoped she might just live through. After all, even if she lost the battle, they could still win the war. A war that hadn't been fought for centuries. Maybe even never.

Reyna

Jump. No, stay and fight. No, jump.

Reyna jumped down into the chasm, bracing herself as the opening above her closed. She tried to muffle her scream as she fell into the darkness. When she saw a black pool of ink swirling under her, before she could think she fell straight into it.

She felt a sharp shock run up her spine, and then found herself on the solid ground drenched in ink. She stood up and realized that she could see Midnight Wolfhart smiling evilly in the same room they had started in. She was on the other side of the pool of ink, only there was no way around it, only through it.

Reyna saw a steel boat on the shore and realized that it was there for her to use. She climbed over rocks and boulders and made her way to the boat. It was a large boat meant for four people with heavy oars to push through the ink. This was her last challenge. It wouldn't be easy, but it would be worth it to finish it. Reyna knew that it would take effort to row the boat, and wondered where she was going to get the energy she needed from.

Reyna saw a bottle of potion on the ground and wondered if she should drink it or not. It could be the healing one that Skyler took, or a different one. It had the same silvery color, but Reyna wasn't at all sure it was safe. *But it might be the only way I can pass this last challenge,* Reyna argued against herself.

Without thinking, Reyna drained the bottle of potion and immediately lurched over, clutching her chest. She felt as though her insides were on fire. Even though Reyna was in pain, she stumbled into the boat and started rowing the oars. Every time she pushed the oars, Reyna felt *unbearable* pain. But the potion had made one thing better: her strength.

Reyna was now able to row the boat with little energy, when it would have been impossible to do before. But with every stroke she made, she had to endure pain that felt like someone stabbing her repeatedly.

When Reyna finally made it across the pool of ink, she felt like giving up. The pain from the potion had been so enduring on her, Reyna was afraid that she might not make it. *C'mon Reyna, get it together. You will be able to finish Wolfhart's test!*

When she got to the other side, Reyna stumbled out of the boat, took one step forward, fell flat on the gravely surface, and the pain vanished.

When she reappeared, Reyna pulled herself up, and saw she was back were she had previously begun. Now this time instead of Wolfhart smirking, she had her eyebrows raised. Reyna took that as a sign that Wolfhart hadn't expected her to pass her test.

"Well, *congratulations,*" Midnight Wolfhart said snarkily, "but don't get your hopes up yet. To pass the test the *others* must make it out too."

Vic

B efore Vic could demand to hear more about her parents from Ūnus, the ghost disappeared. *Seriously? How come every time I find out something valuable, the source always disappears?* But even as Vic was annoyed at Ūnus, she had a feeling she would be seeing her again.

She put her hand firmly on the next doorknob. If something was behind this door, she might as well open it now. She turned it. She walked in. It. Was. Silent. So silent that Vic felt like it would consume her voice if she tried to speak.

"Thud, THUD!"

Vic spun on her heels and turned to see a creature that was at least thirteen feet tall with horns. It had blood-red slits for eyes, and was a swampy-green color. Vic thought it looked a little bit like a Minotaur from the Greek mythology unit at school.

Turning her focus back on getting away, Vic saw that it was carrying a long blade, different from a sword. The weapon looked like a giant lead pipe with a sharp point on the top left. The monster snarled as Vic put her spear and shield up, but it didn't attack.

Vic suddenly realized that when she had picked up her weapons, she never looked closely at them. The shield had a glowing symbol that said II. She realized right away that it was the number two in roman numerals. *This must be my test to get to Duo.*

The monster suddenly charged, taking advantage of the time Vic had taken to think about this challenge. Vic had never been paralyzed with fear, and this wasn't an exception. She had stopped because she felt like *something* was missing.

The monster kept charging at her, coming closer, and closer, until it halted a few feet away from her. Vic pointed her spear at the monster. "Don't come closer." She tried to stay calm.

"Silly creature," the monster snarled. Its hoarse voice sounded like it had a permanent cough. "You have *no* idea how powerful I am, do you?"

Vic knew that there was always a way to beat a monster, but this one made her feel uneasy. She had never met a monster that was so full of itself. Well, actually, she had never even met a monster before at all.

The monster smirked. "Don't think I don't know what you're planning. I know you're waiting for an advantage," it said, as if the monster had read Vic's mind. Or maybe it actually had.

Suddenly, out of nowhere, the monster just, well, melted. Vic couldn't believe what she was seeing. She didn't know whether to be relieved or disgusted. Then, Vic saw the door leading to the next room, and made a run for it.

Amy

As the figure came closer, Amy snuck around the trees. The fallen twigs pricked her bare feet. *Ugh.* She caught sight of a shadowy figure. Amy knew that sooner or later she would see whatever this figure was, so why not make it sooner?

"Hey!" Amy shouted, "who are you, and what do you want?"

The figure spun around. Amy saw it was a girl ghost who was holding wood in her arms. Unlike all the other ghosts Amy had seen, this girl was dressed in casual and modern clothing; a sleeveless shirt and jeans. She also wore square, purple glasses, her bangs hanging over them. The ghost had long hair, not as long as Vic's but longer then Skyler's. The hair must have been brown because even though ghosts don't have any color, Amy could tell that her hair wasn't too dark. The girl had almond-shaped eyes. She looked like a nice person except there was something that made everything wrong. *Something* that didn't match up.

"Are you—Amy?" the ghost asked, still having that peculiar expression on her face. "The one who is on a quest to save Mystery Mansion?"

"Umm, yeah but I wouldn't say our quest is *saving* Mystery Mansion," Amy replied. For some reason, Amy felt like everything this ghost was saying was somewhat—scripted.

The ghost's expression suddenly changed to happiness. There was nothing off about her now. *It was probably just a shadow.* The girl ran up to Amy and tried to hug her, but she just floated though.

"Oops, sorry," The girl blushed, embarrassed. "Well, let me just say, I am so happy to see you!"

"But, why?" Amy asked.

"You know Re—," The ghost stopped looking around. "I shouldn't say his name, so let's just say, the ruler. Well the ruler took control of Mystery Mansion and enslaved, imprisoned, or petrified everyone who wasn't an evil ghost since he was evil. The evil ghosts worked alongside him to do his evil deeds. My brother and I—we were enslaved and have been his servants ever since we died. And we were thirteen at the time." The girl got a little teary-eyed at the end. Amy thought that was a little too much emotion, but who was she to judge? The girl definitely had been through worse times than herself.

"So by defeating the ruler, we're saving Mystery Mansion?" Amy couldn't believe what they were doing was that important.

"Duh!" the girl exclaimed. "And when you said we, do you mean you're doing the quest as a group?"

"Yeah," Amy said, puzzled why this girl wanted to know so much about their quest.

"This is probably Midnight Wolfhart's test, right?" The ghost asked, all knowingly.

"Umm, yeah." Amy told her, surprised. "How'd you know?"

"This is a place Midnight Wolfhart created," the girl answered. "This is where Midnight Wolfhart sent me, but my twin brother isn't here. Wolfhart was bent on separating us."

Amy knew that Mystery Mansion was a place full of evil things, and she should know better than to trust her, but somehow Amy felt like she could trust this girl. Maybe it was something about how kind she looked, or her voice, but there was definitely something trustworthy about her.

Amy relaxed. "Well, it was nice meeting you, but I really have to get back to my test."

Amy saw something glittering at her feet, and realized it was a potion bottle. She reached down to grab it and a sharp pain ran up her arm. *Ugh, I forgot my arm was fractured.* There was definitely something magical about the Mansion because in the real world, Amy would never be able to forget about a broken arm. She picked up the bottle with her unhurt arm and examined it. The bottle was in the shape of a ghost and was a dark green color.

"Hey, where did you get that potion?" asked the ghost.

"It was right on the ground." Amy told her. " You have any idea what it does?"

"Every servant knows what that is," the ghost answered. "It's the potion that gets you back to Midnight Wolfhart. A servant must have dropped it or—" The ghost checked her pockets and came up with nothing. "I must have dropped it," she muttered to herself. "I guess that one's mine," she told Amy.

Amy couldn't believe what she was hearing. The potion would lead her out of Midnight Wolfhart's test, and by doing that, Amy would pass! But it couldn't be that easy, could it?

The ghost seemed to be thinking what she was thinking. "I have to give my kindling to Midnight Wolfhart now." The girl pointed to the wood she had on her arms. " There is enough potion in this vial for two people. You could get out of Midnight Wolfhart's test too, but—"

"'Course I'll come!" Amy interrupted. Amy knew that even if there was a *'but'*, it couldn't be any worse than the test Midnight Wolfhart gave her.

Amy gave the vial to the ghost and she took a sip from

it. The ghost gave the vial back to Amy and disappeared. Amy took a sip from it too. The potion was *disgusting*. It tasted like all things bad in the world had been blended up into green smoothies. And as quickly as she had drank the potion, Amy found herself falling head first a mile above Mystery Mansion.

"WHAT THE HECK IS GOING ON?!" Amy screamed in pure terror as she hurtled towards the Mansion. Amy closed her eyes. Of all the ways to get to Midnight Wolfhart, falling from the sky would be in dead last.

"Don't be scared Amy!" a voice shouted from below her. Amy opened an eye to see the ghost falling a few feet below her. "The potion always brings you to Wolfhart in a way that involves your greatest fear. If you show you are scared, the landing *will* hurt, but if you don't I promise it will be painless!"

Well that explained a lot. "Are you also afraid of heights since you're falling with me?" Amy asked.

"No I'm not!" the girl shouted back. "You can only see me because we drank from the potion one after another. And plus, ghosts can't fall. We automatically float."

Amy, curious as always, wanted to know what the ghost was afraid of. After all, ghosts are supposed to be the ones causing terror, even though this ghost didn't seem like the kind of ghost that was mean. But she seemed in no mood to talk about her fear, so Amy didn't ask.

Calm, be calm, be calm! Amy forced herself to not be frightened. At her school, they had watched a video about skydivers in science. It had really freaked her out at the time, but she still positioned herself in the way the sky-divers do when they are free falling, and just hoped that everything would end up fine. It felt like ages as Amy was falling towards Mystery Mansion. Suddenly she heard a snicker. Amy opened her eyes.

"Well, it's 'bout time!" Midnight Wolfhart rolled her eyes. Amy saw she was flat on the ground, and just like the ghost had said, she was unharmed.

Amy stood up, and then remembered, *My arm is broken!* But when she looked at it her cast was gone, and she could move her arm around just fine. *Thank goodness!* When Amy looked down at her feet, she saw that her shoes had reappeared!

"Amy!" Reyna exclaimed, "finally! You've been on the ground for *ages.*"

Reyna had already passed the test? Amy looked around to see if the others were there too, but it was just Reyna. The other person that was there was the ghost that had helped Amy. Amy shot her a smile, but the ghost had that same peculiar expression on her face again and was looking at Midnight Wolfhart.

"Well, looking for your *friends,*" Wolfhart said, catching Amy looking around. "You might have gotten off easy by finding this servant's potion." Midnight Wolfhart glared at the girl who cowered, "But the others didn't get so lucky."

An image of Vic running away from something in a dark tunnel appeared in the air. Then an image of Skyler holding a sword as ghosts started closing in on her appeared. Amy and Reyna gasped. Midnight Wolfhart was right about one thing. Vic and Skyler hadn't gotten lucky at all.

Chapter 20

Skyler

The ghosts were good fighters. Skyler? *Definitely* not. As soon as the ghosts started closing in on Skyler, she swung her sword expecting ghosts to disintegrate immediately. But the ghosts had anticipated her move and backed away, spreading out, which made it harder for Skyler to defeat every ghost.

Skyler didn't know how to use a sword. As the seconds passed, the sword became heavier, and heavier in Skyler's hand. *Stupid Ghosts! Why do you make this so hard for me?* Just out of spite, Skyler swung her sword, and it hit the nearest ghost. The ghost disintegrated.

Suddenly, the sword felt like it had gained another pound. But unlike before, it didn't keep getting heavier, it stayed the same. She took another swing, but missed and felt it get heavier. The heavier it got, the more tired she felt. Skyler saw the ghosts snickering and before she knew it she had collapsed, but she was still slightly conscious. She heard the ghosts' airy voices.

"I think she's dead."

"No, I thought I saw her move."

Skyler realized that this was her chance. She laid as still as she could, not daring to move.

"She's dead all right," Skyler heard the leader of the ghosts saying gleefully.

"Now she and her little friends won't be able to go on. They might all just die if she is not going to make it through."

"Yeah, their group is useless unless all of them are there!"

Skyler realized what this meant. Each one of them was special in one way or another. They didn't have a chance if one of them got left behind, or died.

Skyler opened her eyes and saw that all the ghosts were turned with their backs facing her. She sprang up and slashed her sword. All the ghosts disintegrated, screaming for their master's help. Then Skyler realized that the leader was still there, but when he turned around he disintegrated, and was replaced by Midnight Wolfhart. Slowly, Skyler saw the room she had started in fading back. Standing next to Midnight Wolfhart were Reyna and Amy.

"Reyna! Amy! You already made it out?"

"Well there," Midnight Wolfhart said before they had a chance to speak, "looks like you made it out. I suggest you get comfortable because it's going to be a while till your friend, Victoria, gets out—if ever!" she said smirking while pointing to an old broken bench in the corner.

Amy took a seat on the ground and Reyna followed. Skyler started walking there when she realized that she didn't have her sword with her and that she wasn't lightheaded and partly unconscious anymore.

"Skyler! We were so worried!" Reyna said, hugging Skyler.

"Reyna got here first. I got there after her," Amy said. "I think we have a lot to talk about, but we should wait for Vic first."

Midnight Wolfhart waved her hand again to show Vic's image. She was still running down a long tunnel when she reached a door and put her hand on the knob to open it.

Reyna

*V*ic. Why did she have to have the hardest test? Why did she have to come out last? All of a sudden, Reyna thought of something.

"Umm, do you guys remember that Vic really had no fear at all?"

"You're right Reyna, Vic probably didn't get a test at all. In fact, she must just be sitting there, relaxing," Amy said sarcastically. It felt good to hear something to laugh about.

"No, I think what Reyna means is that Vic must have a fear we don't know about." Skyler looked at Reyna and Reyna nodded.

"I dunno. I'm worried about her. What if she doesn't pass?" Amy said.

"I heard something that the ghosts talked about," Skyler said, fiddling with her hair. "They said that if one of us doesn't complete the quest with us, then we all might as well—" Skyler trailed off, clearly not wanting to say what she had heard in the end, "—might as well die," she managed to finish in a whisper.

Reyna would never want Vic to die, just because Vic, Amy, and Skyler were her best friends and like her family. But now, she had another reason for Vic to stay alive. If Vic died, they all might perish along with her, and she might lose everyone she'd ever had by her side.

Chapter 21

Vic

Vic ran out of the tunnel and instead of seeing Midnight Wolfhart like she expected, Vic had arrived in *another* room, facing a woman who looked like Ūnus, except she was much taller and thinner with a chiseled face. *Duo.*

"Hello," Duo said, "you must be Vic. I've heard so much about you from my older sister! Well, aren't you a wonder." Duo, unlike Ūnus, was very energetic and floated around Vic with enthusiasm.

"Are you Duo? Ūnus told me about you," Vic said, cautiously.

"Yes I am, and soon you will be meeting my brother Trēs. But first I have to give you a test."

Vic groaned. Wasn't this already her test? How much did Wolfhart expect?

Duo must have read her mind because she smiled and said, "Don't worry, this is just like a pop quiz to move on to Trēs." She waved her hand and a shooting target appeared. "Take your spear and aim for the bullseye. If you make it, the spear will change to be more useful. Now go ahead, take a shot."

What type of a pop quiz is this? Vic aimed at the center and it ended up right where she had aimed. Vic wasn't surprised. She had always been a good shot.

Duo was right. It had changed. Now, instead of a rusty brown spear with a blunt tip, it was silver with a sharp point. But her shield had changed too. Instead of showing II, it showed III. *Three.* It was time to go to Trēs.

"So, before I bring you to Trēs, I have some advice for you." Duo created two chairs and sat down. Vic did too. "Please listen carefully. Do *not* trust *anybody* except for your friends. Unless you are positive that they can be trusted."

Vic frowned. "Does that mean I can't trust you either?"

"Well, that depends what you feel like," Duo told her. "Just go with your gut."

Vic knew the people she could trust. Her friends, Patricia Mister, Aaron, Nina, and now Ūnus and Duo.

"I know I can trust you," Vic smiled. "And I think I can trust your siblings too."

"I thought you would say that," Duo said. "I think my time is over now. Trēs will—"

Suddenly Duo frowned. Then her eyes widened. "There has been a change of plans," Duo told Vic. "You must stay here." Then Duo disappeared.

Vic groaned. *Just like Ūnus! Does their whole family always disappear?*

Then, Vic saw something out of the corner of her eye that she would never forget. The remains of the monster that Vic had thought was dead was forming into some sort of figure, a tree. No, a human. Wait no, a snake. Then Vic gasped. No! It was a dragon.

It wasn't like the kind you see in movies. Instead it looked like a giant floating serpent. It had a gigantic scaly body that was teal, with bits of dark purple on the tail. It was about twelve feet tall. It had one head with cold, icy blue eyes. Its features were so scary, you couldn't even describe the scariness of it. The dragon also had short little arms with huge claws that were almost as big as Vic's head!

The dragon stared at Vic with its evil eyes, and breathed a huge blast of ice. Vic almost managed to jump out of the way before the ice hit her. She stared at her left shoe which was now covered in ice. She sprang to her feet, careful not slip and put her spear and shield up. But the dragon was heading the wrong way! Instead of coming at her it was moving in the opposite direction. Out of nowhere, the monster melted again!

Vic knew what was going to happen next. The monster would regenerate into something that Vic didn't want to fight. This time the remains were forming quicker. Soon it turned into a huge *raven? This isn't a monster!*

Then the raven screeched. It was so loud Vic thought her eardrums might burst. The force of the wind coming from the raven's beak was powerful enough to push Vic back. Vic crouched down and was surprised to see there was no wind pushing there. *If I could just crawl away from the wind, then I might have a chance to attack from behind!* Vic stayed low to the ground and crawled out of the wind. Silently, but quickly, Vic sneaked to the back of the raven. She aimed the spear at the raven's back and the monster melted *again.*

Vic sighed. *The one time I didn't want the monster to melt it has to!*

Well, not for long. Soon enough the monster reformed into a *ghost. This is going to be easy. How can a ghost be a big threat?*

Unlike the other ghosts Vic had met, this one seemed to be a teenager; thirteen or fourteen maybe? He dressed like the boys from school, wearing a sweatshirt that clearly used to be gray and sweatpants. His bangs were artfully styled. Even though ghosts don't have any color in their body, his hair looked jet black and he had almond-shaped eyes. He reminded her of Aaron

For some reason, this annoyed Vic. This definitely wasn't

her little brother, who laughed and made her happy whenever she heard his voice. This boy looked like a teenager who was a disgusting monster, trying to imitate Aaron. But for some reason, she didn't feel like attacking, she just stood there with her spear raised, standing still.

Vic saw the boy walking in the opposite direction, until he spoke to her. Unlike other monsters, his voice was a real human's voice that didn't sound as harsh as the other monsters' voices.

"No, you *can't* do this! It's evil!" The boy yelled. He was still looking away, so Vic assumed that there must be something suspicious.

A voice scoffed. Surprisingly it was a girl's voice, not some creature's. "Like I care! It was a plane crash wasn't it? We can use that to scare them!"

Vic felt like the girl was talking about her. It was bad enough that her parents died in a plane crash, but it didn't help that she had to be born on 9/11. The day when a terrorist group flew three planes into the Twin Towers and the Pentagon. Because of that Vic always felt unlucky, like she had caused the plane her parents died in to crash.

"NO, NO!" the boy yelled again. "YOU'RE CRAZY! Well, what am I saying? Of course you're—"

"Shut up!" the girl retorted. "No one needs to know about that, especially—*them.*" She said the last word in a snarl.

Know about what? And who are the 'them' she's talking about? Vic saw that the boy was shaking his head in regret.

"I can't believe you're evil!" his voice choked. "After all the things we went through together, the things you did for me, I thought you were good! But *no,* you were just hiding your true colors."

"Well, deal with it!" Vic saw a wisp of dark hair near the boy as if the girl had flipped her hair. She heard footsteps storming off. The boy sank to his knees and buried his face in his hands.

A low hum started and filled the area. A voice deeper than the boy's—deeper than anyone's voice spoke out. "Beware!" The boy's image turned black and disappeared and Vic was left seeing the face of Trēs.

Vic was overwhelmed with thoughts. *I thought I was supposed to find Trēs! And how did he find me? Did I defeat the monster? What if it comes back, like when I thought it was dead!*

"How did you find me?" Vic asked Trēs.

Trēs smiled. " I take it that my sister has already told you about me."

"Umm, yes, both of them," Vic replied.

Trēs laughed at this. "Well, why don't we take a seat." He waved his hand and chairs appeared, pulling Vic into one of them, just like what had happened in her encounter with the first sibling.

"I will only be seeing you for a short while, so I must start our conversation and move you to the twins, four and five. Any questions before we start?" Trēs asked Vic while sitting down in his chair.

"No, not really," Vic said, even though it wasn't true. Questions were spinning in her head. *Where exactly am I? How am I going to get back? Will I ever see my family again?*

"Well then, I am here to warn you about something very easy to be misjudged, but I can not tell you this straightforwardly. However, I can give you a clue. 'When given a choice to believe one or the other, only one will be better, but some may believe both, neither, or another.'" Trēs finished. Vic was puzzled, but somehow, she knew she wouldn't forget this.

"I am sorry, but I cannot give you any further assistance," said the ghost, and with that Trēs waved his hand, and vanished. He disappeared like the ones before, but this time transporting her into a room, facing two people. A young man and woman with almost identical faces, wearing the same type of clothes. Vic looked down at her shield, only to see, IV & V. It was time for her last encounter with the twins, Quattuor and Quinque.

The man and woman swirled around her. "Hello, I'm Quattuor," the man said.

"And I'm Quinque," The woman smiled. "I'm the youngest—by a minute. Just so Quattuor doesn't get the satisfaction of saying he's older and more wise."

Vic was puzzled at how different the twins were from their siblings, they were the most energetic ones she had met so far. Vic had to keep turning around to focus on the twins.

"I wasn't going to say it this time!" Quattuor interrupted.

Quinque looked at her brother as if thinking, *'Yeah right'.*

"Okay, *fine* I was," Quattuor admitted. "But let's get back on topic at hand. After all we don't have much time otherwise—"

"Otherwise what?" Vic asked, her eyes wide. Even though the twins seemed very playful and not at all serious, they were here to help Vic. And that means, the *'otherwise'* would be something that could seriously affect the quest.

"Well, we hadn't planned to tell you, but I guess you have a right to know," Quinque sighed. "We don't have much time otherwise—If Regal Seville finds you before you finish the quest, he has the power and right to petrify you. For life. And destroy all good in the mansion, including us."

"WHAT!" Vic shouted incredulously. "And you weren't going to tell me?"

"Well, Patricia was supposed to tell you sooner or later, I guess we just told you sooner." Quattuor said.

"This is all your fault," Quinque argued. "She wasn't supposed to know this early!"

"My fault?" Quattuor asked incredulously. "You were the one who told her. You could have said we can't and left it be!"

Ugh, they said we can't waste time and now they're arguing instead of 'getting back on topic'!

As the twins argued, Vic thought about something Ūnus had said. Something like, 'Quattuor couldn't go on without his sister'. *Wow. I can really tell.*

"Hold on." Vic interrupted the twin's argument. "Ūnus said that you," Vic pointed to Quattuor, "couldn't go on without Quinque. What did that mean?"

Quattuor smiled sadly. "Well you see, my siblings and I were born in the time when the Roman Empire had just taken over Greece. We had to convert to Latin so that is why our parents covered up our real names with Latin numbers. My parents were still very much Greek, and even after the Romans took over Greece, they always followed Greek customs in secret. We also learned to be Greek in secret because we still had a Greek heritage."

Vic gasped. "You're—3,000 years old!?"

Quattuor smiled. "Yes, around 3,000. You see at the time we lived, a cold could be the death of someone."

"Oh," Vic said, seeing where this was going.

"Quinque had gotten the flu when she was twenty, and in the conditions of our city, Quinque kept getting worse. One day she—passed away."

Quattuor took a breath and continued. "I couldn't bear to live without Quinque and just spent my days mourning. Then because I just sat around mourning in a dusty corner, I also got sick and perished."

"Oh," Vic said, not knowing what to say. Then something occurred to her. "Wait, Regal Seville put the curse on you after you guys passed! Then how did you and your siblings get trapped in Mystery Mansion? I thought only ghosts that were in Colorado were in the Mansion!"

"Well, you see, once a person dies, their ghost roams forever on the earth unless a good ghost dissolves in rain and bad ghosts in basilisk blood," Quinque told Vic. "We had stayed in our hometown until our siblings had become ghosts too. Our parents stayed in Greece wanting to see if the Roman Empire would ever go away, but my siblings and I roamed around the world. Unfortunately, when we came to Colorado, Regal Seville had just put the curse on Mystery Mansion and all of us got trapped in the Mansion. Same with Midnight Wolfhart. She was born in the Medieval ages and came to Colorado, but since she was a bad ghost, Regal Seville made her head of the servants."

"So anyone can be here?" Vic asked. "Even Albert Einstein?"

"Yes," Quattuor answered, "but who is Albert Einstein?"

"Never mind," Vic said.

"Well, we are way behind schedule now, so we must give you the last piece of information before you go." Quinque said hurriedly.

"We are the last to give you information, "Quattuor said. "Our information might not be as important as what our other siblings told you, but it is important for you to know."

"My siblings and I are known as the Omega. We were the first people to be trapped in Mystery Mansion," Quinque said. "We wanted to somehow escape the rule of Regal Seville. That's why we created the quest. For years we planned what we would do, the riddles, and then put our plan into action."

Vic couldn't believe what she was hearing! "You created the quest to stop Regal Seville? And the omega symbol we found in the room— it was you?!"

"Yes. We put up the omega symbol when we want to give a little extra help. Well, not exactly us. But we have our people to do what we need to do since we're locked up. If you hadn't pressed on omega then you wouldn't have found out about Regal Seville. You would have had to find out yourself, which would have made your quest much harder," Quinque explained.

"But Patricia had told us about Regal Seville, like she knew we would find it! If there was a chance that we wouldn't, why did she assume that?" Vic questioned, confused.

"Well," Quattuor said, "Patricia picked you for the quest right?" Vic nodded. "That means anything you do related to your quest, Patricia can see. Does that explain it?"

Vic nodded. "One more question. How were you able to hide all of the clues and make all of the secret compartments when you were stuck here? It seemed like you were trapped in the place Wolfhart created."

The twins nodded. "Yes, we are trapped in here, but back when we were putting the quest into action, nobody knew what we were doing. So thankfully, we weren't trapped until far later," Quinque told her.

Quattuor nodded. "Then Regal Seville found out what we were doing. He couldn't destroy what we had done since we put a protective barrier against everything related to the quest. So, instead Midnight Wolfhart created these places and put each of us in different places."

"Except us of course," Quinque added. "When Midnight Wolfhart was about to separate us, I threatened to destroy Regal Seville since we had found the way to defeat him. Of course, they didn't want that, so my terms were to not separate Quattuor and I."

"Since there are two of us," Quattuor said, "we have an item to give you."

Quinque brought out a sapphire in her hand that definitely hadn't been there before. "This sapphire will let you talk to our siblings and ask us for help. *But* you can only use it four times. Every time you ask for help, a different one of us will come to you in order."

"How is that possible? It just looks like an ordinary sapphire. There is nothing special about it!" Vic said to the twins.

Quinque held out her hand with the sapphire, and Vic saw a *tiny* little symbol engraved on the top and bottom of the circular sapphire. Omega. No wonder it was magical. Vic started to finally put together the mysteries of the quest. She clasped her hand around the gem.

"And that is all the information we have," Quattuor said. "It is now time for you to escape Midnight Wolfhart's test."

The twins said a few words in unison under their breath and a portal appeared in front of her, showing Midnight Wolfhart.

"It is time for you to go back to your quest," Quinque smiled.

Vic took a cautious step then went into the portal, closing her hand tightly around the sapphire. As it whisked her away, she heard Quattuor saying, almost like he was shouting from far away, "I know you will succeed!"

Chapter 22

Amy

Amy paced around impatiently. Unlike Reyna and Skyler, she didn't doubt the fact that Vic would pass, but she was just worried about her best friend. Of course, all three of them were her best friends, but if she had to choose her tiers of trust, it would be Vic at the top, then Reyna and Skyler next. Sometimes she even doubted where her parents would be on the tiers if they were still alive.

As time passed, Amy watched Midnight Wolfhart become more and more confident that Vic wouldn't pass, while they become more and more restless. Suddenly, a portal appeared out of nowhere and Vic crashed through and collapsed. After a few seconds, she shook her head as if she was trying to regain her thoughts.

"VIC!" they all shouted, barely before she made it through the door.

Amy ran up to Vic and hugged her. The look on Vic's face was enough to make Amy stifle a laugh, but it made sense. Even Amy was surprised she had hugged someone. She hated hugging people. It just made her feel weird. If you were to rank who was the most emotional of the four, Amy would come in dead last. Reyna would be first *of course*.

Vic still had the astonished look on his face. "For the first time you actually—"

"For the first time and the *only* time!" Amy interrupted her, then punched her arm.

"Ow!" Vic exclaimed, rubbing her arm. "What was that for!"

Skyler and Reyna both ran up now. "You scared us!" Skyler was exasperated.

"Yeah! You took two whole days!" Reyna exclaimed. "What happened?"

Vic looked extremely confused. "What do you mean I took two days?"

"You didn't know?" Skyler exclaimed, surprised. "You would surely be able to notice two days passing!"

Vic still had a confused expression on her face. "But it felt like only an hour had passed! And that's the most amount of time that could have!"

Midnight Wolfhart chuckled. "You don't really think all of your tests could have been passed in an hour, did you? It took all of you *three days* to finish your tests."

What! This is crazy!

The ghost girl who had escaped with Amy spoke up. " I knew something like this would happen. Midnight Wolfhart's tests always trick people."

Amy looked at Vic, who seemed to be staring intently at the girl from Amy's test. "Who is she, and how did you meet her?" Vic asked

Oh, I haven't told Vic about her yet!

But it seemed like no one else had heard. When Amy opened her mouth to introduce Vic to the ghost, Wolfhart interrupted her. "You of all people should know that." Midnight Wolfhart said, going back to the girl's comment. "I tricked you so many times and you still didn't have a clue when I tricked you today! I was going to trap you in there and you would have never found the potion. But then *Amy* came and she found it for you." Wolfhart glared at Amy. "But since you did make it out, you can have your brother back."

"Wait—so that was my test?" the girl asked. "I really passed?"

"Unfortunately, yes," Midnight Wolfhart sighed. She muttered something under her breath and a portal appeared. A boy who had the same jet back hair and looked like the girl except for his clothes, walked out of the portal. He looked at his sister for a moment and he almost looked ashamed for a second. Then it vanished and the expression morphed into joy.

"You got me out!" He floated over to his sister. "I can't believe I'm finally free!" He made his voice sound mockingly happy, maybe to annoy Midnight Wolfhart, who rolled her eyes and looked extremely disappointed.

Amy looked over at Vic and saw she was clutching something bright blue. *That's weird. Vic didn't have that before!* But the expression on Vic's face was enough to make those thoughts disappear. It looked like Vic had just seen pigs fly! Vic's jaw had dropped to a point where it seemed like she was doing it consciously.

"Let's back up," Vic said, "Who are you two?" she asked.

"Well they are—" Amy stopped in the middle of her introduction. "Well actually, I don't know your names! What are they?"

The boy turned to face his sister. "Wedinthin—" he muttered, or at least that's what it sounded like.

The girl muttered something back that sounded like, "Yeswidi!"

"Umm, your names are—Wedi what?" Amy said, causing the twins to look at her.

The girl chuckled. "No, you must have misheard. Anyway, our parents were um, interesting, so they gave us really weird names. But we didn't like those names so we gave each other nicknames. His nickname is We and mine is Yes."

Yes and We? Kind of weird nicknames if you ask me!

We rolled his eyes. "We," he muttered under his breath.

"What are your names?" Yes asked curiously.

"I'm Amy, as you already know," Amy said, nodding towards Yes.

"I'm Skyler," Skyler said.

"I'm—" Reyna started to say but got interrupted by Yes.

"Oh yeah, I remember hearing your names!" Yes exclaimed. "You're Reyna, and you must be Vicky!" She pointed to Vic.

Vic glared at Yes. "It's *Vic,*" she said in a cold, sharp manner.

Amy knew that Vic didn't like being called anything else other than Vic. Especially Vicky, but that didn't mean she had to be so rude to Yes! We, on the other hand, seemed kind of suspicious.

Yes nodded in a friendly way. "Oh I'm sorry Vic. I remember now that you don't like to be called Vicky or Victoria."

There seemed to be a hidden clue in what Yes said, but Amy was too preoccupied by Vic's harsh tone that she didn't catch it. Vic still was glaring at Yes even though she had corrected herself. It was very unlike Vic! But on the other hand, while Amy didn't like being around We, Vic was okay with him, and not her usual sharp self that took a while to trust others. Amy brushed away the thought since they had a more important question to ask.

Amy turned to Midnight Wolfhart who looked almost bored during their conversation. "Well, we did what you asked us to do," Amy told Wolfhart. "So now tell us where Regal Seville is!"

Midnight Wolfhart raised one eyebrow. "Why should I tell you where Regal Seville is after *you* tricked me."

"W-what?" Amy stuttered anxiously. Did Wolfhart know what their secret was? "What d-do you mean?"

"Oh don't act ignorant!" Wolfhart snapped in her Southern accent. "I had known you were questers ever since

I looked at your tests. Normal servants just get tested on doin' chores and housework. But y'all got tested with your greatest fears. And you, Victoria, you met *them* and that's how I knew immediately. Be grateful I'm not imprisoning you right away." And with that Midnight Wolfhart started to disappear, but then she stopped to hear the voice of a lady who sounded old and tattered, but when they all heard the voice, Vic seemed to recognize it.

"Now now Midnight Wolfhart, these girls passed your test and they deserve an answer. That's why *I'm* giving it to them." The voice took a pause. "The answer that you want could be right in front of you. If you search hard enough you will see the answer too. But since that's the hardest to find I will give you another chance. You will find Regal Seville with a potion, but if you do it incorrectly you might end up in a trance." Then Midnight Wolfhart disappeared fully.

Chapter 23

Skyler

Skyler immediately, with her favorite pen and notepad that she always carried in her pocket, started to write down the clue or riddle or whatever the voice had told them.

The answer could be right in front of you. If you search you'll see the answer. But that's the hardest to find so I give you another chance. You will find Regal Seville with a potion, but if you do it incorrectly you might end up in a trance.

Does that mean we can find him with a potion? But what does it mean by: "The answer could be right in front of you"?

The room was so quiet you could hear a pin drop. Skyler waited for a little bit until she decided Midnight Wolfhart was truly gone, and it was safe to talk. But talking out loud made Skyler feel uneasy so she whispered, "I guess we're going to have a lot to talk about later."

"Definitely, but first thing's first, let's get outta here!" Amy said, like she had been holding her breath for a long time. Or maybe she had been.

"I second that," Vic said. "Let's meet up in our room. *In private.*"

"Yeah, what time do you think it is right now? I don't think there's a clock in here," Reyna said.

Suddenly, We spoke up. "It's about five in the afternoon," he said.

Oh right, We and Yes are still there!

"Looks like there is a clock in here after all," Vic joked, winking at Reyna who smiled back while mouthing, *Let's get out of here, now!*

It was weird of Reyna to act that way. She was shy whenever she met new people, but never wanted to get away from them! And plus, We and Yes seemed trustworthy. There was no reason to be skeptical of them.

Yes laughed and said, "Well, I guess we should leave you alone for a while to talk, but let me tell you why we came here in the first place," she smiled charmingly. "We're here to help you on your quest. We will be in the dining hall for breakfast tomorrow at 7:00."

"Okay, bye. See you then." Vic motioned for them to leave and shut the door. Hard.

"Lets go," Amy said, having a silent agreement with Vic.

They walked through hallways, passages, corridors, and whatnot, then finally made it to their room, where they were met by Nina and Aaron.

"YOU'RE HERE!" Aaron said, throwing himself on to Vic.

"Finally! We were *so* worried!" Nina said, hugging them.

"What can we say? We thought we only took like two hours!" Skyler explained.

She watched Amy create a big show of collapsing on her bed. "Yeah, we're completely exhausted," Amy said, barely keeping her eyes open. Or at least *pretending* to be that tired.

"You're right. You guys sleep through dinner. Aaron and I will leave you here and help Patricia in the kitchen. We're making fresh soup, spaghetti and meatballs, and chocolate cake," Nina told the group.

Amy's face lit up as she quickly sat up. She loved chocolate cake and spaghetti. And soup. Pretty much any type of food in general!

"Well that woke someone up!" Nina teased Amy.

"Ha, I doubt the chocolate cake will last long with Aaron in the kitchen." Vic eyed Aaron suspiciously, smiling slyly. "He used to have a sweet tooth when he was just one year old!"

"HEY!" Aaron whined, while Skyler and the others laughed.

"Rest for at least an hour, and we'll bring dinner whenever—" Nina started to say in a motherly fashion, but got interrupted by Aaron.

"No, we have many customers and a busy schedule, we cannot change it. Dinner will be served at 7:00 p.m. sharp. You better be at the dining table by then." Aaron bowed and stuck his tongue out at Vic before walking out with Nina as she shook her head smiling. Vic rolled her eyes.

"He thinks he's *soooo* cool," Vic said, bringing another round of smiles and laughs.

"Hey, it could have been worse," Amy grinned. "At least you didn't have to go through his jokes the past couple of years!" Amy smiled again but this time it almost seemed— sad? Vic also had the same smile.

Amy bit her lip and her eyes lost her sparkle. Basically, she put on her serious/worried face. "So Vic, I was wondering, who are the *them* Midnight Wolfhart was talking about?"

"Can we talk about this later? How about tonight, when everyone else is sleeping, and it's safe to talk?" Vic had an excellent poker face; sometimes no one seemed to ever know what she was feeling through her face. But her eyes gave it all away. Her eyes almost seemed to be *begging* Amy, which was something Skyler had never seen Vic do.

Amy *and* Reyna groaned. "Fine," they said in unison.

"We probably have to go down to the dining room anyway," Amy admitted, looking at an alarm clock. "It's

6:40 and we have to go earlier if we want to find the room
and not get lost."

Skyler snorted. "You know Aaron was just joking around,
right? We rest for a little and wait for them to bring dinner."

"What!" Amy exclaimed incredulously. "You want to *rest!*
We're questers, we don't have time to rest!" She pulled Skyler
out of bed.

Well, there's no arguing with her now!

"*Ugh,* fine." Vic got up and Reyna did too. "But just so
you know, we're not questing now. We're just eating dinner!"

Amy just rolled her eyes, smiling, and walked over to the
door. Skyler shot a glance at the others who shrugged, as if
saying, *Well, we have no choice.*

After all of them got their shoes on, they headed towards
the dining hall. The Mansion was literally a maze and like
Amy said, it took them a *long* time. After a lot of arguing,
guessing, and going through weird passages, they went
through a door next to their room. After wandering in a
circle, that passage became smaller and smaller, and became
steeper and steeper downhill. Finally the passage came to a
stop and the ground became flat. Skyler stood up and saw
there was a trapdoor above their heads.

"Hey guys!" Skyler exclaimed. "I think we finally found
the exit!" She opened the trapdoor, and one by one the girls
pulled themselves out.

They found themselves under a table! They crawled out
and saw themselves in the dining room!

"Finally!" Reyna exclaimed as the girls got up. "We made
it!"

At that moment, Aaron and Nina came in holding trays
of food. "I take it that you guys took the crawling passage."
Nina laughed, looking at the dust on their knees.

"Yeah," Skyler admitted. "We kind of got lost and this
was the only passage we could find!"

"Well it's a good thing you came," Nina told them, "because there's someone waiting for you."

The girls spun around and saw Patricia waiting for them at the dining table. "Hello my girls," she softly spoke. "We have much to talk about."

Chapter 24

Reyna

"We're really glad to see you," Reyna smiled, sitting down in a chair as the girls followed. "We have to talk too."

Patricia seemed to be gathering her thoughts as the others impatiently waited for an answer. Nina and Aaron had brought the soup and the girls had already finished half of it when Patricia finally answered.

"Well, we need to talk about Regal Seville," Patricia started. She waved her hands and squeezed them tight. When she opened them up, a ghostly replica of the soup in the same bowl the girls had appeared. She took a long sip of it, then exhaled.

So that's how ghosts eat!

"I know I had told you that you had to find Regal Seville, and you dears, took that the wrong way. Though to accomplish your quest you must find Regal Seville, you don't have to find him immediately. Just follow the directions you have seen or *heard.*"

Amy nodded. "Yeah, I was thinking about that! Pretty sure the others were too."

Patricia's eyes twinkled. "Now moving on, I have something else to tell you. Though you have successfully finished the first part of your quest much quicker than any others, the next part will be much harder. It will involve more physical challenges and you have to use your intelligence every step of the way."

Reyna wondered if the 'any others' were some of the questers before them. But what could have happened to the others? Surely they would have passed, and if they didn't— where were they?

"What do you mean by 'more physical challenges'? I mean the quest has already been pretty physical. How much worse can it get?" Vic asked. She seemed to have a lot on her mind.

"Ah, that you will have to figure out on your own, but what I will tell you is that this will be where you find your physical *strengths.*" Patricia looked at each one of them.

So we're going to find our strengths. But how? And when?

"Now girls, I know you have a long night ahead of you." She paused, looking pointedly at the girls for enough time to make them realize Patricia was talking about them sharing their information tonight. "So now I must say, good luck girls. Remember to eat enough—you will have a hard task in front of you. I know you'll make it through the quest."

Her last words rung in Reyna's ears, long after she disappeared. It felt good to know that Patricia was rooting for them—not that Reyna ever doubted it. Though there was one thing that made her feel uneasy. How come Patricia seemed to know everything that was happening in their quest even when they hadn't told her, but never asked about Yes and We? It just proved her suspicion against the twins. Unlike the others, Reyna just felt like the twins were extremely untrustworthy. Skyler didn't seem to have the same feelings as Reyna, and if Amy did, she sure didn't show it. Vic meanwhile, seemed to not trust them. Reyna couldn't tell if that was just her imagination—or if it was true that Vic didn't trust them or one of the twins.

Nina walked in with Aaron, bringing a large bowl and

plates. Aaron brought in a domed platter. Nina raised her eyebrows at the girls' faces, which must have shown a lot of confused emotions. Being an artist, Nina could always find the small details in objects and people. "Well, that must have been an interesting conversation!" she exclaimed, most likely trying to lighten the mood.

"Sure was," Reyna muttered out of the corner of her mouth, expecting no one to hear it. Of course, everyone did.

Chapter 25

Vic

Why do I trust this shady boy over a charming girl who seems innocent?

Vic knew Yes wasn't innocent though. Something made her think that. As soon as she saw Yes she just knew something wasn't right. Even her features seemed too perfect, it just wasn't right! After her test, she wanted to spill everything to the others, but she felt like telling them in front of Yes wasn't right. She knew she had to wait till the nighttime to tell Reyna, Amy, and Skyler everything she had heard from the Omega.

"Which way? Right, no, *left.*" Skyler looked around as they tried to find their way back to their room.

"You're just confusing all of us, Skyler. I don't think we'll ever find our way. It's like the mansion changed while we were eating dinner," Reyna said.

"Hey Vic, why are you so quiet? You haven't said anything for the past half hour. Something up?" Amy questioned.

"Nothing is 'up'. I'm just thinking about stuff," Vic said. "Come on, the sooner we get to the room, the sooner we can talk."

"Umm Vic, if you haven't noticed, we're lost." Reyna looked at Vic.

"No, we aren't. The room is right there!" Vic led them down a hallway straight to the room, not hesitating a bit. This surprised Vic herself. She had the same feeling she'd had when she first entered her test. A feeling that she knew what was where.

"How'd you just do that?" Amy asked, wide-eyed.

"Yeah, that would have been more useful just about *half an hour ago!*" Skyler said, opening the door.

"Okay, that was once. I probably won't be able to do that again!" Vic smiled, feeling pretty pleased with herself.

"What took you so long? We already went to sleep!" Nina said groggily.

"Sorry to wake you. We'll just change and head to sleep, but how did you guys get here so fast?" Reyna asked

"You know that if you take that passage, it will take you to where you want to go, right?

"Ughh. Thanks for telling us now, Nina." Reyna collapsed on her bed with Nina.

"You're welcome," Nina went back to sleep.

Good, now we can talk since everyone else is asleep. Everyone else must probably be thinking the same, Vic realized, as she met eyes with them.

Vic went to her bathroom and changed into her electric blue pajamas—*ugh*—then sat on her bed and waited for the others.

"Hey, Vic," someone whispered, making Vic jump. She realized that Aaron was there too, tucked in bed, probably waiting for Vic.

"Vic, do you have your harmonica?" Aaron whispered. When Aaron said that, Vic realized they had almost left all their belongings on the cliff trail! But her harmonica was still in her pocket. It moved from her old jeans, to the blue pants, to the pajamas she was wearing now.

Vic nodded and brought it out to play something, so he

would sleep. After she was done, she checked to make sure he was asleep, then asked Amy if they could use her bed.

"Sure." Amy lifted the comforter over their heads, creating a tent, then beckoned Reyna and Skyler to join them, grabbing a flashlight she had found in a drawer.

"Smart," Skyler smirked as she walked over.

"For once," Reyna added, as Amy pouted.

Vic laughed and turned to ask Reyna to start talking about her test. Reyna took a deep breath and started. She talked about her initial encounter with the creatures, including a snake, then a chasm appeared, and Reyna jumped in it. "I had picked up a dagger, but there was something weird about it, when I dropped it, it made the omega symbol— and that's what caused the chasm to form." Reyna then explained how she had found a potion, and a boat, and had to row across a pool, no, a sea of ink.

"The potion was probably the reason I passed the test," Reyna finished.

"Same," Amy interrupted, clearly looking the most serious Vic had ever seen her. "My test started differently though." Amy started speaking, explaining about her going through three different experiences in her test—all of them relating to her fear of heights. "Just before I got transported, I met Yes. Then afterward I found Yes' potion that lets her go back to Wolfhart. She let me use it too. When I met Yes, she said that she was 'glad to see us,' because we're doing this quest," Amy said, looking directly at Skyler, when Vic realized she was writing everything down.

Vic thought it was kind of fishy that Yes knew about their quest already. Did that mean Yes could have been spying on them?

Reyna stifled a laugh. "You should have seen the way they came. Amy was lying on the ground for literally five minutes!"

The other girls smiled. "Well my test definitely wasn't as dramatic as Amy's!" Skyler exclaimed sarcastically. She told about seeing ghosts that wanted to kill her and remembering how basilisk's blood destroys ghosts. Then she got transported back to when they were fighting the basilisk and collected the blood there. "The sword kept getting heavier and heavier when I had to fight the ghosts. But luckily when I collapsed from the weight of the sword, the ghosts thought I was dead and I got a chance to defeat them. Then after that I came back to Wolfhart."

Skyler didn't write anything in the notebook this time. She probably already had.

"I guess it's my turn," Vic said. The others looked at her, eagerly. *Well, here it goes.* She saw Skyler holding her pen ready.

"Wait, hold on Vic. First tell us, what is your, um, fear? None of us know!" Reyna looked demandingly at Vic.

"Well, I guess I didn't know myself! I mean, it's basically, not knowing what's going to happen, what I'll have to face." Everyone looked at her, shocked. Vic started telling them about being put in a room, and her picking up her weapons, and entering into the room, where she met Ūnus. Then about the monster, the other siblings—Duo, Trēs, Quattuor, and, Quinque—and finally, the Omega and the communication sapphire.

"That's why we keep seeing omega symbols, like Reyna's dagger, that compartment by the bookshelf. Oh and also our parents, they're here in Mystery Mansion!"

"O-our parents?" Reyna's voice cracked. "They really are here?"

Suddenly the room started to shake. Vic, through the covers, saw the omega symbol shining with a bright green light and the room starting to expand. The furniture in the room also started to change, but they couldn't see the

changes well with just a flashlight. The beds also started
to move and shift. Now instead of six twin beds pushed
together to make three, there were six full beds lined up
side by side, each one a different color. The girls found
themselves each on a different bed. *Ugh, not the color
thing again.*

"Come on, not the colors again! 'Least now we get bigger
beds!" Amy said, waving the flashlight around. Vic really
felt like Amy could read her mind now. Aaron and Nina
were still in a deep sleep so they hadn't noticed the changes.

"Seriously, why does everything have to match?" Skyler
rolled her eyes, pointing to her pink and yellow polka-dot
pajamas and the pink and yellow bedspread.

Though it seemed as though Vic's comment hadn't
affected anything, there was tension between the girls. Vic
knew it was about their parents—after all, knowing that the
parents that you barely remembered are in the same place
as you would be a big shocker.

"True," Vic agreed referring to Skyler's previous comment.
"Anyway, I told you my story so I think we should all get
some sleep," Vic said, but after she laid down, she couldn't
fall asleep. Vic soon realized that she was the only one awake.
Things were spinning in her head. Finally she decided to
walk outside the room. Vic knew it could be dangerous,
but she needed to clear her head.

Near the door, there were six pairs of fuzzy slippers. Vic
slipped on the ones that looked the most blue in the dark
and opened the door a crack. The coast was clear. Trying
not to make a sound, Vic squeezed through the doorway
and walked out. She took a deep breath, closing her eyes.

"What're *you* doing?" asked a boy's voice. His voice had a
tinge of sarcasm as if he was regularly sarcastic, but it also
had a melodic curl to his words. It seemed quite familiar.

Vic opened her eyes and jumped back. Standing in front

of her was We, crossing his arms with a "stern and gruff" expression on his face.

"First of all, why do you care? And second of all, why are *you* here?" Vic asked, crossing her arms too.

"I don't really care, but *you* know that it's dangerous to be outside."

"Okay, *fine*. But you still haven't answered my last question."

"Ughhh!" We groaned and ran his fingers through his hair—just as the boys did at Cristobal Academy. *"Look,* I actually came here to talk to you because I know you saw that projection of Hy—*Yes* and I."

Wait, he knew that I had seen the projection of him and Yes? But, how? Unless—Wolfhart told them, but that could mean We is bad! And how come he started to say 'Hy' instead of Yes?

"And—" Vic said, beckoning him to continue.

"And, I don't want you—you four—to lead on the wrong side."

"Meaning—" Again, Vic beckoned for him to continue. *Sheesh, this guy sure doesn't know how to complete what he's saying!*

"Meaning—well, it's hard to say, but Yes is bad, evil, you might say. And that means, well there aren't exactly sides, but I'm trying to help you." We looked down disappointedly, clearly not proud of his word usage.

"And why I should believe *you?"* Vic asked, skeptical.

"Jeez! Why are you like, shooting arrows at me?" he asked, removing his *'stern and gruff'* facade. Maybe he *was* just trying to help.

"I don't shoot arrow! *Amy* does." Vic paused. We rolled his eyes but he stood still. "Look," Vic softened, "it's not like we came here on vacation. We just found out our parents are here after living with someone we thought was a madman, who turned out to just be depressed, and now I have to decide if I can trust you. If you haven't noticed, it's a lot to

take in." As soon as Vic said that, Duo's words rang in her ears. *"Do not trust anybody except for your friends. Unless you are positive that they can be trusted."*

"I understand, I mean, I really do. I've had a whole lot of issues with my parents myself. But that's a story for another time," We said urgently as if trying to cover up a mistake.

Curiosity hit Vic again. *We's parents— who are they? What's his past?* "I— better go to sleep now."

"Okay, but one thing," We said, running his fingers through his hair again. *Ugh, he really has a bad habit of doing that.* "Mind, um, keeping this conversation a secret? Like not tell anyone, not spread the word?" Now that hit Vic like an arrow. How could she not tell the others? She hadn't kept anything important from any of them before. *Ever.* And she wasn't going to let this boy tell her what to do.

"Okay, but don't blame me if it slips," Vic said casually. "Oh, and I know what a secret is." Vic rolled her eyes, as she closed the door to her room behind her back. *I didn't think that would get more complicated than it was.*

But We stuck his foot in the doorway just before it closed. "I know you're gonna tell your friends and you have every right to since I didn't make you promise on an unbreakable promise."—*There was such a thing as an unbreakable promise?*—We ran his fingers through his hair again. "But I've spelled you already so you can't tell the others."

Vic groaned and again tried to close the door softly when a thought occurred to her. "Wait," she whispered so the other girls wouldn't hear. "You stopped the door with your foot!"

We turned around and put his hand out as if to say, *seriously.* "Uh, yeah!"

"What I mean is I thought ghosts floated through everything!"

Now it was We's turn to roll his eyes. "Ghosts can only pass through *humans.* We can spell ourselves to go through walls, but we can touch any inanimate object. Haven't you seen other ghosts doing that?"

Vic realized We was right! They had seen Patricia sit down on a couch and chairs! "It's just that I never thought you could do magic."

"Why's that? Did you think that 'only old ghosts can do magic'?" We asked, almost accusatory.

"No, I just thought you were too dumb to be able to do it." Vic smiled, then opened the door again—it had closed automatically—happy that she had the last say. As she turned around to close it fully, Vic thought she saw We smiling too.

Chapter 26

Amy

Amy could hear Vic climbing into bed and hoped Vic wouldn't notice she was awake. Amy had known Vic long enough that she knew Vic never kept important secrets from them. So Amy wouldn't even bother to ask Vic about her 'night walk'.

Amy laid in bed closing her eyes, though she was awake for the whole night. *Hopefully the others will be awake soon.*

Sure enough a yawn came, "Looks like 'once an early bird, always an early bird'." Skyler groggily teased Vic, who had probably already gotten up, not making a noise.

"Old habits die hard," Vic said. "We should wake the others up."

"No need," Reyna yawned, her bed creaking while she sat up.

"Mhmm, *totally*. Look at Amy!" Skyler said. Amy had been pretending to sleep since she didn't want the others to know she hadn't gotten a wink of sleep. But now she had something up her sleeves.

Amy quickly sat up, raising her eyebrows and smiling. "Actually, I think you were wrong this time!" Skyler scowled. She was usually the least gullible.

"Shut up," Skyler said jokingly. "Anyway, let's get ready. We overslept and the twins will be here to pick us up soon."

Oh yeah! We have to meet Yes and—ugh—We in the dining hall.

The girls sleepily got up—well, Vic wasn't sleepy— and went to their bathrooms.

As Amy went into her bathroom, she remembered something. The box with the riddles and clues, and the potion that Patricia gave them! Amy stepped outside and scanned the room. When she looked up, she saw the box on a bookshelf, and breathed a sigh of relief. But the potion—where was that? Then suddenly she felt something heavy in her pajama pocket. Amy reached inside and to her surprise pulled out the potion! *Well at least I found it! Even if it was kind of weird how it traveled. I guess I probably shouldn't be too surprised though considering how many weird things I've been through.*

Amy quickly walked to the box and placed the potion in the bottle shaped compartment. The compartment was a little bigger than the potion, and more oddly shaped, but Amy didn't think twice.

Amy walked back to the bathroom and saw that this time the clothes weren't all the same color! The bathroom was still all red—even the shampoo, sink, toilet paper, etc.—but now the clothes were more like the ones the would wear everyday! There was a black athletic tank top, gray gym pants with a white stripe running down the side, and regular socks and, er, undergarments.

After Amy got ready she saw that Skyler was already out. Vic and Reyna came out last, both from Vic's bathroom. Just like Amy, they were wearing their regular types of clothes. Vic had on a tank top like Amy's, though she usually didn't wear a tank top, and black leggings that were a high rise. But there was something extra that Amy just noticed. Instead of Vic's hair hanging down, it was pulled into a French braid with some messy strands hanging out, obviously the

work of Reyna. Reyna herself was wearing light washed
jeans, a lavender t-shirt, and earrings. She had her hair in
her signature fishtail braids. Skyler had on an olive-green
V-neck shirt, white shorts with lace, and green gem studs.
Her hair was pulled into a high ponytail. All of them were
wearing socks. Skyler was carrying the box. Amy's eyes kept
wandering back to Vic's hair. For some reason, it almost
seemed like the real Vic had just come out of a shell.

"Hey Amy," Skyler exclaimed, "did you put the potion
in the box?"

"Yeah," Amy answered, "I thought we should keep it in
a safe place."

"Okay. Also, we decided to bring the box along since it
has the jewels and riddles which are probably going to be
important. Anyway, c'mon let's go!"

Vic was frowning at her top. "Hey guys, I forgot something. I'll be right back." Vic jogged back to the bathroom.
Amy looked at the others who gave her a puzzled expression.

Vic came outside, now wearing an overly large, gray
sweatshirt with thumb holes. There was also something
blue peeking out—probably the sapphire Vic had told them
about. Amy groaned. "Seriously Vic? It's summer!"

"I know but it's cold!" she said, as if that was a good
explanation.

"You think everything's cold!" Amy, Skyler, and Reyna
exclaimed in unison.

The girls laughed and left the room. Outside they found
four pairs of shoes that were also not just one solid color
and one type of shoe. The girls each headed to a pair of
shoes and put them on. Amy wore red tennis shoes, just
what she would have wanted. Amy looked around and saw
Reyna wearing black canvas sneakers, Skyler wearing socks
and sandals.

"Seriously Skyler? Socks and sandals?" Amy exclaimed.

"They're in high fashion!" Skyler retorted.

"Yeah, in France!" Amy said, causing the girls to laugh.

Amy looked at Vic and she was wearing—socks? Vic was just staring at one pair of boots. They were black, knee-high boots with *heels*. No wonder Vic hadn't worn them!

"I'm *not* wearing that," Vic said, clearly not changing her opinion.

"C'mon Vic, just put them on! They won't bite!" Skyler put a hand on her hip.

"Not happening, besides, I'll be like a foot taller that all of you," Vic said stubbornly.

"You're already taller than most of us anyway. If you'd rather be wearing socks, then let's get moving!" Amy's impatience was really getting to her. "Oh look! Yes, oh and We are here!"

"Hey guys! Ready?" Yes asked smiling.

"Yeah, but only if Vic would put on her shoes. She's as stubborn as a mule!"

We eyed the high-heeled black boots, and snickered.

Vic groaned. *"Fine!"* She put them on and tried to stand up, but she could barely stand without falling. Skyler had to help her up over five times.

"Vic, the heel is going to—"

"Snap!"

"Break."

Amy looked at the left boot which was now heel-less.

"Works for me!" Vic exclaimed. She kneeled on the ground and broke off the other heel too.

"Great! Now can we get moving?" Skyler asked, clearly annoyed.

Everyone walking sounded like a stampede of elephants., Amy was surprised to see, or hear, that Vic's boots, unlike the others' footwear, didn't make that clicking sound. Instead they were completely silent; and Vic was surprisingly comfortable now that she had gotten used to them. Amy's shoes, on the other hand, seemed to catch the light on the sides of the shoes and reflected it. *Maybe a good distraction for monsters or something?*

Amy noticed that Vic kept on glaring at her sweatshirt. She wondered why, until she noticed We was wearing the exact same one!

Amy leaned to Vic and teased, "Looks like someone's *twinning.*"

"Oh shut up," Vic hissed. "That's why I didn't want to wear this!"

"But you had to otherwise you'd be *cold,*" Amy snickered.

Vic rolled her eyes.

As they entered the dining hall, Amy noticed something different. This time Patricia wasn't there! It was weird since Yes and We came to help on their quest and Patricia was also their quest helper, more like manager. Aaron and Nina were already there. As usual they were already eating. There was a stack of plates, bowls, and cutlery: and laid on the table were platters of pancakes, bowls of scrambled eggs, boxes of cereal, cartons of milk, and baskets of muffins and bacon. Amy's stomach growled. *Mmmm, foooood.*

"Hi Nina! Hey Aaron!" Reyna walked over to them and gave Nina a hug as Vic ruffled Aaron's hair.

Yes pushed her glasses back. "Well anyway, why don't we start eating and you can tell us anything you need to for us to help you on your quest!"

They sat down and started eating their food as We and Yes made their own, just like Patricia had done.

"So, what do you want us to help you with? Anything in particular?" Yes asked, eyeing Vic.

"Actually, we would like to know what *you* want to help us with," Vic challenged.

"We want to be useful for once is what she means." We

spoke up, surprising everyone, except Vic. *Weird, Vic never seems surprised by what We does. I wonder if she really trusts him that much.* Amy's mind wandered. Amy had her reasons not to trust We. He never talked and came randomly into conversations. Plus he seemed so surly. Nothing good could come out of that. Yes, meanwhile, was kind, nice, and had helped Amy pass her test. She had to be trustworthy!

"We were told that if questers met us, we would be obliged to join their quest. Even if they didn't want us to help. And we died so early—Just when we turned thirteen, fifteen years ago. We aren't aging so we're still thirteen and we'll always be thirteen. We felt like if we didn't accomplish anything, we would be useless." We spoke a mourning tone. Now he just seemed *sad* and innocent. But as Skyler would say, don't judge a book by its cover!

Skyler looked apologetically at We and Yes. "I'm sorry to hear you died on your birthday of all days. And we do want you to help. Vic here," Skyler glared at Vic, "can have a hard time trusting people. Don't mind her."

Vic glared back.

"Well it was for a good cause. You need to loosen up, Vic!" Skyler whispered back.

We snickered *again*. Vic glared at him too. Maybe she *didn't* trust him.

"Anyway," Skyler started, smiling at We and Yes, "I brought this box that carries all of the things we have found during our quest."

Skyler told them about the box, the previous riddles, the jewels, the potion they got from Patricia, and the Omega.

Reyna took the riddle from the box and showed it to We and Yes. "This is the last riddle we got. It says, 'Find a ghost, beware the bad. Find a maze, beware the quest has only begun. We thought 'find a ghost' meant to find Regal Seville. That's why we went to Midnight Wolfhart."

"Yeah," Vic jumped in. "But since we heard the voice telling us that we could find him with a potion later, we realized he wasn't the ghost. Maybe the riddle meant the Omega, or you." Amy noticed Vic only looked at We when she said this. We's face became a tint darker. Was he—blushing? Amy rolled her eyes. He wasn't *that* important.

"So anyway," Amy also started talking, "the next step for us is to find a maze. Since we found jewels with the riddles, I think that might be connected to finding the maze. So we should probably split up into groups of two to find anything."

Everyone agreed. They all finished eating and got up from the table and said bye to Aaron and Nina, who went back to the kitchen.

"I wanted to ask, who should take the box? Since we're splitting up, someone needs to take it, but if the person who doesn't have the box finds a lead, then how do we get it into the box *and* contact everyone else?" Reyna pondered.

"Well, I think I have a solution," We said. He squeezed his hands together and six wristbands appeared cupped in his hand. Unlike the food that ghosts make this wasn't a ghostly substance. From what Amy saw, it was something like a smart band. "My magic creates the most up to date items and what the recipient will most like. So take the band that you think is for you."

Amy rolled her eyes. *Could you sound less like an egotistical spokesperson?*

Each of the bands were different, but with the same model and design. There was one that was red with mini soccer balls on the ends. Of course, Amy grabbed that first. There was a blue one with music notes on it, an ombré pink and yellow one with glitter, one with a splatter painted case, one with a dark purple and black band with pop-up lightning bolts, and a gray band with a moon and music notes flying out of it. *Well this should be easy!*

Of course, Reyna took the one with the paint, Skyler took the pink and yellow one, Vic took the one with music notes. To Amy's surprise, though, Yes's was the purple and black one. Amy always thought she seemed like the type to have neon pink since she was so cheerful. And We took the one with the moon and music notes.

Music. Figures. There had to be a reason that Vic got along with We.

"You should be able to call on this so when you want us to come, you can call," We said, then tapped on the black button twice to show them what would happen. When he did that, a giant projection appeared with three options that said call, video call, and text. We pressed on call and Amy saw a list of all their names. We pressed Yes and Yes's band started to ring. "See?"

"Okay, wow," Reyna said. She was right. The highest technology the girls had ever used was the broken microwave back at Mr. Misters house.

"Well, since we have that worked out," Skyler fiddled with her wristband, "I'll keep the box. No offense to you guys, but I've always been the most responsible one."

Reyna shrugged. "That's true. So anyway, we can split up like usual, and Yes and We can—"

"Actually Reyna," Amy interrupted, "since we're the questers, it would be better if I went with Yes , you with Skyler, and Vic with, um, We."

Vic had an expression as if she were thinking, *I should've known.* "Well what're we waiting for? Let's go."

Chapter 27

Skyler

Skyler headed with Reyna down a corridor they had never been in. She tugged at her band nervously. She wished that they had a ghost in their group. Without one—well let's just say the danger possibilities were even higher. No life saving magic basically. Besides, they seemed trustworthy and they were just thirteen. How bad could they be?

"This is so stupid," Reyna groaned. "Splitting up is always the worst thing to do! Mr. Mister has seen enough loud horror movies for me to know what happens."

"Yeah," Skyler agreed absentmindedly. "Anyway, what are we looking for?"

"No clue," Reyna shrugged. "Hey, can I borrow your notepad?"

Skyler nodded and handed it to Reyna, who immediately started sketching something.

Reyna continued drawing as they walked through winding hallways for what felt like an hour. Finally Skyler groaned, "How much longer will that drawing take?"

Reyna made a small line and looked up. "Well actually, I was just about done." She showed a drawing of a door with a little flap, a hand putting something into the flap, opening the door, and a bird's eye view of figures at the entrance of an intricate maze. "I was thinking that since we got the jewels from the first part of the quest and this is the second, the jewels would have to connect. So maybe to get into the maze, you had to 'give' the jewels to the door or whatever it will be."

"That makes sense," Skyler nodded. "But now, we're gonna take a break. We've been walking for like an hour!"

"Maybe we should call the others. I'll call Amy and you call Vic to see if they've found anything, and lets avoid needing to talk to the ghost twins. I feel like we haven't had a lot of time with just the four of us without the twins around lately," Reyna said, recalling the past few days.

"Well, can't we call Yes and We?" Skyler asked. "They are part of our quest now."

"We're going to stick to us four at least for now," Reyna said emphatically.

"Okay," Skyler said, nodding. They both called Vic and Amy, who were already in their contacts along with Yes and We.

"Hey Vic," Skyler said after Vic picked up. "Have you found anything?"

"No," Vic replied. "I'm beginning to think that this search is going to take the full day! How 'bout you?"

"Nothing," Skyler said glumly. "We're taking a short break now. Reyna is calling Amy."

"Good thing."

"By the way, Reyna made a drawing of her idea of the maze entrance. Can you video call me?"

"Yeah, sure."

Skyler showed Vic the drawing and how they would 'give' the jewels to the maze door.

"I guess that makes sense. I have a feeling that the jewels might be, I don't know, magical!" Vic exclaimed. "We'll be sure to search for something like it. But first, do you think we should talk to the 'you-know-who' with the 'you-know-what'?" Vic showed a little of the sapphire peeking out from her sleeve.

"You know you don't have to hide things from me," We called from the background.

"Oh, shut up," Vic replied. "I'll fill you in later!"

Skyler chuckled. "Well, we'll contact them if we haven't found anything by the end of the day. But don't do it before."

"All right, bye!" Vic waved and hung up.

"Took you long enough!" Reyna joked, causing Skyler to turn around. "I finished with Amy way before. She and Yes also haven't found anything."

Skyler groaned and leaned against the wall. As soon as she did so, Skyler felt that there was something wrong. The wall—it was too light, too papery, too—*fake*.

Skyler screamed as the fake wall gave way and almost sent her tumbling into a dark pit. Luckily, Reyna grabbed Skyler's hand and pulled her back up.

Oh! My! Gosh! My heart can't take these kinds of scares!

"Umm, Skyler," Reyna's voice was full of fear, "look!"

Where the wall had crumbled the floor was now crumbling too. Reyna and Skyler started backing up, but they couldn't move fast enough. The floor was crumbling faster than ever.

"Oh no, no! What do we do?" Skyler panicked.

When there was just a foot of ground left to stand on, Reyna said calmly, even though her eyes told a different story, "We're gonna have to jump!"

And then when there were only five inches of floor left, Skyler and Reyna started to jump. In that moment, everything seemed to happen in slow motion. Skyler saw her arms hug the box tightly against her chest and heard a voice shrieking—probably her own. She also saw Reyna reaching out to grab her arm so she wouldn't crash into the rocky pit walls.

Far down below, at least a mile down, was a pool of water. Skyler could only imagine how long it would take to get there, and how hard a landing it would be.

Skyler closed her eyes and braced for a hard landing as the air zoomed past her, stinging her skin. But the landing Skyler expected never came. After falling for quite some time, Skyler heard a splash of water, but nothing hurt.

Wait, did Reyna fall before—

Skyler opened her eyes and she immediately stopped falling a foot away from the water. But Reyna was still falling.

So if opening my eyes made me stop falling then—

Skyler gasped. "Reyna, open your eyes!" But it was too late. Reyna had hit the water. Her head bent back at a frightening angle and now she was sinking in the deep water.

"No!" Skyler screamed. She tried to move and found that it was almost like she could fly. She just couldn't close her eyes. Skyler floated down to the edge of the water and forced herself to keep her eyes open as she plunged into the water. There must have been some magic going on because Skyler could see in the water as if she was in the open air, and she could breathe as well.

Omega, if you're doing this, thank you!

Skyler saw Reyna sinking beneath her and floated/swam towards Reyna. When she came up next to Reyna, Skyler put one hand on her back, another on her lower head and placed the box precariously on the crook of her elbow. Skyler floated up with Reyna, but it took her all her energy to pull along another person. And Reyna was in a critical state, Skyler couldn't do *anything* wrong.

Right now, I'm really wishing that I had taken the lifeguard training course at school during intermission.

Finally, Skyler made it back to the surface. But there was no exit for them and Reyna's time could be running out.

Then Skyler saw a light of hope—engraved on the rocky wall. The Omega symbol.

Thank goodness!

Skyler pressed her hand against it, and an opening wide enough for two people to walk through appeared. Skyler floated through it with Reyna and her knees touched the floor. As soon as she did, Skyler felt her weight settle on the floor. The spell had been broken.

Skyler laid Reyna on the ground and placed the box next to her. Skyler's eyes welled up with tears as she looked at Reyna. She could never forgive herself if something happened to her. Then Skyler remembered that Patricia had given them a potion to cure basilisk blood? Wait, no, it could cure anything!

Skyler frantically opened the box, took the potion out, and found a sign on it that hadn't been there before. *If you see this, someone close is in desperate need. But be warned, the chances of good or bad are as lucky as rolling a dice. So if you use this potion, there will be a guaranteed fix. But the end may result in a price.*

A price—I have to take the risk though. Reyna can't die! Skyler uncorked the bottle and poured the whole thing in Reyna's mouth. Reyna's eyes shot open, and for a second seemed to be pure black, then changed back into her normal gray. Reyna spluttered and threw up a whole lot of water.

"Reyna!" Skyler exclaimed. She hugged her tightly.

Reyna gave a small yelp. "Skyler, the door, a monster, someone screamed," she said hoarsely, almost as if she had lost her mind.

Skyler sat up. "What? You're talking crazy Reyna! Just rest now. You must be confused. We can talk about it later."

Skyler told Reyna what had happened. How she fell in the water, how Skyler opened her eyes and started floating, how she brought Reyna up and into the tunnel that the omega created, and how she saved Reyna's life by giving her the potion.

"Thank you for saving me, Skyler, but listen to me! I saw the entrance, the maze, then someone, something—"

"Y-you, saw the m-m-maze— Wait where?" Skyler stammered.

"At the end of this tunnel!" Reyna exclaimed then coughed. "My throat—what happened?"

"Umm—What do you mean? Nothing happened!" Skyler was confused. Then she remembered. *'The end may result in a price.'* She looked at the bottle and the sign was gone but somehow it had refilled. *The dice—it gave a second potion to the bottle!*

Reyna sat up, grimaced, and looked at the tunnel with Skyler. It was long and narrow, but they couldn't see the end.

"Reyna, look!" Skyler turned on Reyna's band. "It still works. It must be magical, I mean—wait look, Vic texted you!"

Skyler turned on her own band and saw that Vic had left about twenty missed calls, and a text.

'Where are you?! I've called you both like a million times!' The text read.

"Oh no! They all must be worried!" Skyler exclaimed.

Skyler texted back saying, 'We fell down a pit. Reyna almost died, but great news! I think we might have found the maze entrance!'"

Vic immediately texted back. 'WHAT! Are you joking or what? Reyna almost DIED! How did you save her!'

'I used the potion to save her—which reminds me that I need to say something.'

'Okay, but I want clear answers soon!'

Skyler switched the band off and turned to Reyna, who had laid down again and was clearly in pain.

"Reyna," Skyler cautiously said, "does your body still hurt?"

"Yes," Reyna held back tears. "It feels like it's being stabbed repeatedly! My whole body feels weak and my vision is slightly blurry. Skyler—is this the side effect of the potion?"

"I think it is," Skyler said gravely. "The potion could be good or bad and you ended up with the bad one. You ended with a price."

Chapter 28

Reyna

Reyna felt absolutely *useless*. She had heard Skyler tell her to open her eyes, but had waited a second too long, and was now unconscious. If she had just opened her eyes then this whole fiasco wouldn't have happened. Reyna wouldn't be so weak she was unable to move.

"This sucks," Reyna groaned, changing her voice to a softer tone so it wouldn't hurt her throat as much. "Why couldn't I have gotten the good potion?"

"I'm sorry, Reyna. Maybe we could use the potion again and you'll be better?" Skyler said, looking down.

"Hey," Reyna said, making Skyler look up. "You did good. If you hadn't given me the potion, I would have been dead. But we can't use the potion again! In the vision I had, someone got hurt. We need to save the potion for them!"

"I guess you're right." Skyler got up to her feet and brushed away some dirt. "Maybe We and Yes can do some magic to make the pain lessen."

Ugh. Reyna didn't like the thought of Yes or We helping her. Reyna felt the pair would for sure, double-cross them. "Yeah I guess," Reyna lied. "Well, help me up. We need to get going! The maze door is right at the end of the tunnel!"

Skyler grabbed Reyna's hand, but it was no use. Reyna

still wasn't strong enough to get up on her feet by herself. Skyler then wrapped her arms around Reyna's waist and pulled her up. Reyna's legs felt like jelly, but she mustered all her strength and took a small step, leaning on Skyler for support. Reyna felt her legs burning. Her soaked clothes helped her muscles, but didn't make the process of putting one foot in front of the other any easier.

"This'll take a long time, Skyler. Just leave me here and go and open the maze door," Reyna said, admitting defeat.

"I can't do that!" Skyler exclaimed. "What if some monster comes? No way! You're coming with me." Skyler put her arm around Reyna to give her more balance. Reyna sighed. There was no arguing with her now.

The tunnel was dark and humid and had puddles of water on the ground. The slippery floors and the dark made it even harder for Reyna to see and walk. It took them a very long time to make their way down the tunnel, but finally they saw a glimmer of light.

"We're getting close to the end," Skyler said, her voice full of relief and strain. Carrying so much of Reyna's weight must have been really hard for Skyler.

"Sorry Skyler," Reyna apologized. "Do you want to rest?"

"No, c'mon let's go! We're so close to the end!"

Reyna and Skyler managed to stumble all the way to a door. But not just any door. A door that was arched with a huge Omega symbol on it. In the center there was a group of five people, holding something cubed. No, it *was* a cube carved into the entryway.

"Skyler," Reyna gasped for breath, "I think that's where we put the jewels—or anything else."

"Yes, and I think that's the Omega, the people, er, ghosts that Vic told us about." Skyler ran her hand over the carving and studied it. Skyler helped Reyna down to a sitting position. *I feel better already!*

"Well, I guess I'll call the others then?" Skyler said, with a bit of uncertainty in her voice.

"Duh!" Reyna exclaimed. "Make sure it's a video call."

Skyler turned on her ombré wristband and video-called Amy and Vic. She sat next to Reyna so they could see her, and she could see them.

"Well, thank goodness!" Vic seemed to be angry though Reyna could tell she was relieved through her voice. "We've been scared to death! Let's hope you have a good story behind it all!"

"Ditto," Amy said, joining the call. "I can't believe you're talking this casually, after Reyna just 'almost died'. I mean seriously."

"Well, how do you expect me to text you when I have higher priorities. For instance, I would prioritize someone who is dying over four perfectly fine people who have each other," Skyler pointed out.

"Whoa, slow down, I'm fine now, but that's not what matters—" Reyna went in the middle hoping a fight wouldn't happen.

"THAT'S NOT WHAT MATTERS?" Vic shouted, her voice echoing off the walls. *Sheesh*.

"I was going to say that we found the entrance to the maze. We need you all here right now."

"On our way," Yes called. They cut the call, and soon enough, they appeared in front of them.

"Reyna! Skyler!" Amy and Vic took off, and hugged them. Skyler helped Reyna up and let her use Skyler as support.

"Amy! I thought that was your last time hugging someone," joked Reyna.

Amy looked sheepish then said, "Old habits die hard. Isn't that right, Vic?" Amy grinned.

"Oh come on," Vic pushed Amy playfully.

"Anyway, Reyna are you okay?" Vic asked.

"Well, I'm in pain, but if it weren't for Skyler I would be dead. I think that counts as okay!" Reyna smiled.

"Well, just tell us if you need more help," Amy said. "But now let's get outta here." Amy looked around and shivered.

"You mean, let's get in here." Skyler pointed to the entrance which Vic was already studying.

"The Omega," Vic whispered, "they look exactly like how I met them." She said it almost wistfully.

"I've met them too," said We as he joined her at the entrance.

"Well, what are we waiting for?" Yes asked hurriedly.

"Yeah, lets put in the jewels and go!" Amy agreed.

Skyler pulled the jewels out of the box and gave them to Reyna. "Want to do the honors?"

Reyna smiled and limped over to Skyler. They walked over to the square hole and Reyna went to put the jewels in their spots, but just as she did, the jewels reappeared in her hands. She did it again and again, but the same thing kept happening.

"Wait! Vic must be right!"

Amy gasped. "The *clues!*"

Reyna put the jewels back in the box and then took out all the riddles. She placed them in order from oldest to newest and then the omega symbol on the door lit up with a glowing gold light.

"Yes," murmured Reyna, "it worked!"

They heard the noise of a lock unlatching and knew the door was now unlocked.

"Wait," Skyler demanded. "Yes and We, do you think you could make the pain Reyna has go away?"

"I think so," We stepped—*floated*—forwards. "But first—" We drummed his fingers on his thigh and Reyna felt her clothes, skin, and hair become dry. It was nice to not have water dripping on her and the floor anymore, but Reyna still didn't trust We and Yes.

"Hold on We, I can cure her," Yes said smiling.

"No, I think I'll do it," We said stubbornly, glaring. We put both hands out towards Reyna and started chanting something under his breath. A thin stream of light came out and into Reyna's chest. She could feel the heat of it in her heart. We kept chanting and as he did his face got paler and paler. Reyna could feel the pain fading away but it still wasn't completely gone. Then We fainted. His eyes rolled back in his head.

It was weird to see a ghost fall, but the exhaustion must have made him collapse. Reyna gasped. "A-are you okay?" She was surprised to find that there wasn't any pain and she could see better. Reyna took a step. And another. And another as she didn't feel any pain except for a slight ache that was barely noticeable.

"I-I'm cured!" Reyna exclaimed, then felt bad. We had cured her and she had thought he was untrustworthy. Maybe he changed for the better.

We groaned and got up.

"Thank you, We," Reyna said sincerely. "I can never repay you for this. Are you okay though?"

"Yeah," We said. "My magic is mostly drained so I won't be able to do big spells for a day or so. But you should be fine Reyna. Once my magic wears off, the price you got from the potion should be gone too."

We turned to Skyler who was carrying the box. "I think I have a solution so you don't have to carry the box. Can you look at the side and press a button if there is one?"

Skyler did so, and the box shrunk down to the size of a needle. "Thanks! It would be a pain to carry things in my arms all the time." She slipped the now tiny box into her pocket.

Reyna could see Vic's harmonica was also in her sweatshirt pocket. So was Skyler's notepad. There was a pen in her back pocket. Reyna smiled at that.

"Well, let's go." Reyna strode over to the door with the others following behind. Together they pushed the door open. A cold rush of air greeted them as they prepared for the hardest part of their quest. The maze of ghosts.

Chapter 29

Vic

The maze was *huge*. It was cold—cold enough to make goosebumps appear on the girls' skin. The maze wasn't outside, so it should have had a ceiling, but it felt like the girls were looking up at a cloudy, night sky. The maze wasn't filled with cobwebs like Vic expected, but still was quite dusty. On the walls there were fire-filled lanterns that provided enough light for them to see. Vic had expected the walls and floor to be a gray cement, but instead, the walls and floors were silver with a shimmer in the dust-free areas.

Vic felt something appear in her hand that wasn't there before. She looked down and saw her spear from her quest, gleaming in her hand. She looked around and saw Reyna holding a knife, no a dagger. Skyler—obviously—did not look happy to be holding the sword she hated. And Amy— Vic had to stifle a laugh.

"Oh c'mon!" Amy sighed. She was holding a shoe with lava on it, but instead of the lava destroying the shoe, it stayed at one spot. "Just because I threw a shoe with lava on it doesn't mean it's a weapon! This is so not—COOL!" A bright flash of light appeared and Amy was now holding a polished wooden bow. There was a quiver filled with sharp arrows slung across her back.

"Well, looks like you'll have to learn how to use a bow and arrow then!" Reyna grinned.

"Yeah, just don't hit us." Skyler backed away.

"Don't worry. I took archery at school, remember?" Amy said, rolling her eyes at Skyler. "I just hope this is magic so I don't run out of arrows.

"It probably is, considering that it just appeared and it probably knows you'll waste a couple of arrows trying to shoot them," Vic teased her.

Reyna and Skyler put their weapons in their sheaths which had appeared with the weapon. Amy slung the bow across her back, and Vic just held it.

"Let's get going. We don't want to make the monsters—I mean the quest— wait!" Yes said, pointing to the left.

"Let's go this way. It looks—" We started, but Yes cut him off.

"But it's always safer to stick to the left side in a maze," Yes chimed in.

"How about we decide. We are the questers, after all." Reyna looked at her fellow questers for support.

"Yeah," Vic agreed. "We can survive a few things by ourselves."

"Actually, I think we should go with the people who have been in Mystery Mansion the longest." Amy pointed to We and Yes. "And I'm pretty sure I heard that if you stay to the left you will find the exit—"

"But what if we're supposed to find the center, you know like that story in Greek mythology where the Minotaur that had to be defeated was in the center of the maze?" Vic interrupted. She was desperately trying to find a way not to go with Yes's idea, but it was true. Vic had heard something about staying to the left—or maybe it was right—helped you get to the exit.

Yes laughed. It was a kind, tinkling laugh, but her eyes

showed no signs of kindness. "Of course we wouldn't go to the center, Vicky."

"It's Vic," Vic muttered.

Yes continued. "Oh sorry, *Vic,* but that just seems kind of foolish, don't you think! How about we take a vote. Who votes for my idea?"

Yes, Amy, and Skyler raised their hands. Yes glared at We, then We unwillingly put up his hand, almost as if he was being possessed! Or maybe he was.

Vic gasped at We. "I guess it's our only real option," We said, though he didn't seem to like it.

"Majority wins!" Yes smiled. "But sorry Vic and Reyna, I'm sure you'll understand later."

Both Vic and Reyna glared at Yes. When they had first met Yes, Vic was doubting herself for thinking Yes was bad. But now—Vic knew Yes was bad for sure. *Well if she thinks she's being deceptive, she's not. If she thinks she's going to lure us into a trap, she's not because we'll catch her.*

"Well, sorry to break this amazing moment of utter silence, but we should probably get going." Amy was impatient, *again.*

Vic tightened her grip around her spear—she was *definitely* going to need it.

"Come on." Reyna walked in the back with Vic, who was on her daily dose of being ticked off about Yes.

"Oh look! Here we are! Told you this was the right direction!" Yes gave a sickly, sweet smile. It was directed towards Vic "Aren't you glad you listened to me?"

This can't be right." Vic shook her head. "It's too easy. This has to be a trick!" It was true they were looking at the exit of the maze and there was a portal right there to bring them to wherever they had to go next. And there was a clue right there. But this was too easy! The maze was supposed to be challenging! That's what Patricia told them.

"Too easy? Aren't you glad, Vic? Do you want to go out there and fight those monsters?" Yes smiled again. " You are brave Vic, but very reckless, and slow thinking. You-"

"If you think I'm slow thinking and careless, I can't imagine how you think of yourself. *I'm* the one speaking logically! Do you think Seville will just let us exit the maze so quickly?"

"Umm, sorry to break the argument, but Vic is right. This isn't the exit, look!" Reyna pointed to the doorway. Sure enough, that wasn't an exit, it was just a reflection.

"Okay, but if that's a reflection, the exit must be on the opposite wall! And it's clearly not." Amy pointed out.

"Well, who knows. It's probably magic, but wait, what if—It's reflecting what's on the other side of the maze?" Skyler suddenly realized, and as she did, the maze walls became transparent, and they could see a faint exit on the opposite side.

"Told you so!" Vic exclaimed. "We can't stick to the left in a magical maze. Plus, I'm pretty sure it was supposed to be the right. We just need to go wherever we feel is the right path!"

They heard a rumbling. The floor they were on was lifted off the ground, high enough so they could see a bird's eye view of the maze.

"Oh, no. Oh *no,*" Amy quivered. Though she had passed Wolfhart's test, her fear of heights was still there.

Reyna gasped. "Guys look!"

They all looked down upon the maze. Well, everyone except Amy.

"I see it too!" Vic marveled at the sight below her. The maze was a very intricate circle maze. You couldn't even spot the exit! But around it was a gold wall that was part of the maze. A gold wall in the shape of Omega.

"*Amy,*" Vic rolled her eyes and pulled Amy towards the edge. "Just look!"

Amy opened her eyes a crack and gasped the same way Reyna had before. "Then it's clear. We need to make it to the center. Then we should pass the maze!"

Suddenly—with a lot of rumbling and creaks—the maze started to shift. It kept speeding up until all they could see was a blur of silver. Then as suddenly as it had started, the shifting stopped and they were brought back down in the maze.

This time the maze had left them looking at a fork in the road. *A fork in the road— The maze surely must be planning something.* Its plan was as clear as day. One of the paths was pristine and basked in a gold glow that made it feel warm and homey. 'Come here,' it was saying. 'There are no monsters here!'

Meanwhile the other path was pitch black. The only way they knew it was a path was that a small crack of light from the other path showed the entrance. The entrance was extremely hazardous. There were thick, thorny vines growing everywhere, and the opening was extremely small. Vic and the others could fit through, but there would still be the danger of thorns poking them.

Vic looked expectantly at Yes, but to her surprise, Yes was doing the same thing!

"Go ahead, Vic," Yes urged her on. "What's your plan?"

Weird. "Well, we should take the pitch black path." She pointed to the path. "I know, I know. You think it's danger—"

"Of course it's dangerous, who would even go that way?" Yes asked, almost evilly. "I mean of course it's dangerous, but if you guys want to go that way, I'm cool with it." Yes changed her tone so forcefully that Vic almost agreed with her. But when Vic saw her smiling at Amy, she hated herself for thinking that for even a moment.

"Actually, do you guys remember when we went up? I remember something. The one that looks good is actually good, except it's all a dead end, you can go in as far as you want, but it will lead nowhere!" Reyna said as if recalling something she had heard just a minute ago.

"She's probably right," We said. "But it's becoming night time. We need rest. Why don't we rest and start again the morning?"

"Yeah, let's set camp here for the night. We'll get a fresh start in the morning," Skyler agreed.

"Sure, but are you positive that there won't be any monsters or anything?" Amy shivered at the thought.

"Well, it is a better option than staying in the dark tunnel in the night."

Vic and the others stepped into the homey tunnel, gripping their weapons, ready to fend off an attack, but they felt a sensation of an enclosure put around them—a sensation of a locked room.

"You did it again, Reyna!" Amy patted her on the back. "This is the perfect place to stay."

Vic was happy that they had found a sound home for the night, but she felt like this was too easy. What if a monster showed up at night while they were sleeping? What if they all don't make it back? Vic quickly put that out of her mind and looked around the area. There was no furniture or anything like they had in their room in the mansion, but it somehow felt comfy.

"Hey guys, over here!" Amy called. She had explored further into the enclosure already. Amy brought them into the back corner of the enclosure. There standing was a cracked mirror that had a scary blue tint to it.

The mirror was big enough that the group of six girls could all see themselves in it. We was looking puzzled, and it was the first time Vic ever noticed. It was odd to see We without a hint of surliness in his expression. Yes was just looking normal, but that could all be an act. The girls were also looking normally at their expression. But their reflections were *not* looking normal.

Their reflections were just—*off.* According to *science,* their reflection should be exactly the same! But it wasn't—Vic just couldn't explain what was different. Was it the freckles on Amy's face? Was it her eyes? Was it Skyler's blond hair? What *was* it?

They walked back to the center of the empty area and immediately started feeling sleepy. And no, it wasn't a spell—they were just pretty tired from searching. And since We had a watch, they could see that it had already become midnight. Time flies when you're, er, what? Monster hunting?

Vic and We had encountered another basilisk while searching for the maze. Vic looked over at We and felt sorry seeing his tired face. We had saved Vic's life from the basilisk since she didn't have a weapon at the time. He used so much of his magic to save both Vic and Reyna. And after defeating the basilisk he had even gotten some of its blood. '*Just in case we have to defeat an evil ghost,*' he had said. Vic wished she could somehow return the favor.

"Um guys, just a question. Where are we gonna sleep?" Amy asked.

"Let me take care of it." Unlike We, Yes didn't put her hands forward or do anything like that. She just stood there doing nothing.

"Nothing's happening. Yes, are you—" Skyler started. A random wind came out of nowhere, and before they could even blink, there were six sleeping bags in the area. They were all in a staggered line going from the mirror to the entrance of the dead end enclosure.

Show off. She's just trying to seem better than We.

"Whoa!" Amy raised her eyebrows. "That must have been a whole lotta magic!"

"Don't worry." Yes threw herself on a sleeping bag. "Now

let's get some rest. Gotta get through this maze as fast as possible."

But no one except Vic seemed to care. Her self-doubts started coming back. Maybe she was *too* worried. Maybe she was just looking at random signs that didn't mean anything. Maybe Yes *was* good! Or maybe *Vic* was the one who shouldn't be self-doubting. And Vic knew that she had to trust her first instincts. They were telling her that Yes was bad.

The girls and We laid back in their beds, er, bags, and immediately Vic could hear Amy's soft snoring. She must have been more tired than they thought. Vic found herself a sleeping bag next to We and Reyna. She did this on purpose because she was planning to pass them a message tonight: about how Yes was leading them the wrong way.

Vic laid there in silence, and found herself thinking about what all had happened since they ran away. Vic knew this would be another sleepless night. She turned over and saw We standing by the mirror again.

What's up with that?

Vic got up with her spear and walked silently over to We. Vic was good at not making a sound. "Hey," she whispered. We jumped.

"Why are you awake?" We asked.

"I should be asking *you* the same question," Vic challenged.

We was silent and that just made Vic shiver. The silence was eerie and it felt like the silence was closing in on her.

"It's just that this mirror—it's *different.*" We frowned. "I don't get it. Ghosts' reflections don't show in mirrors for some reason. But it does here. And I know for a fact that this mirror is not a ghost mirror."

This sent chills down Vic's spine. Vic felt We move closer to her as he reached out and gently touched the mirror. The mirror stayed the exact same, making Vic feel even worse.

It didn't help that a second later Reyna tapped Vic on her shoulder with her dagger.

"Reyna!" Vic took a shaky breath. "Sorry I woke you up."

"I couldn't sleep either," Reyna admitted. Now tell me, what are you doing at this mirror? I did have some doubts about it, but what can a mirror do?" Reyna leaned against the glass then pushed away. "Look, it's just normal!"

It may have just been Vic's overactive imagination, but she swore she heard hissing whispers. They seemed to be saying, *Finally!* The mirror seemed to be getting darker.

"Guys we should go—" But Vic couldn't move. She just watched in horror at the mirror as a pale hand with sharp, long, blood-stained fingernails started to materialize at its edge. Soon a lady with a sunken face, long, black hair, and blood stained clothes appeared. She lifted her head and the true horror was revealed. She had sharp teeth with something that looked horribly like flesh stuck in it. Her eyes were a dead black with no sign of anything living.

Reyna, We, and Vic stood there transfixed at the lady.

"It's time." She made a low growling voice in her throat as she spoke. She swooped from the mirror into the air and was falling as fast her hands reached out to grab.

They screamed and Vic faintly remember someone yelling, "RUN!"

Yes and Skyler had already gotten up from the screaming and started to run away. Surprisingly Skyler had brought her sword. But there was someone missing—*AMY!*

Vic ran as fast as her long legs would take her and yanked Amy's arm, which got Amy up immediately. Luckily Amy still had her quiver and bow on her back. That raised a question: how did she sleep? But there was no time to think about that. "W-what!" Amy looked up and saw the creepy lady flying towards them from the mirror and screamed.

"Just RUN!" Vic yanked Amy's arm again and this time Amy ran too.

With the others close by her, Vic shouldn't have been scared since she knew that six people to one meant their chances of winning were high, but this was something scarier than Vic had ever experienced. And now, she didn't know what was ahead. *That* was her greatest fear.

Chapter 30

Amy

Amy couldn't believe that she had slept through all the chaos. Maybe she was a heavier sleeper than she thought. Amy was surprised she was still able to run. A psycho lady coming out of a mirror had her paralyzed in shock. But still, she was running on her feet with Vic still grabbing her arm as so called Bloody Mary was flying after them screeching.

Wait—Maybe it is Bloody Mary! But the last time I checked she couldn't fly. It's probably some Greek hybrid.

Amy always thought if she was put in this kind of situation, she would be scared to death. But surprisingly, Amy was calmer than she expected. Of course she was worried for their lives, but Amy knew that they could get through this.

Vic didn't seem to be like that. Her face was ashen gray and her eyes were a spiral of terror. That was the most emotion Vic had ever shown in her eyes. *Ever.* Amy tried to never be that serious about something. She preferred to add a touch of humor and happiness to everything. It helped her deal with the problems.

"Vic, don't worry. We'll be fine!" Amy said, out-of-breath.

"I'm not worrying about anything! Just the fact that the so called 'fake' Bloody Mary is hunting us down for our lives! Why would I be scared?" Vic's voice leaked with emotions

Amy never wanted to hear again. They shouldn't have done this quest. But now with the hope of reuniting with their parents, Amy wasn't going to let anything stop her and the others.

Amy opened her mouth to say something, but was interrupted by more psycho *thingamabobs* coming out of the mirror. They were pitch black blobs of darkness that had sharp, scary teeth.

"RUN!" Reyna screamed.

Skyler, on the other hand was too terrorized to scream, or for that matter, say anything.

Suddenly, out of nowhere, Vic spun into a clear dead-end as everybody followed her. Skyler started to say something, but Vic cupped her hand over Skyler's mouth. Finally, the ghosts or whatever they were, lost them and floated into the midst of the maze. Vic collapsed onto the rough ground.

"That was close," Skyler breathed.

"Ya think?" Amy looked down at Vic, who was still paler than Amy had ever seen her—and that's saying a lot.

"You guys," We started, but Reyna cut him off.

"Wait a second, do you smell that?" Reyna asked sniffing her shirt.

"Smell what— Oh. My. God," Skyler smelled her shirt and looked scared and sick.

"We—we smell like blood!" Reyna was shaken.

"Yes! You did it, you did this to lure the monsters!" Vic jumped up from the ground.

"Vic, let's not jump to conclusions—"Amy started.

"From now on, *we* choose the direction we go, *we* choose the weapons we use and the monsters we defeat, and *we* ask for magic if we need it." Vic stormed directly toward Yes.

"I agree," Reyna said, facing her.

"Sorry Yes, but I have to agree too," Skyler said it like she was sorry for her. Amy realized then that Skyler trusted her too. Amy couldn't see why the others didn't.

"I guess I agree too," Amy shrugged, but as they left Amy shook her head as if to say sorry.

Yes couldn't have done that! I mean, I don't think she would have—

"You know Amy," Yes started innocently, "you can come with me. We can go the right way."

"I'm sorry Yes," Amy apologized, "but I have to stick with my friends." Amy trusted Yes, but she knew Vic and the others better. No matter what, she would stick by their side.

Amy ran through the glowing silver path, her shoes rubbing against the rough ground. She caught up to Vic who smiled a reassuring smile at her. Besides, what are friends for?

* * *

They continued to walk down the maze in the darkness with only fire-lit lanterns hung on the rock walls. Once in a while when Amy looked into the lanterns, she would see images of terrifying ghosts and monsters growling. The others seemed to have noticed too because they were moving in closer to each other in tighter groups.

"I don't know about you, but I have a feeling we should start moving fast." Amy shivered looking at the lanterns.

"Ya think?" Skyler returned the favor of lightening the mood.

Amy knew this was not a time and place to laugh, but she couldn't help it. Soon the others were laughing infectiously along with her. We chuckled. Then he frowned.

"Where's Yes?" We asked. *So he does care.*

"Probably exploring another path. Why, 'you worried?" Amy asked casually.

"No, Yes can do some magic and get through the walls to find us. I just wanted to know." He tried to look casual, but

Amy could see he had some hidden intentions. Something he said also caught Amy's attention.

"Wait, you said Yes can do magic to get through the walls. How come—YOU HAVEN'T USED IT FOR US!" Amy shrieked. This whole quest could have been a lot simpler with that!

We sighed and ruffled his hair. The others had heard their conversation and now started listening intently. "We can use magic on you, but not *for* you," he said, as if he was teaching a four year-old "Get it?"

"No," Amy said wryly. "Explain."

"What I'm saying is, Yes and I can't get you through the walls!"

"Ohhhhh," Amy widened her eyes. "Teach me more, great teacher!"

"Not funny." We crossed his arms, talking dead-pan. "I'm a wonderful teacher."

Now the others were doubling over in laughter. Amy and the others all laughed super easily. Vic suppressed her laugh and imitated We. "I'm a great teacher. I teach people how to be impatient." She and the others burst out laughing.

"Oh, shut up." We's mouth twitched. " Let's keep going."

Amy smiled and elbowed Vic in a friendly way. She still didn't trust We as much as Yes. But she owed him for curing Reyna when he could have done nothing, especially since Amy was glaring at him. And when someone does something like that, you can't help but trust them.

Chapter 31

Skyler

*L*eave it to Amy to make everyone laugh in a dangerous situation. A smile was still plastered on everyone's faces. Well, except We, who was trying to hide his smile. And Yes—*Where was she?* Skyler believed Amy, but they welcomed her into their quest. If anything went wrong, Skyler would never *ever* forgive herself. Yes was sweet, kind hearted, and so much more they would never find out if something happened.

"Well, hasn't this been a peaceful walk?" The five of them spun around to see Yes smiling.

"Yes," Vic said dryly. "How ever did you find us?"

"I can go through walls, duh!" Yes put her hands in front of her.

"I'm done here." Vic rolled her eyes. *No need to be rude!*

"Wait, then where were you, and how come you can't take us?" Reyna glanced at Yes, skeptical.

"First of all, I just needed to check on a few things, and second, like We was explaining, we can go through walls, but we can't bring you through them." That comment was a little eerie.

"How long have you been standing behind us?" Skyler asked. She trusted Yes, but eavesdropping is frankly kind of creepy.

"Never mind that." Yes changed the subject. "Let's keep searching!" Her enthusiasm made Skyler want to keep going.

"Fine!" Vic crossed her arms.

So they kept going. The humorous mood had faded. The pictures in the lantern kept popping up—pictures of shape-shifting monsters and evil ghosts. Skyler yawned and felt her eyelids droop. She realized that they had not had a good sleep in a long time.

She heard talking and turned around to see Vic talking to We.

"You know Yes put the blood on us. You have to do *something!*" Vic hissed.

"Well, I know, but you're not helping the fact that she's too powerful for anyone, and I'm completely out of magic!" Skyler listened to We and Vic bickering. Skyler looked around and saw that no one else had noticed the talking. She lagged behind to let them go in front of her so she could listen to them. For someone who just said eavesdropping was creepy, Skyler was really contradicting herself.

"Well, I guess there's probably a better time to confront her. We can't rush into it." Vic looked at We like she was in deep thought. Suddenly, Vic froze in her tracks, causing her to bump into Skyler, who went down to the ground.

"Oh my god, Skyler! Are you okay?" Vic reached down to grab her arm and pull her up.

"Hey, were you listening to us talk?" We asked defensively, crossing his arms at Skyler.

"Cut her some slack. I'm sure you would be eavesdropping if you were her too," Vic said. They saw Yes smirk from where she was standing.

"And I'm sure someone can relate." Vic shot Yes a glance that quite straightforwardly told her to 'keep your mouth shut'.

"You okay?" Reyna ran back to Skyler after everyone started to move along.

"Yeah I'm fine," Skyler nodded.

Skyler and Reyna ran back up to Vic and Amy.

"Hey," Reyna turned to Vic and Amy, stopping the girls. Skyler resented herself for feeling left out. She knew that Reyna would never try to not include her. "There's something I want to do."

She grabbed Skyler and pulled them into a hug. Skyler's doubts immediately went away. She loved Reyna just like a sister. They all stood there, hugging each other. Skyler couldn't remember the last peaceful time they had enjoyed since they left Mr. Mister. They all felt like her sisters. She had never known anyone closer to her. Even her parents seemed a long way from close. Skyler could feel tears forming. It had been too long since the last time she felt loved.

Skyler pulled away. "I love you guys. You're the only family I need," she said and immediately felt cheesy. But that disappeared when she saw the other girls' even more cheesy smiles and Reyna's glassy eyes.

"I love you guys too," they said, overlapping each other. Even Amy looked emotional.

"Well, now that you've had your embrace, can we move along?" Yes looked irritated.

"Like we said before, *we* make the decisions, not you, so I would appreciate patience." Vic wasn't glaring anymore. She was smiling smugly.

Skyler glanced at We, expecting rolling eyes. Instead Skyler was in for a surprise. We was actually hiding a smile! Turns out he was more emotional than they had thought.

"Well, I know what we should do next," Vic spoke out like a leader. "We need to find another place to sleep. They looked around themselves, but there wasn't an open space.

"Maybe we should try looking in another place," Amy suggested, looking at the creepy lanterns.

"Yeah, that's a good idea!" Reyna also looked at the lanterns in fear, unlike Amy, who looked pretty chill.

"Actually," We said, reverting back to his emotionless tone. It kind of reminded Skyler of her old math teacher, but Skyler knew that this surliness was just an act. She could see through his barrier. "I think we should just stay here. And maybe we should take turns keeping guard. I can try and make some blankets at the most."

"Well, that a good idea." Vic pondered the idea. "But your magic—it's too low!"

"I should be fine." We shrugged, but Skyler knew he was lying. Apparently Yes could too.

Yes looked at her brother in worry. "Are you sure G—We? Maybe I could make some."

"No!" Reyna shrieked. "And Yes, what was with that slip-up?"

Yes took on a blank face. "What?"

"You called We something starting with a G. You're hiding something from us."

"No, I was just about to call him our really long name. It's actually pronounced with a G, but to make things simple we use different pronunciations." Yes's prominent smile faltered for a moment.

Reyna still looked skeptical. Even Skyler thought that was weird.

"Well, while you were arguing, I made the blankets." We brought their attention to six fluffy blankets. They were even thicker than winter comforters.

Skyler almost felt emotional. In Mr. Mister's house, they never had these—luxuries. They learned to make do with the worst of things, the littlest of things—the scraps. Skyler was always jealous of the people who had nice things, but she learned to adjust. Skyler was so sleepy she could just fall on top of the pile of blankets (which were also color coordinated). So that's what she did. Only when she fell on it, she felt hard ground sooner than expected.

"Ow!" Skyler winced, rubbing her head. Reyna gave her a hand and pulled her up.

"I'm sorry, Skyler. That's the most my magic can do here in the maze. There's some kind of barrier holding it back. The looks of our magic might be deceiving, but it won't feel as great as it looks." We looked at the blankets disappointedly. Skyler was disappointed too. But she was still grateful for the rough but warm blankets she was laying on. And she suspected it was more than just the maze. We's magic still hadn't fully returned and everyone knew that.

Skyler got up and everyone grabbed their colored blankets. No surprise, We's was also blue. Just like Vic's—Although it was probably a shade duller from Vic's bright electric blue. They were so similar and while the other girls would say it's odd, Skyler thought it was cool. Their friendship was sarcastic, but it always made Skyler smile a lot, to be honest. It was a good thing Skyler was a talented actress, otherwise her friends would think she was going crazy. And yes, she included We and Yes in that list.

But soon, she started to doubt that. We and Vic took guard—We didn't want Vic to guard alone— Maybe We was good, and Yes was bad or maybe Yes was good and We was bad. Skyler heard We talking to Vic. She turned around to see them sitting together against the stone walls.

"Look I'm sorry." He sounded ashamed. "But I had to do it. It was the least I could do with Yes controlling me."

Skyler heard a gasp. "You mean—" Their conversation faded away to muted whispers. Then it continued after a while. "You should've told me!"

"I'm sorry," We apologized again, maybe for the tenth time in their muted conversation. Everything went quiet. Skyler cracked open an eye. We looked like he was in pain—an emotional pain. Their muted conversation must have been more serious than Skyler thought. Then Vic turned towards where Skyler was and she glared. "Why?" she hissed. "Skyler, you're not supposed to eavesdrop!"

"I-I'm sorry," Skyler was taken aback, and she sat up.

"You did it once, and I let you get away with it, but this time? No!" Vic walked towards her. Skyler felt like backing up.

"Vic, you can trust me." But Vic didn't stop ranting.

"Vic—she didn't mean—" We tried to intervene but Vic interrupted.

"How can *I* trust you if you *keep* breaking my trust?" Vic's piercing blue eyes were glassy.

"You sound like our ELA teacher." Skyler tried to bring some humor, but Vic's stare just became more deadly.

"Fight, fight—" The three of them turned around to see Yes watching them evilly.

"Oh, so now we have to deal with two eavesdroppers." Vic looked like she was going to throw her spear. She did, and it clattered on the ground next to Yes' feet.

Skyler was taken aback. She never thought she could be hurt by Vic so much, but it was shattering her. Vic's face was hardened in anger, but she suspected that anger was more directed towards Yes.

"I'm sorry," Skyler whispered.

Vic's face softened for a second and Skyler thought she saw her apologize quietly. She turned towards Yes. "I can't accept *you.* "

"Oh, then you'll learn how to," Yes shrugged like it was no big deal. She vanished with a snap.

And that shattered her to even tinier pieces. Skyler could feel Vic's pain hurting her too. Skyler felt tears slipping from her eyes for the first time in years. She felt bad for Vic. She hadn't only lost her parents, but she had lost a baby brother who she only knew for less than a year. Then she came here and maintained her lively attitude even when she had been breaking down. Skyler realized that now it probably felt like she was losing her only friends in the world.

Vic looked like she was going to retort back to Yes, but instead she collapsed onto the ground, leaning on a wall as she sobbed into her hands. Skyler got up and ran to Vic and put an arm around her as Vic gave in. Skyler just then realized that Vic was much softer and fragile on the inside. All the years Skyler had known her, Vic had been bold and strong, and never let comments get to her. No matter what she faced. But Skyler was sure of something. No matter what Vic faced, her best friends would always, *always* be there for her.

Chapter 32

Reyna

Reyna jerked up and saw something even worse than a monster. A crying figure, hunched over with Skyler next to her. *Vic!* We was floating towards her and Yes was nowhere in sight. Reyna nudged Amy who immediately woke up. *I guess she could sense Vic's pain too.*

"Why does everything have to be so awful!" Vic sobbed. Reyna saw Skyler pull her limp body in to hug her as they jogged over to Vic. They wrapped their arms around her, and Skyler turned her head in fright, probably thinking it was a monster. Then her eyes went calm and she hugged Vic as her sobs softened.

"I'm sorry Vic," Reyna's eyes were glassy. "We promise to never let you feel like this again"

"Yeah. I guess we all feel this way once in awhile," Amy gently whispered.

Reyna always thought Vic was so fierce. At school, no one would mess with the girl with electric-blue eyes and long, dark hair. Even though Vic was fierce at school, she was always kind, caring, clever, and fun anywhere else. But now Reyna saw an even deeper side to her, a side that maybe needed support, a side Vic had been hiding for years.

The peaceful silence was broken as an inhumane sound came from behind her. The girls turned in terror, but instead of a monster, it had been We's mangled scream. Reyna always felt that a scream in silence was something people definitely didn't do automatically, but there was something about it that sounded authentic.

Vic smeared her tears and got up, taking a shaky breath. "What is it?" she asked, her voice was still choked up.

We shook his head in disbelief. "No. What? And— how? I-I didn't think—"

"What is it?" Vic replied more calmly than Reyna thought she would.

"A-after all t-those bad e-experiences—I c-can't," We broke off, shuddering.

Reyna tried to get a glimpse, but she couldn't see anything. "A what?" Unlike Vic, Reyna was slightly annoyed.

We took a breath, a fearful look in his eyes. "I-it's a—ugh, a s-squirrel."

Reyna couldn't help but scoff. Vic gave a smile. Unfortunately it still looked sad. "Really We? You? You're scared of squirrels?"

Reyna could finally see a small, brown squirrel looking like it was going to scamper away. Soon it stood on its hind legs and stared at them with its beady eyes. The other girls had to hide their smiles.

We exhaled. "Yeah, not in the mood to explain those horrible experiences though." He smiled and stepped closer to the girls (well, it wasn't so subtle that it was meant for Vic). "I could make a good comeback, but I don't think now is the time or place for that."

Vic's eyes welled up with tears; not sad, but happy and relieved tears.

"Thanks," she said. Vic took a step closer to the squirrel and kneeled next to it. The squirrel placed a tiny hand on Vic's as if comforting her. Something about it felt wrong though.

"Vic—" Reyna trailed off. The squirrel's hand was growing larger. No, not just the hand, its whole body! The eyes turned red and the teeth were growing larger and sharper, as if they were beaver's teeth that turned into fangs. *Help me. Can this place get any weirder?*

It was weird to be scared of a squirrel, but this one was okay to be scared of. Vic jumped up and ran to get her spear, which was a couple of feet away. But before she could get it, a twenty foot squirrel with unproportionally big hands and feet, with fangs and red eyes, blocked her path with a *STOMP.* The ground erupted. Rocks and rubble sprayed everywhere, covering Vic's spear. Vic jumped out of the way before she could get hit by rock shrapnel.

Reyna felt something drip onto her head. The foaming drool of the possibly rabid squirrel started dripping foam onto Reyna's head. It was like flowing water, only this was more horrible and disgusting. "Ew!" Reyna slipped away from the squirrel and wiped away the foam. The only problem was that it was now on her hands. She wiped them on the walls. Reyna gripped her dagger and caught Skyler's eye at a distance.

"What are we gonna do? Vic can't fight now," Skyler mouthed, but it ended up coming out as a loud whisper..

"Who said I can't fight?" Vic mouthed back, struggling with the ruble that covered her boot.

Amy stood next to Skyler and stared pointedly at Reyna. *"You're the leader Reyna. What's the plan?"* she mouthed.

Reyna felt like a hundred pounds were dropped onto her shoulders. She felt the pressure of deciding what to do weighing her down. Or maybe that was just her tiredness, but Reyna knew she had to act, and *fast.*

"On three we'll charge," Reyna mouthed, gripping her dagger even tighter. Amy and Skyler did the same with theirs. "One, two, three!"

They charged. Vic managed to get her boot out of the rubble and lunged herself at the monster just as Reyna and the others did the same, but the effort went to waste. With a *THUMP,* the girls were sent flying back. Amy winced and placed her arms over her stomach, bending over.

"How can we defeat it?" she cried.

Reyna realized how dire the situation was now. "I-I don't think we can defeat it!" Her body ached from the impact, but nothing seemed to be damaged. Skyler looked as good as her, and Vic seemed to be limping. Reyna would have to figure out what to do about Amy later. Right now, they had to take action.

"What do you mean, we can't defeat it?" Skyler shrieked.

"It's too big," Reyna said, shaking her head. "We'll never be able to defeat it without a proper army."

"Uh, guys, look!" We pointed to a horrid sight. The squirrel's enlarged foot was rising above their heads. If they didn't move soon, it would crush them like ants. "Run!" he yelled.

They scrambled away, running as fast as they could. *THUMP!* This time, the squirrel's foot had made an indentation in the ground because of the impact, splattering rock and rubble everywhere. Reyna saw Vic sneak behind the monster, and stab the monster behind its leg. The monster buckled with pain, but soon, it was mended. Vic's eyes turned as icy as the monster's eyes were when the monster turned towards her in rage. Vic screamed and rolled between its feet, just missing the squirrel's bloodied hands.

That split second was all the girls needed for Amy to shoot an arrow in its direction. Amy was perched on top of the wall, surprising all of them, including the squirrel. The arrow hit the squirrel on its arm this time, but before they knew it, it was mended again with the arrow still embedded, looking like a splinter. Reyna racked her brain. She knew they were missing something. Reyna saw Skyler swing her sword at the squirrel, but the force sent her flying into the wall. *Great, now what?* Reyna took her dagger and tossed it in the opposite direction of the squirrel, distracting it from Skyler. Reyna ran after the dagger, reaching it just before the squirrel did. That's when it hit her.

"Vic! Can you distract the monster?" Reyna watched Vic nod to her, as if calculating something.

"Amy! Shoot an arrow towards that wall!" Reyna yelled, pointing to the opposite wall.

"Reyna, what should I do?" Skyler yelled, sword fighting the squirrel beside Vic.

"Come help me!" Reyna yelled back. Skyler dodged the foot of the squirrel and ran towards Reyna. That was the first time Reyna had seen Skyler so close up since they had started fighting. Skyler's knees were scraped and cut, blood staining her shorts. She had a bruise on her arm and a cut across her cheek. Her ponytail was coming out, and strands of hair were falling over her face.

Reyna heard a cracking noise when Amy's arrow hit the wall. Then, a scream. The type of blood-curdling scream where you know something is drastically wrong. It was Amy, but that didn't make any sense! Amy shot the arrow. How could she have gotten hurt?

Reyna turned to the top of the wall. Amy wasn't there. Reyna looked down, expecting the worst. There, laid Amy passed out in a pool of blood.

Reyna screamed. Skyler and Vic ran over to Amy as soon as possible. The squirrel had been shot straight in the heart by Amy's arrow. It stumbled, surprised, and crashed into a wall, killing itself. But it didn't matter that the squirrel was defeated. Amy was more important. Reyna couldn't remember stumbling to Amy, half falling down. Skyler caught her by the arm.

"She's alive," Skyler reassured Reyna, though all their

faces were pale. Reyna caught a glimpse of Amy and felt like gagging. There was a huge gash near Amy's stomach, probably what she was clutching before. Her clothes were blood soaked, and judging from the cracking noise they had heard, several of her ribs were probably broken. A trickle of blood ran down her face.

Reyna was in shock. The last thing she could remember was a huge stone hitting her as she fell backwards, hitting her head on the stone wall and blacking out.

Chapter 33

Vic

Vic felt like crying again. Amy was severely hurt, and who knew what state Reyna was in. We had brought the four of them into an enclosed area—no one knows how he found it— and put blankets on the ground. Skyler, who was supporting Amy, laid her down on the blanket, but it was no use. Before they knew it, it was soaked with blood. Reyna's head was also bleeding; she had hit it on the stone wall, just when they thought they were going to lose Amy.

"Vic," Skyler sputtered, tears rolling down her cheek. Vic hugged her and watched Amy and Reyna as their breathing became more shallow.

"The potion. We could save one of them," Vic glanced at Skyler's pocket, as Skyler pulled out the box, watching as it enlarged. Skyler opened it and took out their silvery potion.

"But which one do we save?" Skyler asked. Her tears were pouring down faster.

"Wait, there's one more option," Vic added, as she pulled out a glistening sapphire. "Ūnus."

Vic and Skyler watched as the sapphire began to swirl around. Suddenly, a figure of an old lady ghost showed up. It looked like a hologram.

"Is that—" Skyler couldn't finish her sentence.

"Yes dear, it's me." said Ūnus. She smiled sadly at them. "I know your situation is dire, but it's not hopeless. You will know which one you will save when the time comes to make a decision. Or should I say, the potion will tell you. Just try to pour it into their mouths. Only one will come through, the other might not." The image flickered out of view, as the sapphire turned back to its normal color.

"Skyler, I think she means—that the potion will only work for one person. I guess we won't be stuck in a conundrum, but it's only one—"

"No—it can't be," Skyler cried. Vic felt a tear running down her own cheek as she held the potion to Reyna's mouth, but nothing happened. The potion was solidified.

"Wait, do you think a person can only use a potion once?" Vic murmured, sorrow filling her soul. She held the potion to Amy's mouth. This time it worked. As they trickled it into her mouth, the two of them watched the color return to Amy's face. Her cuts and bruises slowly disappeared. The only sign something was amiss were her blood-stained clothes,

Amy bolted upright. "W-What's going on! I just had the weirdest dream that I was knocked unconscious, and—" Amy looked at the concerned faces of her friends. "Oh, was that real?"

Vic and Skyler squeezed Amy as tight as they could. "All that matters is that you're safe."

We coughed. "But, what about Reyna? Even if I make bandages, there's a possibility that she might not be healed.

"Wait, what happened to Reyna?" Amy looked like she was going to cry.

"Actually Amy, it was Reyna who was knocked unconscious. You had a huge gash in your stomach and you had broken your rib cage. Because of the pain, you became unconscious." Vic looked down.

"Wait, why didn't you split the potion between the two of us?" Amy looked bewildered and frightened.

"Because, Reyna could only use the potion once." Skyler looked at Amy sadly.

"What? You can't be serious!" Amy wasn't a crier, but her eyes welled up. She stood up, wobbled a little, then readied herself. Amy walked over to Reyna and with determination in her eyes she said, "We, get ready."

"For what?" We looked a little nervous.

"Don't worry, it'll be something that will make your parents proud." Amy gave a smile. "You're gonna be the doctor."

"Wait, what?" We practically screamed. Vic felt like doing the same thing.

"Amy," Vic raised her eyebrows at Amy, "you're not planning to make this unqualified teen act as a doctor, right? And just to point out, *this* unqualified teen?" We glared at Vic.

"No, of course not! Reyna is too important for that. We just has to use some magic on Reyna so we have a chance of healing her."

We floated over to Amy's side quickly. Vic wasn't sure if whatever Amy was planning would work, but they needed to trust each other. She and Skyler ran over to Reyna's side.

"We, do you think you could wake her?" Amy asked, kneeling over Reyna.

We exhaled and passed his hands over Reyna's eyes. Reyna gasped, her breath quickening.

Vic breathed a sigh of relief. "Reyna, calm down. You're going to be okay." She said it more like she hoped so than she knew so. Reyna's breath stayed at the same pace, but didn't slow down. Maybe that was good. At least it showed she was alive.

"We, can you do something to like scan for injuries? And make bandages and an ice pack?" Skyler seemed to be calmer, but even she looked like she was going to be sick.

"Yeah, my magic should be back to normal." Soon enough, bandages and an ice pack appeared by Amy's side. We closed his eyes and held his hands over Reyna. When he finally opened his eyes, they were more relieved than the girls had expected.

"Well, she has minor injuries like cuts and scrapes. The only thing that's major is that she has a head injury. There doesn't seem to be a concussion. She also has a small gash on her left elbow."

"I can take care of her. I took first-aid remember?" Amy said. Vic suddenly realized that her ankle was hurting. She looked down at it and saw that it was swollen and bruised. She was going to say something, but stopped herself. *Reyna is more important.*

Amy checked for rocks and materials and used a gauze to clean as much as she could. Reyna winced, but they couldn't do anything about the pain. She pressed a bandage to the wound and for five minutes they waited in a nervous silence.

Reyna muttered, "I'm sorry."

Skyler sniffled. "Don't be, you didn't do anything. You're going to be fine Reyna."

Amy removed the bandage, and only a small trickle of blood was left. Amy took the bandages, wrapped them around Reyna's head, and applied a little pressure. Then she wrapped them around her elbow too. "Reyna, sit up." Amy sounded so authoritative, Vic felt like standing up.

Reyna—with a lot of groaning—slowly sat upright. She put a hand to her head and winced. "Y-you guys did a great job, but do you have anything to make my head hurt less?"

Amy handed her the ice pack. Reyna stood up, pressing the ice pack to her wound. Vic felt like hugging Reyna, but changed her mind at the last moment. *I better not. It could hurt her.* She settled for patting her on the shoulder and saying, "I'm glad you're okay."

"We *all* are," Amy corrected.

"I'm sorry I couldn't do better Reyna." We gave a sad smile. He looked truly sad about it.

"Don't say that!" Reyna looked mad for a second then smiled. "Like I said, I can never repay you for what you did. You just gave me more debt. Without you all," Reyna looked around, "I wouldn't be me." It warmed their hearts to hear Reyna say that. For once in the maze, they felt at peace.

"Well, let's continue before another—" We frowned and pointed to something above them. "What's that?"

The girls looked up —well except for Reyna who didn't want to move her head too fast— and saw a bird. It looked normal until you saw its wings. The bird was black and the wings were white, but looked like they were held together with metal and golden wax—wait, wax? It flapped around, doing little dives, then started heading down the middle of a path. There was something about it that made Vic curious. It had to be special.

Vic caught the others' eyes. She looked at the determined look on each face and knew they were ready. "You all know what we have to do now, right?"

Amy sighed, then gave a sly smile and pointed upwards. "Follow that bird!"

* * *

Vic took the lead and started running, grimacing from the pain of her ankle. She winced and looked back to see the others.

"Looking for someone?" Vic turned around and saw Amy smiling, not even breathless. "Y'know I was always the fastest runner!"

"Congratulations," Vic said sarcastically. "I was looking for Reyna."

They both looked back and saw Reyna running with We and Skyler, who were jogging alongside her. Reyna had never been a fast runner, but Vic suspected she was more cautious now because of her head wound.

Reyna saw them and sprinted over, panting. "Go ahead, you follow the bird. I'll catch up."

Vic looked up and saw the bird flying away. Soon, it would be too far away to catch up. But Reyna was already hurt and she was a priority. That's when Vic couldn't stand it any longer. She collapsed onto the ground clutching her ankle.

"Vic!" Skyler shrieked. "Vic, are you okay?"

Do I look like I'm okay?

Vic shook her head knowing if she made a sound, she would collapse in tears from the pain.

"Her ankle!" Reyna said, pointing to the bruised, swollen ankle.

"Vic," Skyler chided, "why didn't you tell us? C'mon We, I think we need your help again."

We nodded. The process went faster this time. We first did his scan as Vic tried her hardest not to move. "It's a hairline fracture, and the bruise must make it hurt worse. Running, and that huge fall must have caused it. Especially if you did a lot of running at your school."

Vic shrugged, grimacing as Amy spoke for her. "The only sport Vic did was lacrosse, and that was all year round with barely any breaks and a game every two weeks."

"Just try and take it easy, okay?" We looked sympathetic. "I know I'm not a doctor, but I've done my research."

Vic gave a small nod again. She trusted We, and it seemed the others did too. We did his 'squeeze and stuff appears' thing to get a cast. Not just jumbled items to make one, but the actual item, a cast that strapped onto the lower leg and ankle. Amy took the lead again. She straightened out

Vic's ankle, touching it lightly, and moving slowly. Spoiler: It could have been the worst pain Vic had ever experienced, but she put up with it as Amy strapped the cast on her ankle.

Vic stood up. There was still some pain, but the cast did help. She took a few tentative steps and was surprised to see to see that she could walk properly. She walked with her full weight this time and everything felt normal!

"Magic?" Vic asked We.

"What do you think?" We gave a half-smile.

Amy rolled her eyes. "Wow, *wow*. You are literally the most annoying people I have ever met. And I've *lived* with annoying people."

"Thanks Amy!" Reyna looked at Skyler and gave a knowing smile.

"No problem!" Amy stepped backwards, which was forward in the path. "Well, c'mon guys! We're all up and alive so let's get a move on."

Vic smiled at Reyna and Skyler. "Amy's right! Let's go!"

Suddenly, Vic remembered. *The bird!* She looked up and gave a sigh of relief. The bird with the wax and feather wings was still there! "Thank goodness! I had forgotten about the bird. I can't believe it waited for us—"

The others froze midway through their sigh of relief.

"What's wrong?" Skyler asked cautiously.

They all were looking at Vic now. Vic backed against a wall and thought for a second. Something was tugging at the back of her mind. It was *something* important. The others formed a semi-circle around her. Then it clicked.

"The omega, they're Greek!" Vic exclaimed

"Yeah, we know," Amy said as if saying, *Get to the point!*

The gears in Vic's head were already turning. "The bird had wax wings—I saw a creature that looked like the Minotaur in my test *too*, and the maze—*The maze!*"

"Vic, just explain your complicated thinking!" Amy groaned.

"It's the myth!" Vic exclaimed. "It's Daedalus!"

We's jaw dropped. Then he nodded in appreciation to Vic.

"Repite, por favor?" Reyna said. Reyna loved interchanging Spanish and English phrases. She hadn't done it for a while, so it was good to hear it again.

Vic smiled. "Remember the story of Icarus and Daedalus?"

Skyler gasped. "Oh, you're right!"

Reyna shortly came to the understanding a few seconds later. Even Amy remembered after a lot of sighs from the others.

"Oh, yeah! I remember that story. It was about that boy dying because he didn't listen to his dad that wax wings melt." Amy shook her head.

Vic tried to hide her amused face. "His dad was Daedalus the inventor! His dad made wings with wax and feathers. He also created the labyrinth in Greek mythology. Inside that maze was a Minotaur, which I faced in my test. Because a hero escaped the labyrinth, Daedalus and Icarus were locked away. That led to them trying to escape with the wings and you know what happens next."

Reyna furrowed her eyebrows. "But that's just mythology! It's not true."

"We met so many mythical and 'fake' creatures and things! Do you really believe that?" Vic challenged.

"I guess you're right," Reyna said, giving in.

The bird cawed, and flew in circles—warning them to hurry.

Skyler glanced at the bird. "Explain later Vic, let's go!"

They didn't run this time. The bird still flew ahead, but it seemed to stay at their pace. As they continued on, Vic felt happy. They cracked jokes, made puns for Reyna. Skyler had tears slipping down her cheeks.

"Skyler, it'll be fine." Vic reassured. "Don't worry about the maze."

"It's not that," Skyler smiled, "I'm just happy."

The others understood and smiled too. Except for We and Amy.

"Could you be any cheesier?" they asked in unison. They looked at each other, just plain surprised.

"Did we just agree?" Amy asked almost too genuinely.

"Did we?" We turned too.

The moment passed, and they continued pacing through the winding paths. Each turn seemed to get darker, and darker. The lanterns kept getting brighter, but filled with more pictures of monsters and ghosts. Vic fiddled with the Omega sapphire. The Omega said they created the quest. Vic assumed that meant the maze too. But what if it was Daedalus! The Omega never mentioned him though. Could that mean Daedalus was working with Seville and created the maze so it would be harder for them to succeed? Vic hoped that wasn't the case.

The ground became cracked, tiny pebbles and rocks were scattered all over. The atmosphere had again become tense. The girls knew they were close. They had to be! The bird cawed again, but not for them to hurry. It sounded like it was in distress.

"You guys hear that?" Skyler looked distressed. They watched the bird flap its wings, but it didn't move forward. A drip fell to the ground.

Wax! They wings were melting in record time, with tiny feathers falling in clumps of wax. Reyna lunged forward, and caught the black bird in her hand before it hit the ground. Vic felt a jolt of worry that Reyna hit her head again, but everything was fine. Reyna could take care of herself. Vic needed to learn that.

Reyna looked puzzled. "How did this happen?" She set the bird down. It seemed to be struggling to get out. Reyna stood up. "We still need the bird to guide us, and its real wings are too tiny to fly."

The bird flapped its wings as if it was giving an example. "Or—maybe this happened for a reason," We said. "Look!"

The girls looked at where We was pointing. There was a sign on the wall. The Omega. They couldn't be sure where they were, but they all knew they were in the center, the last part of the maze. There was something else written in the middle of the omega: The Lair of Icarus.

Chapter 34

Amy

I think I'm dying of information overload.

Amy couldn't even congratulate the group for getting to the middle by themselves. Okay, maybe that was a lie, but they had accomplished something! Now, they had learned about the Daedalus thing and the Lair of Icarus! Amy hadn't heard about anything called the Lair of Icarus in Greek mythology. This was something new for sure.

Amy sighed. To be honest, Amy felt a little left out. It seemed like We and Vic were identical. It made Amy feel like Vic didn't care about her now that We was there. Then again, Vic trusted Amy more than We. Amy knew that she needed to trust Vic too.

Amy walked over to We and Vic. Vic traced her finger over the Omega. Traces of rock lingered on her hand.

"I don't understand!" Vic backed away from the Omega, frowning. "It should be working! Isn't the Omega supposed to help us?"

"The lair of Icarus—" Amy's thoughts were racing. Vic and Skyler were usually the ones to give all the answers, but Amy had one this time. "That has to be affecting the Omega!"

Vic tucked her hair behind her ear. "You might be right. But all things aside, what do we do next? There's nothing waiting for us here like we thought!"

Reyna and Skyler stopped alongside them.

"Well, I guess you're out of luck then!"

Amy turned to glare at Skyler and Reyna but then stopped. *They said, "you're" Reyna and Skyler would say "we're"! And it sounds like someone else—*

They turned around and saw Yes floating, her hands on her hips.

"Yes—" Vic sounded like she was ready to punch Yes. *"Why are you here?"*

"Aw, does *wittle Vicky* want to know?" Yes asked, mockingly.

Vic glared at Yes. "Answer my question!"

Yes rolled her eyes. "C'mon Griff, we don't have to pretend anymore. Let's ditch them. They'll never get through the quest from here."

"Griff"? What's going on?"

Amy looked over at Vic who looked hurt. "We, what is she talking about. You're with her?"

"Tell her *We,*" Yes cackled. "Tell her *all* the lies you told her!"

We sighed in defeat. Vic looked over at Amy, and Amy wished Vic had said this: "I guess you were right Amy," Vic said, glaring at We. "You were right about him all along."

But this is what she actually said: "This can't be right!" She told Amy, then glared at Yes. "We told me—"

Yes just laughed. "Turns out *We* is a better liar than me! Or should I call you your real name *Griff?* The name you didn't even bother to tell the person that trusted you no matter what!"

"We, she's not telling the truth!" Vic seemed confident.

"We helped us so many times and you weren't even there!" Skyler jumped in. "You can't expect us to believe you!"

Reyna also jumped in. "We saved my life! And I owe him for that." Reyna looked at We and smiled. "If that means trusting him, I'd do so."

The girls looked at Amy. *C'mon brain! Think past the overloading information and say what you need to!*

"Yes, you literally just told everyone you're evil! If we didn't have We, we could all be dead! You might have helped me pass my test, but now that all seems like a ruse for your actual plan!"

Vic leaned into Amy and whispered, "Nice vocab."

"Who's the one not being serious now," Amy whispered back.

Yes swirled up and rose above their heads. She laughed maliciously. "I'm tired of being the nice teen when I can show my true self and leave you to wither and die." She spun around in a sonic speed. They heard ripping noises and saw a gruesome sight. Yes was peeling back her skin, and a different body was emerging.

Suddenly, the Yes that was standing there had become a completely different person. Instead of the girl with long hair and fashionable glasses, this one had short, cropped, black hair with purple highlights. Her face was still the same shape, and her eyes were the same, except they were teal. Her clothes weren't a sleeveless shirt and jeans, but instead fishnet stockings with ripped black shorts. She wore a black bomber jacket with a purple t-shirt underneath that said, *Embrace the Darkness.* It had a lightning symbol in the corner. The only color she really saw was purple—Wait, *color?*

"How—" Amy trailed off.

Yes just laughed again. "And I thought you were actually prepared. Turns out you know *nothing* about ghosts."

The other girls had the same confused expression. They watched as Yes came down to the ground and smirked at them. "Well, since you're about to die anyway, I might as well give you an explanation! We have *magic.* We can do anything with that magic. If that means giving ourselves color, we can do it. Show them!" She pointed to We.

We sighed. It looked like he wasn't going to comply, but he did. He passed a hand over his eyes and it flashed teal for a second until it returned to the normal gray ghost color. "We just don't choose to give ourselves color since it takes up most of our magic space, but for certain ghosts, it's easier for them."

You didn't have to be a mind reader to know what We was saying. It was easier for bad ghosts to give themselves color even though they don't most of the time.

Amy turned to Yes and glared. "How could you do this? I trusted you!"

"Haven't you learned," Yes smirked, "to never trust anyone?" She floated down to Amy and tucked a piece of her hair behind her ears. Amy was still in shock.

Yes smiled nicely, but it looked odd on her face. "Why be transparent and not able to touch humans when I have the power to do so! We are stronger following my dad, and you can be too! You don't have to die with your *friends*. If you choose, you can be powerful. You can finally take revenge on Mr. Mister who never treated you properly. I know you're smart Amy, so I'm hoping you'll make the right choice." Yes's smile withered away at that last sentence. Yes put her hand out. Amy's head was spinning. She sighed and looked at the others.

"Amy—" Vic looked at her. She didn't say anything more.

Amy looked at Yes. "I knew you would make the right choice." Yes smiled evilly at the others.

Amy put her hand out, then slapped Yes' hand away. "I could never betray my friends!"

Reyna gave a silent cheer. Amy felt like doing the same. The look on Yes' face was enough to make everyone cheer. Amy's head was still spinning though. There was something Yes had said that had caught her attention. *My father.*

The others realized too because her expression turned stony as Amy said, "Your father, you mean, as in—"

"Yes *Amy*," Yes glared, "my father is Regal Seville, owner of this very mansion. The mansion that you will *die* in."

Chapter 35

Skyler

*W*ait, what? Regal Seville? Father?

"Don't be so surprised, Reyna." Yes wrinkled her nose at Reyna like she was something not worth looking at. Skyler felt a surge of anger at that. "Everyone knows you're scared. You don't need to impress your friends by being brave. Come on, show them. Run away—Reyna. Just like you always do." Skyler noticed that Yes's voice had changed too. Instead of the sweet innocent tone, it now had a sharp, cold tone, like the one you would hear in a horror movie.

"You think I'm going to run away?" Reyna asked defiantly. "After all that has happened, you think I'm still that same old coward? I've changed Yes. Just like you just did. But unlike you, I did it for a good reason."

"I don't appreciate being called Yes. Call me Hydrangea," Yes, er, Hydrangea sneered.

Vic turned to We, ignoring Hydrangea. *"Griff,* if that's your name," Vic looked at him with no expression. "if you have to transform now too, do it. I don't want to be seeing the fake version of you, the version that *lied* to me. I trusted you when you told me you were good. Turns out I shouldn't have."

"I'm not under a disguise like Hydrangea," Griff said apologetically. "But I haven't told you everything—Ghosts

195

can touch humans with magic. We can have color." He looked ashamed. Griff looked down his feet

"I'm sorry," he added. It was what Vic needed. She didn't move, yet Skyler could tell something changed. Griff continued. "I'd never do anything to hurt you." Griff's voice was filled with more emotion. "I could have done so much more! —I thought giving my true appearance was enough—turns out it wasn't."

"It's fine," Vic gave a half-smile. "You did so many things. All I ask is that you be on our side. Don't be neutral."

Griff turned to Hydrangea. "Hyd, you have a choice to change. This isn't the sister I remember!"

Hydrangea scoffed. "First of all, I'm not *Hyd* anymore. Also, I've always been like this, I've *always* been what dad wanted. *You* were weak Griff. You'll never get anything from being kind. Dad told me you always lose what you want no matter what! THIS IS MY CHOICE GRIFF!"

Griff backed away.

Hydrangea sneered. "If you want to go with them *fine!* A real brother of mine would have been with me! *You're not my brother.* Now you'll pay the price." With that, she vanished.

Skyler had a bad feeling in her stomach. *She said there was a price to pay. She said we would die! There's something we can't see—*

CRACK!

"What the heck is happening?" Amy shook her head and tumbled backwards.

A rip had appeared right in the air. Skyler didn't know if that was even possible, but something was happening. They heard a roar coming from the tear. In the blink of an eye, a monster started tumbling out of the hole in the air. No, not *a* monster, *many* monsters.

Monsters of all sorts started to appear. The minotaur,

mini basilisks, ghosts, and a lady with snake hair: Medusa. There were too many monsters to count.

Vic grabbed her spear. Her face was grim. All of a sudden, Skyler did not want to be on the wrong side of Vic. Vic was dull, and probably angry, but one thing wasn't. Her blue eyes were glistening, maybe with the look of craftiness?

Suddenly, they heard something cawing. Skyler looked up and saw a bird made of wax like the one before, only this one was much, *much bigger*. It cried out a battle call that echoed all around the maze.

"Skyler!" Reyna shouted across the clearing. Skyler was worried when she saw Reyna sprinting towards her. *Was something wrong?*

"Skyler, I need a piece of paper," Reyna gasped. *We're in danger—and Reyna wants paper?* Reyna must have noticed the look on Skyler's face. "Just give it to me, there's something important!"

Skyler tore a piece of paper from her notepad and handed it to Reyna.

"Pencil." Skyler handed Reyna a pencil that she randomly found in her pocket. Reyna ran and hid behind a wall, sheathing her dagger. She looked like she was ready to draw, write, and fight.

"Skyler!" Vic shouted. "Grab your sword! We need you to fight!"

Skyler unsheathed her sword and dodged monsters coming her way.

"Skyler, where's Reyna?" Amy asked, looking around.

"She's drawing something. I don't know what but it seems important."

"Watch out!" Vic screamed. Vic pushed Skyler out of the way, right before Medusa hit her.

"Oh my god. Thanks Vic! I don't think I'm going to be of much use—WATCH OUT!" Skyler pushed Vic out of the way of a ghost. Skyler, who still had basilisk blood on her sword—somehow it was the same from the fight in the test—cut across the ghost's leg, making it disintegrate into thin air.

"Not much use huh?" Vic winked at Skyler and ran towards the opposite side. Skyler watched her jump over a monster, sliding under a second one. *Where did she learn this stuff?*

Skyler saw another ghost backing up on her. She side-stepped to avoid its knife, then turned and cut across the ghost's arm. Griff and Amy then joined Skyler. Griff used his magic and Amy used her arrows to pin ghosts to the wall. Skyler then could disintegrate them before they escaped from the arrow.

Skyler saw Reyna join Vic and show her the drawing. Vic pulled Reyna out of the way as she stabbed a basilisk—smaller than the one at the portal, a little bigger than a cobra—with her spear. Reyna joined the fighting. She cut across Medusa's back, who cried out in terror of the literal backstabbing act.

Suddenly, Hydrangea appeared out of nowhere. Something from her power flew Griff through the air. He barely had time to use his own magic to fall on the ground, a couple feet away from where Vic was standing. Griff glared at Hydrangea and helped Vic fight off a huge monster lumbering in their direction.

"Well, well, *well.* Is this too easy for you?" Hydrangea sneered. "How about a taste of this?" She flicked her hand and more monsters piled out of the air.

"Hyd, *please!*" Griff pleaded. "I know you would never do this! You're here because you care about *me!* The Hyd I know is still in there!"

Hydrangea's face seemed to soften for a second. Then she gave a deathly stare. "You'll never learn Griff. I might be here for the reason you said, but I've changed for the better! I know you changed for the worse Griff! Learn to listen Griff, YOU NEVER LEARN! Right now I'm happy if you die."

Griff looked angry, but Skyler could see tears in his eyes. She couldn't imagine if family ever said that to her. It was enough to break a person.

"You need to learn *Hyd!"* Vic said her name mockingly. "Griff hasn't done anything wrong. He might have held secrets, but it was because of you! I can't blame him for trying to trust his sister. Griff's one of us." Vic eyes looked a bit glassy as she gave a smile to reassure Griff.

"Skyler!" Skyler jumped back and readied her sword. Amy looked overwhelmed as she shot ghosts. It didn't do any good. "Did you forget we still have ghosts and monsters to fight!"

Crap, I forgot!

Ghosts had started circling Amy. She shot them back, but without basilisk blood it was no use. Skyler looked back at Griff, Hydrangea nowhere in sight.

"Griff!" she yelled. He looked back, still shooting magic blade-like-things. "Can you use magic to help Amy?"

He nodded and in a blink Skyler's sword jumped out of her hand. It shot as fast as a torpedo towards the ghosts and went straight through the clump surrounding Amy. There were cries as loud as a bird's as they disintegrated into nothing.

Speaking of birds, the giant bird was circling over their heads. Its talons were clutched—perhaps around monsters.

With Hydrangea nowhere in sight they had their good moments of battle. The group was fighting like a machine, each part playing an important role. Skyler didn't want to brag, but she felt like she was one of the most essential parts—for once. Without her, the monsters would have been hard to kill, and the ghosts, *impossible* to kill.

The bird swooped down and stabbed the heart of the
many headed monster Vic, Griff and Reyna were fighting—a Hydra. The name reminded Skyler of Hydrangea.
She gagged at the thought of Hydrangea being killed like
that. She might have betrayed them, but Skyler couldn't
imagine killing her. Even monsters and ghosts were hard
to kill. She knew they wouldn't stop to kill Hydrangea,
especially because of the way it would hurt Griff.

Skyler saw Vic roll under another monster and stuck her
spear into the monster's knee. She cringed as she watched it
fall, a vein spewing blood, and ran away to the other side.
Vic nearly ran straight into Griff. He smiled and Skyler
saw Vic's face turn pink. *Does she really have time to be
embarrassed now?*

He ran over to another ghost—Skyler followed away from
the chaos— and with a flick, the ghost was dust. Skyler
took a breath. Somehow doing it herself didn't make her
as queasy as it did now.

Skyler suddenly heard another loud boom. She turned
around to see nothing but just a few more monsters.
Rephrase— A *lot* more monsters.

Hydrangea cackled, appearing out of nowhere. "Oh, this
is fun! Come on, don't give-up just yet!"

"Give up? GIVE UP?" Vic had a cross between a snarl
and a grin. "I promise you that's the last thing you'll ever
see from us." Her mischievous smile soon turned into anger
when she saw what Hydrangea had in stock for her. A ten
foot tall monster looked down at her. *Horns, red eyes, sharp
weapon— I think that's good enough to be classified as* <u>scary</u>.
Skyler saw Vic's face and knew she was thinking the same
thing. The monster was holding something that looked like
a toothbrush. Only it was a hundred times that size and
each bristle was made out of pointy, jagged, sharp metal
pieces, each about a foot long.

"Have fun, *Vicky!*" Hydrangea gave another of her evil laughs.

Skyler turned around and saw more monsters awaiting the rest of them. There was a monster that looked long and slimy with blue blood oozing out of the corner of its mouth. One was coated fully in rusted knives with only its green eyes full of fierceness and hatred showing. One more monster appeared, which didn't seem dangerous until it started doubling itself without any explanation. Suddenly, each one of them was trapped in something that felt like a bubble, with another monster. Skyler was trapped with the blue blood one, Reyna with the doubling one, and Amy with the one coated with knives. Griff was battling all the monsters that were still left that Hydrangea had first conjured.

Skyler looked at her monster, which was surprisingly calm, circling around her quietly, then turned and watched as Amy's monster pulled a knife out of its body, coated with blood. When she turned again she saw Vic fiercely dueling her monster, dodging all its aims to stab her with its toothbrush.

"SCREEEEE!"

Skyler spun and faced her monster. She looked down at her sword skeptically. It was her best chance and Skyler knew it. In a blink, she brought her sword down cutting through the whole monster with one slash. But surprisingly, it just fused back together. *Now that's disgusting.* Skyler continued jabbing and slashing but nothing seemed to work.

Reyna was the only one actually getting somewhere. Every time she killed one of her monsters, half of what was left would disappear. The only thing stopping her from defeating the monster was that the rest of the monsters wouldn't stop doubling. For Reyna, it was a race against time.

Amy seemed confused. So far she had figured out that every weapon on its body could only be used once.

Skyler brought her focus back to her own monster. It was calmer than the others, but only because it knew that there was no reason for it to attack back unless Skyler did. That's when it hit Skyler.

This time, she was quick with her movements. Instead of lashing through the body once, she made an arc, cutting through it twice and cutting it into three pieces. Instead of fusing back together two of the pieces disintegrated and made the monster smaller, a third of its original size. All Skyler needed to do now was keep dividing until it was too small to do anything.

Reyna had already finished and was bending over, panting to catch her breath. She waved to Skyler as she finished off her own monster and joined Reyna on the ground.

The two of them watched Amy and Vic fight. They knew that if they tried to help the other girls fight, Hydrangea would bring more monsters for them. Amy seemed to be getting somewhere and Vic—Well, let's just say she wasn't the most tolerant when it came to monsters.

Vic was getting more agitated by the moment. The more she fought, the harder it became to defeat her monster. Skyler was afraid of what may come for her; she always seemed to have the worst fate.

Amy had figured out all she had to do was make the monster mad and it would waste its weapons. Soon enough, Amy finished too.

"Well, what a surprise! Vic gets the hardest challenge yet again," Amy sighed and joined the two of them on the ground.

Griff kept turning back to look at Vic. Something told Skyler that he was also worried for her.

Vic had a face that was now filled with anger and slight terror. Suddenly, the monster started to light up in flames. The whole area started to get warmer and warmer—soon enough, they could feel it too.

"Umm, maybe I was understating it when I said, 'the hardest challenge'. Amy looked more scared than Vic was and will ever be.

"I hate feeling useless, and that's exactly what we are right now," Reyna said. Skyler noticed that Reyna was crossing her fingers behind her back. She did the same.

Vic's last straw had just been taken. She threw off her sweatshirt, facing the monster with no sense of doubt in her blue eyes, which stood out in the ring of blazing fire. Vic let down her shield—which in Skyler's mind, was completely the wrong thing to do— and tested her spear on the stone ground. Out of nowhere, from ten feet away she ran and jumped. In Skyler's eyes, it all seemed like slow motion. Vic jumped on to the monster's head and held on to its tall horns to keep her balance.

Amy just stood there, blinking. "That was low-key cheesy. But right now, it's just plain scary." Amy tilted her head, giving an afterthought. "A little too movie-like though."

The monster screeched.

"Yup, definitely movie-like."

Griff's weapon had dissolved back into the ghostly mist as he stood, shocked. He looked at the scene, giving another reason for Amy to give them another 'told you so' look.

The monster seemed confused for a few split seconds, just enough time for Vic to pull on its horns, making the monster scream in pain. The monster fell to its knees in pure pain and collapsed, disappearing in a cloud of yellow dust along with its toothbrush.

As for Vic, well, she was lucky the monster had disappeared on the ground instead of ten feet in the air. She collapsed almost as drastically as the monster.

"VIC!" Skyler and the other two yelled in unison as they ran towards her.

"Vic! Are you okay?" Reyna looked scared.

"Do I *look* okay?" Vic whimpered.

Well, at least she can talk!

"You're burning up. It was probably the fire." Skyler said, feeling her forehead and helping her up.

"Shocking Skyler, just *shocking.*" Amy rolled her eyes.

"I'll be fine, don't worry about me. As for now, we have another matter to deal with." Vic gestured towards a basilisk, silently waiting for them.

Chapter 36

Reyna

Reyna was still a *little* bit in shock. Vic could be scary. No, *very* scary. You always knew when Amy smirked at something Vic does, it's *not* going to be what you expect.

But now—yet again—nothing but another problem. *I think we've faced one too many basilisks for a lifetime already.* Reyna sighed. She couldn't remember the last time they had slept or eaten. For the record, they didn't even know what day it was.

The basilisk swiveled around the girls, studying their every move. The only person that seemed to have an idea for their next move was Skyler.

"This isn't any ordinary basilisk. Something about it is off." Skyler removed both of her earrings and faced away from the basilisk. Skyler used the metal back to reflect the basilisk. Then she used the other earring to reflect the metal's image again—probably in case something could happen to her even through a reflection. Then carefully, she looked at the reflection's eyes.

Skyler turned around to the others. "It's kinda weird. In the myths, the eyes are usually yellow or brown but these are teal—"

Griff had a grim expression on his face. "That's not any basilisk, that's my sister." The others looked slightly stunned.

He looked grim and the girls all gave him a reassuring smile; they were a team, and teams had to support each other.

Reyna twirled her dagger in her finger. "Well, what's she waiting for? She's even missed a chance to get us from behind!"

Griff hurdled them together so Hydrangea wouldn't hear them. "It's her plan. She is waiting for us to give up and be unarmed. You know what that means right?"

Amy nodded. "We need to drop our weapons." She took her quiver and bow off her back and was about to drop it on the ground when Griff stopped her.

"No!" he hissed. "I have a plan that *won't* leave you defenseless. Can you sheath your weapons?" Amy put her quiver and bow on her back again, Skyler and Reyna sheathed their blades, and Vic strapped her spear to her boot. It seemed weird, but if she could walk it probably wasn't a problem. Griff conjured his blade away.

He went around and tapped their weapons twice. Slowly, they all faded away.

"Whoa," Reyna and Skyler breathed in unison. Their blades had turned invisible!

With a flick that Griff made, a clattering noise came and replicas of their weapons fell to their feet.

Vic gave a small smile. "We're definitely going to have to do some acting."

"Yeah," Skyler replied. "Seriously! how long is a stupid basilisk going to wait to attack us?" Skyler sighed, acting. "I'm giving up." Skyler backed up to a wall and slid down to sit. *She's such a theatre nerd!*

The others followed her lead—well expect Griff. It would be odd for a ghost to slide down a wall! Soon enough, Hydrangea attacked. She swung her tail like a rope, nearly hitting Reyna.

The five of them got up and started fighting back.

Hydrangea, utterly confused as to why she couldn't see weapons, kept hitting back. The dueling went on for a while longer, Hydrangea finally realizing the truth about their weapons. As the group went on fighting, the basilisk writhed with every cut. Not much later, the basilisk turned back into Hydrangea— a very exhausted Hydrangea.

"Fine. *Fine!*" she snarled. " I *surrender,* but I'll be back. Your fight isn't over yet. You haven't won just yet."

Griff stepped forward. "Yeah, you're right about that *Hyd.*" Tired, Hydrangea looked confused. "The battle is *not* over yet. *You're* still here." The weapons all became visible. His magical, mystical blade turned into something much longer, shaper, and frankly—more scary. His expression seemed to scare the girls.

Reyna was also worried. Griff had been betrayed too many times but—was too much enough to fight your own sister? To kill her?

"Griff, you—you can't." Reyna called out. "Griff she's still your sister, and even if she betrayed you—don't be like her. Don't fight."

The meaning seemed to kick in for Griff. He looked at the blade and a look of shame washed over his face. The blade slowly shrank and became its regular size.

Hydrangea smirked. "Just like I thought. You're just a wimp who isn't brave enough to fight his own sister!"

Griff blade now fully disappeared. "No, you're wrong Hyd. You've *always* been wrong. What you're doing, your manipulation, it isn't right and I'm finally telling you the truth. Take a look around Hyd. You're the one who has lost."

Hydrangea looked around in fury. "Believe what you want Griff, but *this* isn't over." With that she disappeared.

Griff exhaled, his boldness all gone.

"Hey look, though I don't know what's happened in your past, we're all in the same boat. We'll all get through it together. I promise," Vic reassured them. The rest of them nodded along.

"Thanks!" Griff brushed back his hair with his hand. "It really means a lot. But seriously, I've had enough sentimental moments for a lifetime!"

"Can we seriously stop with the sappy stuff?"added Amy.

Skyler laughed and nodded. "Yeah, this maze is making us sappy! The sooner we get out of here, the better!"

"We should really get to work now," Vic gestured over her shoulder to the Omega. "Reyna do you have your—"

"My drawing!" Reyna said before Vic could finish her sentence. Vic nodded with an unreadable look on her face. Reyna's mind traveled back to when she was drawing.

Reyna brought a crumpled piece of paper out of her pocket. As Reyna unfolded it, the first thing the group saw was the Omega symbol and some markings.

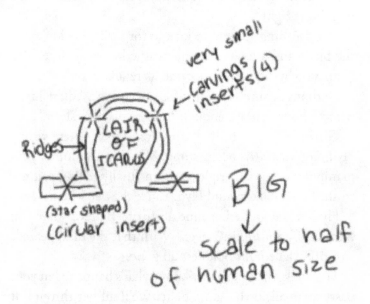

All five of them studied the drawing.

"Wait, I didn't notice the ridges before this! It's so clear now, I can't believe I didn't see it!" Amy exclaimed as Vic nodded.

"So—there has to be a reason for them," Griff said thoughtfully.

Vic rolled her eyes. "Duh!"

"Vic and I think it's for the jewels. It has to lead to the next part of the quest," Reyna paused. "You know, Regal Seville."

Griff's expression became dark. *"Regal Seville."*

Completely oblivious to Griff, Amy said, "Thanks for reminding us we have even more do, Reyna! Haven't we done enough? Ugh, we need a break!"

"Well, it's true, but the faster we get this done, the faster we get out of here," Vic said.

"Hey Vic," Skyler got Vic's attention, "remember what you were saying about Daedalus and Icarus?"

"Oh yeah! I almost completely forgot my train of thought!" Vic's face lit up. "Basically— Come here," Vic said, leading the group to the carving. She traced her finger over the word "Lair".

"What about it?" Reyna asked. From her memory, it wasn't something they had talked about before.

"Look," Vic said, as Reyna traced her own hand over the word. She felt something she hadn't before. Next to each letter, there was a smaller letter in the upper left corner.

"I never realized that before!" Vic nodded deep in thought.

"What is it?" Skyler and Amy asked in unison. Griff looked at them weirdly as they shrugged.

"There are small letters in the upper corner of each letter."

"What do they spell?" Skyler joined them by the wall, feeling the carving for herself. " T-H-E-O. Theo? Wait no, it's not an O, it's Omega."

Amy groaned. "I bet you there's probably another hundred Omegas carved on the floor."

"The Omega? What does that mean?" Reyna's confusion was really getting to her.

"It's obvious isn't it? It means 'The Omega' as in the five siblings." Vic said. But to Reyna, something was still missing.

"A little too obvious if you ask me," Skyler replied, thinking the same as Reyna.

"Yeah. *Very* obvious. We didn't just navigate the whole maze and fight hundreds of monsters and feel the whole carving to figure this out." Amy looked at them with sarcasm.

Reyna sighed, thinking about the whole experience. "Well maybe there is another meaning to the Omega. The letter 'Omega' existed far before these people— er—ghosts did. Omega is the last letter in the Greek alphabet."

"Reyna's right! 'The Omega' as in 'The end'!" Vic said as if they had just finished a puzzle.

"Wait, so it's the end of the quest? Knowing— I mean, Regal Seville is probably not that easy to find." Griff said.

"Easy? EASY? DID YOU JUST SAY EASY?" Amy stared at Griff upset.

"Whoa, calm down Amy." Vic put her hand on Amy's shoulder. But suddenly, something seemed to hit her. "Oh no. I don't think it means the end of our quest. I think it means—the end of Icarus."

Suddenly it all seemed to fall into place. *The end of Icarus.* Reyna shivered at the thought.

"You—you mean, Icarus' grave is here?" Skyler eyes widened at the thought. As she said that, the carving started to shine brighter and brighter until it glowed.

"I would take that as a yes," Amy wrinkled her nose.

"So now what?" It seemed to Reyna as if they were getting nowhere.

"Let's try putting the jewels in." Skyler pulled out the miniature brown case with all the jewels. As soon as it was in her hand, it grew back to the original size. She opened it and took each one of them out carefully. "I think there are four—one for each of us."

"Wait, why have I never seen that before!" Amy exclaimed.

"Seen what?" Vic asked.

"The four stones. Each is one of our birthstones! Reyna's is an emerald, Skyler's is a topaz, Vic's is a sapphire, and mine is a ruby!"

"Yeah! Wow, how did you get so smart?" Skyler teased her as the others laughed.

"When did you get so good at 'pretending'?" Amy smirked, referring to Skyler's acting.

Reyna smirked. It was good to hear the normal joking between the group, but they needed to finish the last part of the quest before Regal Seville figured out where they were.

"Should we put them in on the count of three?" Reyna asked as she started to count. "One, two, three!" The four of them pressed the stones into each of the carvings around the Omega. They waited in suspense for about five seconds until suddenly, the stones burst out shattering.

The girls—and Griff—watched as the shattered pieces rose into the air and merged together and hovered above their heads. The girls looked closer and saw a silver key shining, with the stones at the end.

"Wh-what just happened?" That was all Amy could say.

Amy speechless? Now that doesn't happen often!

But what happened next was something that Reyna would have never have imagined could happen. The key came and hovered in front of her.

"Reyna, I think you should take the key," Vic said softly.

Reyna stammered. For some reason, it just didn't feel like her job, but she was the one who had almost died—two times. Reyna was the one who had grown up the most. Maybe that made her the one who needed to do the final step. Slowly, she held her hand out and the key gently came and landed in her hand.

Not knowing what hit them, they were suddenly swept out of the maze, their weapons left behind, going through another portal—yet again.

Part three:

The Library of Legends

Chapter 37

Vic

"*Food.*" It seemed right that Amy was the one who said that. The first thing they saw when they came through the portal was the grand dining hall, filled with all sorts of food waiting to be eaten. Vic tried to think back to the last time they actually had a proper meal.

While walking through the twisting tunnels, Griff had given them hard crackers and water at times, but that wasn't having a meal. It almost seemed like it had been weeks since they had eaten something hot. But it probably hadn't been long.

"VIC!" Vic spun around to see her little brother running at her at full speed.

"Aaron!" Vic kneeled down and hugged her brother. He hugged her back just as tightly.

"Thank goodness you're okay!" Vic saw Nina rushing into the room to hug Reyna.

"Did you fight a lot of monsters?" Aaron acted out a little scene of swinging a sword. "Patricia told us all about you guys!"

The group laughed and Griff high-fived Aaron.

"Come on, you guys should eat! You look exhausted." Nina looked at them with pity.

"You don't have to tell us twice!" Amy sat down without question as the others joined with a smile.

All of them sat down to eat, enjoying the moment and telling Nina and Aaron what all had happened, as Aaron acted it out. Vic smiled, thinking about how grateful she was to have her friends and her siblings. But something still lingered in the back of her mind. *Mom and dad.* It wasn't something she used to always think about, but for some reason, it was fixed in her mind.

As they all finished their meal, Skyler asked unexpectedly, " Hey Nina, do you know how long we've been in the maze?"

"You've been in there for seven days." Nina told them.

"Pause. Seven days? It feels like 36 hours!" Reyna said, taken aback by Nina's answer.

"The mansion has that effect sometimes. How do you guys think you survived with no real food?" Nina replied to Reyna's comment.

"The Mansion always seems to surprise us," Vic said, sounding more thoughtful than she had meant for it to come out.

Amy laughed. "If only it didn't sometimes!"

Nina smiled and tucked a piece of hair behind her ear. "Well, me and Aaron are just going to tidy up and we'll meet you back in the room. Is that good?"

"Wait!" Reyna stopped her sister. "We can help you guys. I kinda feel bad for not doing anything."

The others nodded in agreement. Nina just shook her head. "*Not doing anything*? Really Reyna? You've been doing so much over your quest! Plus, you need some rest and have you seen your clothes! Next time," she added, the last part with a smile.

Reyna looked like she wanted to do something else but then agreed. "Next time."

"I better be heading back to my room," Griff said as the girls were about to head out.

"Okay then! See you tomorrow!" Vic waved back to Griff.

The four of them crawled to the trapdoor underneath the table—not taking the long way this time—Vic leading the way, they opened up the trapdoor and were just about to go in when Vic stopped in her tracks and kneeled next to it.

"What's going on?" Skyler asked the others, now making a circle around the entrance, sitting down.

Vic didn't say anything. She just pointed to the trapdoor. There was another clue, taped on with *Scotch Tape.* When the others realized what was happening, their expressions quickly changed. How were they feeling at that moment? Vic had no idea. She peeled the clue off the trapdoor and began to read it. "With the key, unlock a mystery. Something beyond imagination. Filled with help and mysteries.

With the key, unlock a mystery
Something beyond imagination
Filled with help and mysteries

"Key? Reyna you don't think—" Skyler trailed as Reyna searched her pockets and pulled out the same key that had transported them.

"I should have figured," Reyna twirled the key around, gently, "teleporting us back apparently wasn't the important part of the key."

"Um guys, maybe we should be discussing this somewhere else—somewhere that's *not* under a table." Amy said dryly.

"Ha, true. Let's just get to the room and figure it out there." Vic led the way through the trapdoor.

The passageway was narrow and steep. The girls held on to the gray walls, trying not to slip. Soon enough, they reached the entrance to their room.

"I never thought I would be so relieved to be sleeping on pink and yellow polka-dots again!" Skyler laughed with a new sense of happiness and calmness in her eyes. It occurred to Vic that ever since the quest started, they always had something or another to stress about.

"So true!" Amy collapsed onto her bed. *Seriously, how many times has she done that?*

Skyler wrinkled her nose a little. "Ugh, we're literally covered in everything from the maze and now we're sleeping!"

Vic rolled her eyes. "You're such a germaphobe, Skyler! But this time, you're kind of right."

Vic took in the state of herself and everyone else. The braid Reyna had done on Vic's hair had become a nest, and the running and fighting had left marks and holes in their shoes and clothes. They were covered in dust, dirt, water, spit in Reyna's case, and who knows what else. Vic wasn't like Skyler about things like dirt, but this was more than enough to make her gag.

Without saying a word, the girls took one look at Vic's face and headed into their color-coded bathrooms. The look on Vic's face must have struck them since it was almost half-an-hour later when they came out, fully changed, cleaned up, and ready to go to sleep.

Vic collapsed on her bed—the room layout had stayed the same from the last time. It was relieving, considering the last time they tried to sleep, they had been attacked by a Greek Bloody Mary. Vic probably got the least sleep out of them all, looking back at the moment.

Vic felt calm for once. She fiddled with the Omega sapphire and noticed Skyler writing something down, using the box as a flat surface.

"What's up, Skyler?" Amy asked, noticing Skyler writing. Reyna also sat up, waiting for the answer.

Ugh, if Amy was asked this she would say—

"The ceiling, duh!" Skyler gave a humorous smile.

Exactly that!

Amy laughed and high fived Skyler. Reyna crossed her arms but you could still see a small smile.

Skyler ripped the paper off the notepad and showed it to them. It was the same paper with the words the Omega had said after they all finished the test:

> *The answer could be right in front of you. If you search you'll see the answer. But that's the hardest to find so I give you another chance. You will find Regal Seville with a potion, but if you do it incorrectly you might end up in a trance.*

But there was also more. Skyler had written the words of the clue and some other thoughts.

> *With the key, unlock a mystery*
> *Something beyond imagination*
> *Filled with help and mysteries.*

The answer right in front of us was Hydrangea! But that was the hardest and she's gone, so that means we need to find Regal Seville with the potion.

Maybe where it says, "unlock a mystery" it means we need to find the keyhole and it'll led us to the next part.

"Filled with help and mysteries" could mean this is where we make the potion!

Vic couldn't help but smile. There were so close to the end! If Skyler was right, then the last part of their quest would be coming up. But deep down inside, she knew it wasn't going to be easy. If anything, it would just be much, much harder.

"That's great and all Skyler," Reyna said, "but how are we going to find a keyhole in this huge mansion? And not only that, there are so many floors! It'll be like finding a needle in a haystack!"

"Wow, where did you learn literature?" Vic teased. Reyna glared back as everyone laughed.

"We really have no idea, do we?" Skyler stated, veering them back on topic.

"Unless—" Reyna turned to Vic. Vic reluctantly nodded in agreement, slow to respond.

The mood settled back and Vic brought out the sapphire. She knew what they needed to do. "The Omega. That's the only solution we have."

Vic clutched the sapphire tightly in her hand. *Duo.* The sapphire started swirling, creating a misty illusion. Duo appeared in what looked like a misty hologram, the 'mist' twinkling like stars.

"Hello girls!" Duo gave a warm smile. "I see you're in need again."

"Duo," Vic looked at the others. They gave her a nod. "We—"

"I know what you need," Duo waved reassuringly. "Look at the key, and you will see, those colors mean something other than what they seem. If in despair, look over there, to where the jewels lay, those colors will guide on your way."

And with that, Duo's figure turned to mist, falling gently on the ground.

"So, how is this helping us?" Reyna asked after Duo's remains completely dissolved.

"Ugh, I should've taken notes!" Skyler shook her head, as she learned over to the bedside table to grab her notepad and pen.

As Skyler opened up to a blank page to write down what she remembered, words suddenly started appearing on the page in Skyler's handwriting. From what Vic could remember, it was exactly what Duo had told them.

"You know, I sometimes forget this place is magical—then something like this happens!" Skyler commented.

"Hey Reyna, can you bring out the key?" Vic asked.

"One step ahead of you!" Reyna exclaimed, the key already in her hand.

Everyone gathered on Vic's bed. Reyna gently placed the key down in the middle of their circle. They stared at it for what felt like an eternity until Vic broke the silence.

"Skyler, can you repeat Duo's clue?" Vic asked, brushing a strand of hair behind her ear.

Skyler cleared her throat. "Look at the key, and you will see, those colors mean something other than what they seem. If in despair, look over there, to where the jewels lay, those colors will guide on your way."

Ugh, how are we supposed to get anything from it when the advice is so vague? Wait, there might actually be something—

"Duo mentioned the jewels," Vic pondered, "and she

mentioned the colors and how they would guide us—But what could that mean?"

Just as Vic finished her sentence, the jewels on the key started glowing; dimly at first, then brighter by the second. The girls started at them in shock, their faces becoming illuminated by the growing light.

"*Whoa,*" Skyler breathed. The others nodded, agreeing.

Vic reached forward to pick up the key, but before she could, the door burst open and Nina and Aaron walked in. They hurried to hide the key, and Amy quickly threw it under Vic's pillow.

"Hey guys!" Nina exclaimed. She and Aaron were carrying glasses of milk; Aaron carried an empty glass, a milk mustache above his lip.

Reyna groaned. "Nina! Making us have a curfew is fine, but glasses of milk? That's gone a little far."

Nina put one hand one her hip. "I get that you're *older,* but you haven't had anything in that maze. You need to drink some milk! Plus, it's already curfew, this'll help you sleep."

As the others groaned but gave in, Vic noticed a shadow out of the corner of her eye. The shadow moved smoothly, hovering over their glasses of milk.

Unnoticed to Nina, she brought the glasses over to the girls. Vic felt a rush of peace and calmness come over her. She eyed the glass, then drank the milk. As she did that, nothing bad seemed to happen to her or the other girls. It was just a glass of milk. Maybe there was nothing to be worried about.

The girls all went to get ready to sleep. Skyler put the key back in the box and when it shrunk down, put it in her pocket. They went to their separate beds as Nina switched off the light.

"Good night!" Aaron exclaimed, going over to Vic bed and giving her a hug. Vic felt a little emotional—she hadn't realized how much she had missed her brother in the maze, and before going to Mystery Mansion.

After everyone said their goodnights, the girls tried to get some sleep but they were unable to drift off to sleep. Vic tossed and turned, and it seemed the other girls where having the same problem, but gentle snores came from Nina and Aaron.

Vic felt more awake than ever, which didn't make sense considering how little sleep she had gotten. Her eyes landed on her pillow, which wasn't doing anything to block the light. *Screw this key.*

Vic pulled the key out from under her pillow, and as she was about to shove it in a drawer, she noticed something peculiar. Before, all the jewels were glowing. Now as she held the part with the jewels in front of her, the yellow topaz was the one glowing. As the light blinked, Vic noticed a thin, barely noticeable, stream of yellow light. Vic's eyes followed the trail.

"You don't think—" Reyna started

"Yup." Vic looked at the key. "We need to figure out where this key's leading us."

* * *

The girls got dressed and soon enough they were all back on Vic's bed. Reyna had started writing a note to leave for Nina and Aaron. The girls didn't want to worry them, and it was sad that they were leaving again only a few hours after they had found them again.

"So far I've figured out that the topaz signals forward, the sapphire stands for right, the ruby stands for left, and the emerald stands for back," Vic said after a few minutes of playing around with the key.

"Well, according to your discovery that means we have

to go out the door." Reyna pointed to the streak of yellow leading out the door. The girls got up and started towards the door when Amy stopped them.

"Wait one second." Amy ran back to the drawers and pulled out the flashlight they had used a while ago under the covers.

"Good thinking Amy, we're going to need it." Skyler said.

"Wait—What about the bad ghosts that are supposed to be roaming around at night?" Reyna asked; a glint of her old fears showed in her eyes.

"I guess we'll just have to deal with them as we go." Amy shrugged it off as if it was no big deal, but the others glanced at each other, concerned.

The girls opened the door, careful not to make any sound. They put on their shoes in the darkness, spooked by how quiet the corridor was.

"Wait, look!" Reyna motioned toward the key. The light had changed from yellow to blue, coming from the sapphire on the right.

"Guess we have to go right next," Vic sighed as she glanced down the long dark corridor that looked like it wasn't going anywhere good. The four of them followed the key for a while longer without hesitation. With each step, their journey seemed to be getting spookier and spookier.

"Hold on. What about Griff?" Vic asked around, looking at everyone. "We should go get him."

"But how do we know where his room is? We have—" Before Amy could finish, the key started to change color. It went from red to green.

"We have to turn around and go back," Skyler said. The girls turned around suspiciously.

"Is this who you were looking for?" Griff came out of the door on the left, grinning in the dark.

Chapter 38

Amy

I'm utterly confused.

Griff tossed the girls their weapons, reaching for them through a portal he opened. Amy didn't question how he knew where to get them since they seemed exactly the same as the ones in the maze. She strapped her quiver and bow on her back, and Vic did the same with her spear. The others sheathed their weapons.

"Okay, hold on. How'd you know to come?" Amy raised an eyebrow.

Vic rolled her eyes at Amy. "Griff, you remember when you had gotten—"

Griff grinned again and pulled out a vial of basilisk blood from his pocket. "I got it. We'll definitely need to use it. Skyler, do you still have that basilisk blood in your sword?"

Surprised, Skyler checked her sword and just as Griff had said, there was a compartment containing basilisk blood. "I guess we're ready then," she said, sheathing her sword.

Griff nodded and they headed on their way, Vic leading. Amy sighed; though whatever was in that milk made her energized, she could give anything to just—chill. Whenever they did something that seemed like the end of the quest, it just kept on going. The only thing that made her keep going was that she knew she had to do this—for Patricia, for the Omega, for the ghosts in this mansion, and most importantly for their families. Amy shook the thoughts out of her head and jogged to catch up with the others who were already turning corridors.

Suddenly, the questers stopped dead in their tracks. Amy couldn't stop in time and ran into Skyler. "Ahh, sorry!" Amy exclaimed.

Skyler turned around and glared, "Shh!"

That's when Amy saw their situation. Ahead of them was more of the corridor, but that wasn't all. Where they had stopped, the darkness had become a cold, pitch black that looked like the hall was filled with tar. They could barely see the yellow stream of light leading them. If that wasn't bad enough, the blackness had glimmers. It was almost like the evil ghosts were waiting for them.

Amy took a step forward, and showed everyone in the group the flashlight. They all just looked at the flashlight, then Griff nodded, slightly reluctant. Amy took a shuddering breath. *Okay, we're really doing this.* Nervously, she turned the light on. The light was dull in the blackness, but Amy could still see. Amy shined the flashlight towards all corners. They saw nothing.

Reyna exhaled. "I think it's safe to—"

As if wanting to contradict what Reyna was going to say, the temperature rapidly dipped. The group looked at each other and got their weapons ready. A pressure was building in Amy's ears and weirdly, in front of her. The group stumbled back into the less dark part of the corridor.

Skyler slashed her sword in front of her as if checking for something invisible. "What—Is—Going—On?"

Again, as if responding to Skyler's question, the blacker than blackness started clumping up and rose up to the railing, becoming some kind of blob form. It was just swirling darkness, creeping closer to them.

"H-how are w-w-we supposed to d-defeat i-it now?" Reyna asked, shivering from the cold.

"Look," Griff pointed to the darkness. He didn't seem to be affected by the cold since he was already a ghost. "I don't think you guys can see this, but I know that this is an evil ghost from being here for so long. Evil ghosts can do different things with their magic, and they always have a silver tint." He pointed to an area that glimmered more noticeably.

"Okay—" Vic said. "And the basilisk blood?"

Griff nodded and gave her the vial. Vic smeared just a few drops on her spear. She did the same thing with Reyna's dagger, and a couple of Amy's arrows. And with that Vic pocketed the vial, and they headed to fight the dark.

Amy was skeptical about making progress, but surprisingly the darkness behaved differently. Amy's arrows could cut through the darkness and the other's weapons could do similar things. Griff was making the most progress since his weapon had the power of his magic and a normal blade. The more slashes, cuts, and jabs they made helped them move further through the evil ghost tar.

Amy felt a rush of dread overcome her and she couldn't understand *why*. Bad memories of what had happened in the past few years rushed back to her. She pushed the thoughts away and looked around. *Nothing.* Nothing except the rest of the group furrowing their brows. Out of nowhere, the fighting paused.

"Is it just me or—" Vic trailed off.

"No, I feel it too," Amy's eyes widened. "I think we're in trouble. *Bad* trouble."

"When are we not?" Reyna tried to joke, but the mood caused it to fall flat.

The feeling confused them and they just stood, frozen—which was the wrong thing to do. Out of the corner of her eye, Amy noticed something. No, not *something*. It was a blur of an evil ghost hurtling towards them.

What the heck?

Amy barely had time to respond or tell the others to move. Out of instinct, she drew back the arrow that was already in her bow and quickly shot it, not taking the time to aim because she knew she didn't have it.

And just as expected, Amy missed! Missed by hardly an inch—it was a little embarrassing. By this time, the others had noticed what was going on, but so had the evil ghost. The ghost hurdled towards them faster, almost passing through them. But what the ghost didn't suspect was that it was about to pass through five people with basilisk blood all over their weapons. With a crumbling sound, the ghost disintegrated in a cloud of purple dust.

"That—was—close," Reyna said through heavy breaths, finally letting the shock get to her.

"Ya think?" Amy asked breaking the mood. But inside, she felt dark, almost as if an evil ghost had passed through her. *Yeah, I know. The irony.*

Amy shook it off as the group continued silently, following the silver key.

"Umm, any of you feel different?" Vic asked. Amy could sense something was wrong. If Vic didn't know something, the world had definitely turned upside down. Almost as if answering her thoughts, the five of them walked into a clearing, relieving the girls after walking single file in narrow corridors, except something was wrong. The sofas, lamps, pictures, everything for that matter, was hanging upside down from the ceiling.

"Either we're upside down, or we just walked into an upside down room," Skyler said, clearly confused.

Amy snorted. "I wouldn't be surprised if both of those were possible in this place. But— for real, what is going on?"

"Um, guys," Vic pointed up. "Look!"

Amy couldn't see anything important at first, then it became clear. If you looked straight up, the furniture turned into a geometric omega. Not only that, there was a circular table in the middle with two lines extending from the bottom on the carpet. It might have looked normal looking down at it, but looking up, Amy saw it looked like a keyhole.

Griff shook his head. "Is this really it?"

"Well, we'll have to see." Vic put her spear back and Amy and the others did the same. A blue light came from the sapphire, pointing right towards a thin strip of brick wall. They all shared a glance.

Amy pointed her flashlight to the wall. The wall looked normal. There wasn't anything magical about it, but that was the way the key was leading.

"Well, how are we going to get up there?" Reyna looked around at the group.

"Griff, can you open the keyhole with your magic?" Skyler asked him.

"I can try, but I don't know if it will work." With that, Griff held his hands up to the keyhole, channeling a streak of silver light through the keyhole. But as it went through the hole, the light died out and did absolutely nothing. "Well, that totally worked! Not!"

Amy stared up at the keyhole. Thoughts flew into her head as she thought of what to do. It felt like ages until she finally said, "No. Magic isn't going to work. We have to physically get up there. As Amy said that, the key's sapphire started to glow brighter.

"Well the key agrees with you," Vic said a-matter-of-factly. The key shined even brighter.

"Okay cool. We know what we have to do, but not how we're going to do it," Reyna said pointedly. The key's shine diminished.

"Wait look! The key gets brighter and dimmer depending on if you say the right or wrong thing! When Reyna said that, it got dimmer. That means that what Reyna said was wrong. The answer must be right in front of us!" Skyler exclaimed. The key shined brighter.

"Well, now that we know that that's right," Amy watched the key intently. Something inside her felt like they were missing something.

As if answering her thoughts, Vic said, "Wait, look!" Vic went to the wall and put her hand on it, tracing a few ridges like steps up the wall. Amy's eyes wandered up the wall to the ceiling and into the geometric patterns.

"We're going to have to climb."

* * *

Soon enough, all four—no five— were climbing up the wall. Amy sometimes forgot Griff was with them because he was so quiet at times, though she had to admit it was worse before. The gravity was different since they were literally walking up the wall.

As they climbed, er, walked, Amy's fear began to come back to her. She tried to forget about it, but she kept looking down, accidentally scaring herself more.

"Amy, are you okay?" Reyna whispered so she wouldn't attract too much attention.

"I'm fine, thanks."

Finally, they reached the top. It was weird how once they put their feet on the ceiling, they stuck there and it *looked* normal. It definitely didn't' feel like it. The girls found four ledges to sit on. Griff just stood awkwardly on the stairs, not bothering to look for a place to sit down.

"Hold on, how are we just sitting on the ceiling without falling down? It's almost like gravity has flipped upside down!" Skyler said it almost as if things weirder than this hadn't happened before.

"At the moment, I honestly don't care. Let's just put the key in already and go into whatever this place is. Any longer and I'm going to be nauseous." Vic didn't look too good. She looked as if she was going to throw up any second.

"Skyler, the key?" Skyler handed Amy the key and Amy bent down and inserted it into the keyhole. With a click, the key snapped into place and a small door opened. The four of them stepped down into the opening.

Griff tried to enter, but something repelled him and he fell—well, floated to the ground.

"Griff! Are you okay?" Reyna shouted. *Reyna— he's a ghost.*

"I don't think I'm supposed to come. This must be the part where you four have to be alone. Don't worry, you guys go ahead. I'll catch up to you sooner or later." The girls nodded reluctantly and the door shut behind them.

As soon as they turned around, they were immediately taken by shock. They entered what seemed to be a library. It was musty, dark, and surprisingly cold. *Vic actually has a reason to be cold now.*

Amy looked around at the tall bookshelves lining the walls. Each wall was about thirty feet tall, and the bookshelves covered all the walls fully. The library seemed to continue on for ages. Amy noticed that the ceiling was a full sky-light. Amy looked up and saw the sky was a dark, midnight blue with sprinkles of stars and shimmering mist. Amy's focus returned to the ground where there were couches and armchairs, tables and desks. Then finally, there were the books. Amy couldn't even count how many were on the first bookshelf, let alone all the others. They all seemed to be old but contrastingly in perfect shape.

"Imagine how long it would take to read all those books!" Skyler exclaimed in a whisper.

"For you, maybe a couple of days. For the rest of us? Wake me up when I turn seventy-seven," Vic joked.

Amy took the first step into the big—no, *huge* library, not knowing where to begin.

"Wait, we totally forgot!" Skyler dug in her pocket and brought out the miniature case. The girls watched as it grew to its normal size.

"Forgot what?" Amy asked.

"The clue!"

"I actually can't count the number of times we've said that!" Vic smiled.

Skyler pulled out the clue. "With a key unlock a mystery. Something beyond imagination, filled with help and mysteries."

Amy looked disappointed. "Seriously Skyler? That's the part we just solved. We used the key to unlock a mysterious library. It was beyond imagination, and it's definitely filled with mysteries. I don't know about the help part though." Amy shrugged as if it was all old news.

"You're right. I thought I remembered it being more useful." Skyler looked dejected.

"It's fine. Maybe there's another clue we have to find," Vic kneeled down next to Skyler and studied the clue.

"And where are we going to find another clue here?" Reyna gestured at the massive bookshelves. Just as the girls were about to lose hope, the clue—now in Vic's hand—started to almost erase itself as a different clue started to appear.

"Just when we thought it couldn't get weirder."

"What does it say now?" Amy asked, all of a sudden more interested.

"Books hold stories, books hold mysteries. Ghost beware of the good, for an old legend can perish one or all." Vic read it aloud suspensefully, making the tension even worse.

Books hold stories
Books hold mysteries
Ghosts beware of the good
For an old legend can perish one or all

"I bet that clue is going to be the darkest clue we'll ever read." Reyna looked slightly scared.

"An old legend? I have a feeling that's what we're supposed to be looking for." Vic comprehended the clue one more time.

"But where?"

"Let's just start with the bookshelves," Skyler said, not moved at all.

Amy thought differently, "Are you serious?"

* * *

Amy knew when Skyler said something, she meant it. And no. In some circumstances, that was *not* a good quality to have.

After about twenty minutes of searching, the girls had still not found anything. Just old books about the History of Czechoslovakia and "The Anatomy of the 57th Species of Insects."

"Okay, I give up Skyler. I'm sorry, but this isn't going to get us anywhere. There has to be another way!" Vic's pleading seemed too desperate to be true.

"Yeah, okay, fine." Skyler gave up quicker than Amy expected. The four of them sat down on the couches, facing each other to make a plan.

"So what now?" Reyna asked. "Just ask the Omega?"

Vic sighed. "If only it was that easy." She showed the sapphire to the group and gave it a rub. The gem got darker; their faces fell. "I don't think it'll work guys. *We* need to figure it out ourselves."

Amy nodded. "Guys, we've come so far already, do you really think this'll be our stopping point? All we need is a plan." She fiddled with her hair. "And I think I've got one. It's a legend, right? That means—"

Skyler gasped. "We shouldn't just be looking for a normal book. We need to be looking for a legend. There'll have to be something different about it—"

Amy nodded. It wasn't the greatest plan but it was the only one they had. She looked around and in a dark corner spotted a hazy outline of words on that shelf—one of which looked like an L.

Amy looked at Vic and saw her staring where Amy was looking. They met eyes, then Vic gave a knowing smile.

"Well, I think we know where to start," Vic said, pointing over to the dark corner—their first step in the final part of their quest.

Chapter 39

Skyler

Skyler couldn't believe how fast everything was going. It seemed like yesterday that they'd left Mr. Mister's house and run away. Now they were so close to the end of the quest. Skyler suspected once they found the legend it would give them some clue to finding Regal Seville.

The girls walked over to the dark corner and all the jewels on the key started to glow, illuminating the bookshelf.

"Well, c'mon! The search continues!" Amy exclaimed, and started scanning the old, worn-out books.

The girls went to different corners of the bookshelf. Skyler found a sliding ladder and moved it to where they needed to search. She rummaged through the top shelves of scrolls and books while the others went through the other shelves.

Skyler couldn't believe *how* many books there were. They didn't even know how big the library was and they were already overwhelmed! Skyler would have loved to be surrounded by thousands of books—after all, she loved reading and writing stories—but right now they needed to work fast, and Skyler knew she didn't have time to read.

L: Lizards of the North, Lemons Versus Limes, Leonardo Da Vinci, Last Lute, Minnesotan Legends— okay, now that's M. Lockhart Magic, Letters of Greek; maybe useful, Skyler threw it

237

down onto a table. *Lost keeper, Legend of the kangaroos—Are you kidding me!*

"No luck here," Skyler sighed. "What about you guys?"

Reyna and Amy shook their heads.

"Nope."

"Nope."

"Can anyone say something other than nope?" Vic groaned. The three gave her a look. "Okay fine, nope."

"Seriously, why is this so hard? I thought we found the right place!" Reyna leaned on the bookshelf, accidentally pushing a book far into the bookshelf. It was almost as if a lever was pulled. Skyler heard a click and Reyna fell back. The girls rushed forward and Amy caught her right in the nick of time. That's when they noticed it.

The girls watched the bookshelf swing inward like a door. No, it *was* a door. Once the door was completely ajar, Skyler could see what looked like a round room. A really *tall* circular room.

Without hesitation, the girls walked in. Okay. The room was *much* taller than they saw on the outside. It was filled with books. *Yeah, no-brainer.* In the center of the room was a small oak carved table with a long, thin pot painted orange and black. As the girls got closer, they could see figures and symbols intricately painted on it.

"It's an urn."

The girls spun on their heels. Patricia was standing there. Reyna looked like she was about to faint with shock. For some reason instead of being a transparent milky white, sometimes gray, Patricia had an aura of green illuminating her.

"From desires within did he cometh, desires within that he couldn't fulfill. But thou's vow from else behalf, risking a life though no regret. The end shall cometh if end shall revive, but one unwanted life back might break thy's end," she said, then disappeared.

What <u>happened</u> to Patricia?

Reyna blinked. "What just happened?"

Skyler shook her head, trying to make sense of what had just happened. "I didn't think that riddles could get any more complicated. But on top of that, Shakespearean? Now that's a whole different story!"

"If we had seen this coming, I would have warned you to keep your notebook ready." Vic grimaced.

Skyler sighed, getting out her notepad and pen. "Does anyone even remember parts of it?"

"How about 'idk-eth, we're stuck-eth hopelessly. Yeah don't judge thou's poetry'?" Amy joked, not getting the group anywhere.

"Real helpful." Skyler flipped to the next empty page as she sighed for like the hundredth time. But to Skyler's amazement, the page started to fill with words.

"Wait, look! The riddle's starting to appear on the page! Just like last time!" Reyna's face grew a smile.

"Convenient! Now let's get solving." Vic was always one step ahead of the group. *In most cases, that's good,* Skyler thought.

The four of them gathered around the small table stools that magically appeared out of nowhere for them to sit on.

"First of all, does anyone know why Patricia was green instead of clear, white, gray—whatever she usually is?" Reyna asked.

"I never really thought about that until you mentioned it," Amy admitted.

"Maybe the answer will be in the riddle. Hopefully the answer—whenever we find it—isn't bad." Vic motioned Skyler to show them the riddle.

"Okay, here's how it goes: 'From desires within did he cometh, desires within that he couldn't fulfill. But thou's vow from else behalf, risking a life though no regret. The end shall cometh if end shall revive, but one unwanted life back might break thy's end.'" Skyler read aloud, hesitating on nearly half of the words.

The girls glanced at each other, not knowing where to start.

"Maybe, we should just start with the first line. Desires within did he come—" Vic went into her deep-in-thought mode.

"He? Who's this he?" Amy questioned, looking around the other three.

"I don't know. What's the next line?"

Skyler started to read again. "But thou's vow from else's behalf—"

"Well, thou means you, it probably means us." Amy said, surprising Skyler. Amy always said she fell asleep in English class.

"But what does it mean by 'Your vow from someone else's behalf?" Skyler almost expected the answer to come from Amy.

"Someone made a promise that *we* will do something." Vic answered instead.

"That makes sense. What's the next line?" Reyna nodded.

"Risking a life though no regret," Skyler recited, not mentioning that this was actually part of the same line.

"The promise made about us is risking someone's life." Amy said a little too bluntly, only realizing what she had said meant after it came out of her mouth.

"If we don't do something someone promised we will do, someone will die," Reyna repeated.

"But who made this promise, and who did they make it to?"

The girls sat there contemplating for almost five whole minutes, thinking through that single line of the riddle. After their session of contemplation, Reyna finally said, "Patricia."

"Huh?" Amy looked confused.

"Patricia made the promise to the Omega that we will beat Regal Seville."

"That means if we don't, Patricia will—die." Vic finished off Reyna's sentence.

Skyler couldn't believe what she was hearing. How could the Omega let her make that decision if she could die from it? Did the Omega really have that much faith in them? Did Patricia really have that much faith in them?

"Well, that's just more reason we have to do this. How about we start by just solving the other parts of the riddle." The four took deep breaths and steadied themselves as they proceeded to the next line.

"The end shall cometh if end shall revive, but one unwanted life back might break thy's end," Skyler read aloud.

"The end will come if the end stays? That makes no sense whatsoever." Vic silently judged the creator of the riddle.

"But one unwanted life back might break the end? Maybe there's something there." Amy was the only one there who even had a spark of hope.

"So an unwanted dead person coming back will break our end?" Reyna asked.

"I guess. So basically, we just have to make sure that we don't bring this person back. That seems easy enough." The girls gave Vic a look. "Well, you know what I mean. Easier than the other things we've done."

"Wait. No. I think you're wrong. One unwanted life back will *break* your end. So it will stop our end from coming." In response to Amy, a gray smoke billowed out of the urn in front of them. But the cloud was sucked back in just as fast as it came out. Silence fell over the girls, spooking them out at the eerie sight.

"Okay then. That was not scary at all." Vic shifted in her seat. If something scared Vic, something was really off.

Suddenly a flash of blue light appeared somewhere on the top shelves of the bookshelves.

"Wait look up!" Skyler said. The girls turned their heads up and looked at what Skyler was pointing at. Painted above them on the high ceiling was a sign made of jewels. It read *Room of Legends*.

The blue flash happened again. The girls turned and saw a book sitting on the top shelf surrounded by other tall books.

"Might be a wild guess, but I'm pretty sure that's the one we're looking for." It had been a while since anyone had been so confident. Even Amy. The book glistened one more time.

"Yeah, but question. How on earth are we supposed to get that?" Almost as if on cue, the book came floating down. Vic's look was surprising. Instead of being in awe, she looked as if she had expected it to happen. "Hey, after all the other weird things this mansion has done, this is nothing."

"True." The book landed on the table with a soft thud.

The girls gathered around it. The title said, "The Legend of the Basilisk."

Skyler opened to the first page and blew off some dust on the page. It was an old book with yellow pages, yet it still managed to hold together. The girls looked at her, waiting for her to start reading, yet she couldn't seem to get started.

Skyler looked over at Reyna, who shot her a smile. She felt a little less nervous and cleared her throat. "The Legend of the Basilisk. Regal Seville, keeper of Mystery Mansion, lays a curse on the mansion, the curse coming with a guard. The guard of the mansion was guard of the portal, the portal being the guard of the mansion. Seville had his eyes on the guard of the portal."

Skyler paused for a moment, took a breath, then continued. "If anyone passes through without an encounter, punishment is the reward; the reward of death, the reward of escaping the master's lock. But that punishment isn't enough for just the guard, but the one who passed without encounter. The one who passes without encounter, falling into the portal, falling into the clutches of the master, the clutches of being the new guard. Once the transformation happens, the cycle repeats again. For those who pass with an encounter, pass with luck. Those who don't see the basilisk, turn into one after only sight of luck."

"But something comes of the master's curse, the something being another curse on himself. His ghost remains, but lifeless, soulless, the soul that disappeared held in ashes. The urn of Thanatos holds the master's remains. A cloud of gray may be all that stays. To revive the soul and unite with the ghost may be the one way, the only way, to break the untied ends. But what comes with hope, comes with danger Coming with danger is the fear held inside. The solution is held inside a solution. A solution of the potion, waiting to be created. A library is where the room of legend stays. The room of legends is where the room of potions stays. Under the ashes is what is above decision, for that may be the only way. The potion will revive an unwanted soul, but will prove necessary for those who've proved."

"Now who is the basilisk you may ask? The answer is in between what you already know. Your promiser, your vower, your mother of sorts, holds lies she knows will be exposed very soon. She says you're her daughters, she says you're the only ones. But soon you'll know what may really be lies. Her son fell into the portal of doom, or more so *to* his doom."

"Now back to Seville, why you may ask. Soon you will see what you never predicted before. Your close truster and his related evil spirit. If you are a hero, she is a villain. One trusted brother, one the sister, the other neither, the last one both. The four traveled unwantedly here, to defeat the evil Seville and to meet two more. Brother and sister, son and daughter of who you seek, but who you don't, son and daughter of the soul before you—"

"Now let's tie the two stories to create this legend—the Legend of the Basilisk. Brother and sister in charge of son of vower, one with care, one with hatred. Hatred threatens the life and soul of Brent—Brent Mister. But instead of him, her brother was gone. With fury of her mistake she too becomes a ghost. Now the fate of Brent you already know. Now he is the one you battled to get here—the one you battled to save his life."

"Now you know what to do, revive a life, a soul, a curse of sorts. But the curse and life must be destroyed once more, but by the hands of those who've been promised by else's behalf. Now it continues to—" Skyler finished. "It just ends like that! And it's horrible grammar."

Vic looked pale, not that she usually wasn't. "The soul before us—" She looked at the urn and Skyler and the others did too. "It's Regal Seville—in the urn."

Skyler held her breath. It was getting way to creepy for her. "Y-you mean—Regal Seville's soul is in the urn?"

Vic slowly nodded her head. They looked at it in silence, overwhelmed by the newfound information. Suddenly something struck Skyler.

"It also says he laid a curse in the first paragraph. The curse came with the guard—" Reyna trailed off.

"We're missing another important point." Skyler looked back at the text as the girls looked at her. "Your close truster and his related evil spirit, if you are a hero, she is a villain. One trusted brother, one the sister, the other neither, the last one both. The four traveled unwantedly here to defeat the evil Seville and to meet two more. Brother and sister, son and daughter of who you seek but who you don't, son and daughter of the soul before you."

"It's Griff and Hydrangea—" Amy trailed off. "But what's so important? We know this already."

Skyler shook her head and started reading again. "Now let's tie the two stories to create this legend—the Legend of the Basilisk. Brother and sister in charge of son of vower, one with care, one with hatred. Hatred threatens the life and soul of Brent—Brent Mister. But instead of him, her brother was gone. With fury of her mistake she too becomes a ghost. Now the fate of Brent you already know. Now he is the one you battled to get here—the one you battled to save his life."

She looked at the others. "Brent Mister! He's the basilisk. When it said he fell into a portal to his doom, and we battled him to get here—don't you get what that means? Hydrangea hated Brent and because of that—Griff died and Brent fell through the portal without an encounter, becoming the basilisk. And then with anger Hydrangea died herself."

Reyna took a breath. "That's a lot to take in."

Amy furrowed her brow. "But why were they in charge of Brett or whoever?"

"It's *Brent*. But anyway, yeah I don't know," Skyler replied. "Vic, you haven't said anything in a long time."

"No—no. It's just that there's a whole lot about this we had no idea about. It's all like a big puzzle. If you think about it, there's a mansion that's cursed by an evil owner, who set up a basilisk to guard the portal to get here. His son and daughter, one bad and one good, were in charge of the son of a woman who later died and became a vower. But before she died she found us, the questers, who she vowed on to the Omega about us defeating Regal Seville. She mentioned we were her only children even if we weren't blood related, but she was lying. Before she found us, she had Brent, who was being watched over by the brother and sister. And things happened, he became the next basilisk

because he didn't have an encounter with the previous basilisk. So then years later when we came by, we had to fight
him and get to the portal. So that's how we ended up here,
reading the Legend of what all happened." Vic finished and
took a deep breath. Vic looked up and saw Skyler writing
down everything she said.

"But we still don't know why Griff and Hydrangea were
in charge of Brent, who the last basilisk was, and why Regal
Seville really put a curse on this mansion," Skyler said, jotting everything down as she talked.

"And don't forget, we still don't know why there is a guard
of the portal, and why Patricia lied to us about not having
any children," Amy said, looking up after staring down at
the book for a long time."

"We also don't know why the Omega are so involved,"
Reyna added to the long list. "And why Patricia was green
when we saw her."

After Skyler wrote everything down, she looked up and
sighed. "What now?"

"I guess we have to find out how to make that potion to
revive his soul," Vic said, staring coldly at the urn."

"Umm, have you guys noticed something? There are still
so many more pages in the legend." Amy looked at the book.

"Yeah, but it says the end." Skyler looked confused. She
tentatively touched the page, ready to flip it. She slowly
turned it, half expecting something to jump out at her.
But instead, the girls stared down at a bottle with a piece
of parchment rolled inside it. The pages were neatly cut
so it looked like it formed a box made of pages of a book.

"That was not expected." Amy lifted the bottle slowly. She
lifted the cork and carefully pulled out the piece of parchment. She unraveled the scroll to see what looked like a list.

αστραπή

νερό

τέφρα

ρόδι

κλαδί ελιάς

φτερό

χρυσός

φωτιά

ασήμι

σταφύλια

σιτάρι

αίμα

"How on Earth are we going to translate that?" Amy asked after she tried to read the words.

"If I was to guess, it's probably Greek," Skyler said.

"Yeah. It most likely is," Vic said.

Almost as if on cue, right as she said that, twelve books started to light up all around the tall room. Some on high shelves, some on lower ones.

"Whoa. This room can do a lot more than we realized," Reyna said. Suddenly, right after she spoke, the door that was wide ajar slammed shut. Skyler ran to the door and tried to pull it open, but it was locked.

"No! We're stuck in here!" A look of panic spread over Skyler's face. She had never been claustrophobic, but at this time she really did feel like that.

"Maybe, as soon as we solve this and do what we're sup-posed to do, we'll be let out." Vic took a deep breath, like she was definite that would be the case. As fast as the door swung shut, suddenly the lights turned off. The only source of light were the twelve books glistening bright blue all around the room.

"Whoa," Amy said.

"I guess we're going to have to get them down somehow." Skyler knew she was stating the obvious, but that *was* what she did.

"Skyler, you take the bottom, Amy and I can take the middle and Vic, you can take the top," Reyna said.

After a moment of Vic looking annoyed she whispered, "Sorry."

"It's fine, I guess. We just have to work together to figure out how to get them down."

The girls got to work, collecting all the books. For a while, Vic just stood there. Skyler had already collected the three books in the bottom. They were glowing in her arms when Vic finally approached the bookshelves.

She used the shelves like a ladder and started to climb, coming dangerously close to Reyna's head. Vic slowly inched towards the top of the twenty-foot bookshelves, collecting the books. Thankfully, Vic didn't fall before she climbed back down to the eighth shelf and jumped into a crouching position.

Amy smiled and rolled her eyes; Skyler did the same. After all, it was something the girls liked to tease Vic about since she always landed on her feet—of course, it wasn't everyday she jumped from a bookshelf though!

Soon, the girls stood in a circle, the books in the middle. *So, what now?* Skyler bent down to look at the book. Vic picked one up.

"*Αστραπή,*" Vic said in a halting voice, trying to sound out the word. She opened the book and look of puzzlement came over her face. "It's—blank!"

Skyler looked at the other books, all of them having similar Greek names. Then, an idea struck her. "Hey Amy, can you show us the list again?"

Amy nodded and unscrolled the paper.

Αστραπή, νερό, τέφρα—

She looked at the books and the same words on the list appeared on the books too. "You guys, the books have the same names as the words on the scrolls," Skyler exclaimed. She picked up a book to show to the others. "That must mean—"

Suddenly, a blinding flash of white light appeared in the dim room. Skyler shielded her eyes until all she could see was her hand. As she cautiously let down her hand, she noticed the lights turned back on and more importantly, the book she had been holding—was no longer a book. Her hand dropped to her side as the saw realized all the books in the room had turned into glass container holding unknown substances.

"That must mean—" Amy started, finishing the sentence of Skyler's. "It's the ingredients we need for the potion."

Vic nodded. "Look." She held out her bottle with the label, *Αστραπή*. Inside, was something flickering—something that almost looked like lightning.

"It's lightning," Vic said, as if answering Skyler's thoughts. "I think that's what the Greek word means. With all the other 'ingredients' we should be able to finish the potion."

Skyler nodded, and together they started gathering the ingredients—the ingredients that would bring back Regal Seville.

Chapter 40

Reyna

Reyna was finally feeling excited. They were close to the end of the list, and had finally figured out what the ingredients were through Skyler jotting them down. After she was finished, the girls finally got the full list.

αστραπή = Lightning
νερό = Water
τέφρα = Ashes
ρόδι =Pomegranates
κλαδί ελιάς = Olive Branch
φτερό = Feather
χρυσός = Gold
Φωτιά = Fire
ασήμι = Silver
σταφύλια = Grapes
σιτάρι = Wheat
αίμα = Blood

Blood. The thought sent shivers down Reyna's spine. She knew it would defeat Seville but—she couldn't help but feel a chill.

"So—" Amy started. "When it says blood, it means basilisk blood. Right?"

Vic hesitated. "Well, we'll have to hope."

That definitely did not help Reyna. She couldn't help but feel pessimistic. She felt like they would mess up the ingredients. She felt like they wouldn't be able to defeat Regal Seville. Reyna shook the thoughts away—she *didn't* want to think about that.

"I guess that's it. Those are the ingredients," Reyna stated. "So—"

"—Wait a second you guys," Skyler interrupted. She looked at one of the bottles. "The bottle with ashes—it's empty now."

"What?" Amy asked. "For real?"

Skyler nodded, looking worried. "It's the third ingredient too. We need it fast."

A feeling of dread overcame the girls. Reyna looked at her bottles and saw the second ingredient, water. She looked at Vic, who was also peering at a bottle, but hers was lightning. Then she looked up.

Vic started walking to the urn. "We forgot something you guys. It said Regal Seville is in the urn—that might mean—"

Reyna gasped, "It's his *ashes.*"

Vic nodded and the girls walked over to the urn where Vic was standing. Reyna didn't even want to look inside. Neither did the others.

In the silence, Vic uncorked the bottle and motioned to Reyna to pour her bottle into Vic's. It blew Reyna's mind that you could "pour" lightning, but she decided not to pay attention to that now. Reyna uncorked her bottle and poured the water in. Just like that, everyone added the ingredients in their bottles: pomegranates, a small olive branch, a feather, gold, fire, silver, grapes, and wheat. The only thing left was the blood—the basilisk blood.

Vic took the vial from her pocket and the girls gave her a nod. Vic took a breath and poured the blood in, drop by drop.

For a moment, the ingredients sat there, motionless. Then, slowly the base turned into a shimmering liquid with colors like gold, silver, black, purple, and more. Slowly, all the ingredient turned to a liquid.

Reyna gave a sigh of relief. "Vic, do you want to do the honors?"

Vic gave a small smile and walked forward to the urn, but before she could pour it in, Amy interrupted her.

"Wait!" Amy exclaimed. "We don't know what's going to happen after we pour it in. We better get out weapons ready."

Our weapons! I totally forgot about them. They obliged and unsheathed their weapons. Vic gave a nod and got ready to pour the mixture. For a second, she hesitated, then dumped the contents into the urn.

There was silence. It felt like an eternity as the girls waited for something—*anything*—to happen.

"Did we something wrong?" Skyler asked. "Maybe—"

As if replying to what Skyler had said, something immediately happened. The room got darker and darker again, and this time a light shined over the urn. Reyna slashed her dagger in the air, nervous something invisible was coming. Well, something *was* coming.

A soft buzz started coming from the walls and something started rising from urn. It wasn't misty like a ghost, it looked like—a coffin. It was rising slowly. Reyna could only see a couple centimeters of wood. It didn't make sense how it was possible, considering the narrow opening of the urn, but somehow, it was coming out.

"Is that—" Skyler trailed off.

"Regal Seville in a coffin?" Amy answered. "Yup."

Skyler looked pale. The girls shot her an encouraging smile, but they felt the same. Suddenly, something flickered. It wasn't a light. It was almost as if air flickered.

"What the—" Amy got an arrow out and ready. Reyna held her dagger with a shaking hand.

That's when the figure of a boy appeared. It didn't seem like a ghost though. It looked more like a hologram. He looked to be around Griff's age, and looked slightly familiar. *This is not Regal Seville.*

"W-who *are* you?" Reyna asked.

For a second, the boy looked puzzled. He then switched to having a blank face. "My name is Brent—Brent Mister. I'm not exactly sure what's been happening but—I'm here because you are the questers who are going to defeat Regal Seville. His body will fully emerge in three minutes. That's three minutes to get prepared and I'm here to guide you."

Vic looked wary. "And why should we believe you?"

Skyler looked slightly shocked. "Vic, he's the person from the legend! He's Patricia's son! I think we can trust him. Right?" She turned towards Brent.

Brent nodded. "You can trust me. And it's true that I am the son of Patricia—" He suddenly looked sad. "M-my mother. Is she guiding you too?"

"Yes—" Skyler started then got cut off by Amy pulling on her hand.

"Skyler! I don't think we should give this kind of information to him. We aren't sure about him." Amy glanced at Brent, who didn't give any type of reaction.

"Well, how do we know he's *not* trustworthy?" Skyler snapped. "He's Patricia's son you guys!"

Reyna didn't want to step in but she felt like she had to. "Well, take a look at Griff and Hydrangea."

Skyler shook her head. "Seriously? No one believes me?"

Amy sighed. "Skyler, it's not that we don't trust you. It's just that Vic was right about Griff being good and Hydrangea being bad. What's to say she isn't right again?"

Skyler looked frustrated and opened her mouth to say

something, but Vic spoke first.

"Let's not argue about this—we're just wasting time. And one thing's for sure, Regal Seville *is* coming and arguing won't help anything!"

Reyna didn't know what to do. They did need more information, more tactics to defeat Seville, but from Brent? Reyna just wasn't sure.

Vic turned to face Brent. "We're not sure that we can believe you. But tell us what we need to do."

Brent took a deep breath and said, "Four girls, one brave, one smart, one strong, one artistic, destined to beat Seville once and for all. Behold this image of the story beforehand. The way to defeat holds within your hand." Once he finished, he waved his hand and an image appeared in front of them. There was a man, or ghost, sitting at a table that looked like the one in this room. He had an urn on top of it and he had a number of potions beside him. Next to the table was a mirror and a ghost lady with a kind face, but a face that was scared. Suddenly, it was like a movie started.

"Don't do this Regal, don't do it!" The lady yelled.

"Mysteria, don't worry so much. All that matters is that after this, we will be together. It may take a year or so, but after that, we will be inseparable!"

"No, we won't Regal. Don't do this. You're going to cause more harm than you're going to save! Please Regal, don't do it!"

"Save it. You'll be grateful once it's over."

"No I won't. If it means anything close to hurting Hyd or Griff, I won't be happy."

"Mysteria, it might hurt them on the inside, but they'll be in perfect condition," he scoffed.

"No they won't. You'll be a bad influence on Hyd. You know she already looks up to you." Her eyes were pleading as she reached to touch Regal's hand.

"Yes, she does. Like she should be doing. Maybe one day Griff will learn that from her." Regal retracted his hand and rubbed his forehead before Mysteria could reach him.

She sighed. "Oh don't be so hard on him. He already has a hard time fitting in. He doesn't need his father after him too."

"At least his mother won't be." Regal Seville casually put down the potion in his hand and uncorked it. Before Mysteria could stop him, he poured it in. "One last step, and it will all be over."

"NO!" she screamed. The mirror beside him flew to the ground and shattered, sending blue dust into the urn.

"No, no, no! NO! The potion!" Her face, once made up of beautiful features, twisted into nervousness and horror.

"Don't do it Regal, DON'T DO IT!" Of course, he did. He floated up and put one foot into the urn. Suddenly, the whole image dissolved.

The girls sat in silence for a moment. They couldn't believe what they were seeing. Reyna re-thought what she had just seen. *Mysteria? Is that Griff's mother?*

"That's all my job is for now. But don't worry, I'll be back. There's a lot more that has to be done." With that, Brent disappeared in a flash.

"What do we do now—" Skyler was cut off by a rustling sound. The girls turned to see the coffin slowly open. Inside, there was a pile of ashes. Suddenly, with a glow of light, the ashes started floating up and turned into the figure of a human. Regal Seville was the figure that walked out.

He didn't look like how he did in the image. His hair was trimmed perfectly. It was jet-black, like Griff and Hydrangea's. He was wearing different clothes too, now wearing a dark purple suit that just screamed, *"I'm rich"*. There was something off about him though. His features—slightly like Hydrangea's—were different. The only word to explain it would be— dark. His almond shaped eyes glistened with contempt for the girls.

He smiled—dark and cruel. "Well, well, well, what do we have here?" Regal Seville examined himself, smiling almost *more* evilly. "My my, it does feel good to be back in the form of a human." He smoothed the wrinkles on his suit with bony hands.

He looked Reyna dead in the eyes. "Reyna Aztec, Victoria Harper, Amy Pierre, Skyler Aeroluet—I see you're my questers." He looked at the other girls as he said their names. Then he sneered. "I can sense you've been with that disgrace of my son. Tell me, has he convinced you I'm some sort of *demon?*" He gave an evil chuckle. "And my daughter, Hydrangea. How did *she* fail as miserably as my idiotic son?"

"Your son is not the disgrace, *you* are!" Vic spat. "Now *tell me,*" she said mockingly, "why would someone like you *ever* do such a thing?"

He smiled. "Oh Victoria, I don't think you understand these circumstances." His face hardened. "I only had hope for Hydrangea, but even then, I knew she would never be what I wanted—just like Griff. I knew I would always love Mysteria, so how, *how* could I ever let us be separated?" He started walking towards the girls then stopped. "I put myself in the urn so I could put a curse on Mystery Mansion. So me and Mysteria could stay here as ghosts forevermore, and with no one else to stop us—"

He started walking over to Vic, looking angry now. Reyna pulled Vic's arm and dragged her over to the other girls. He wrinkled his nose. "And I thought you were smart enough not to get involved girls. I thought you were smart enough to listen to Hydrangea. Then I suppose we'll have to do this the hard way."

Skyler started talking, stammering. "Why would you put

so many people at risk? We saw you talking to Mysteria. Why would you go against her word if you really loved her?"

Reyna stood in shock. She knew that was a big blow. Seville's face becomes colder and angrier. "After all I have done for my wife, you say I don't love her? YOU SAY I DON'T LOVE HER? I didn't *care* about anyone else because they never cared for me either! I was just the person who bought the mansion. I was the 'bad' father—I tried being a good father, but my own son hated me from the beginning! Only Mysteria cared about me the most. And I'll do whatever it takes to keep her." He reached into his pocket and pulled out a red liquid. "And the only way to do that—is to get rid of you."

Chapter 41

Vic

Vic couldn't believe how similar Seville and Hydrangea were. They both kept saying the girls would die, and they both liked purple for some reason. But there was no time to focus on that. At the moment all she could think about was what an idiot he was and how dangerous he was. She thought about why he hated Griff so much. Why did it matter to him if all the dead bodies turned into ghosts and got trapped in the mansion? How did that help with him and Mysteria being able to stay together if he was already trapped in the urn? And where did the Omega come in?

But soon, Vic snapped back to reality.

"Looks like someone's daydreaming," Seville sneered. "What's it about? Or is it a who?" He started to laugh and Vic turned red. She didn't know if it was because of anger or embarrassment. Reyna looked at her concerned, getting ready to hold her back.

"Well, looks like no one else has anything to say." Seville smiled down at the vial with red liquid. It wasn't red like blood. It was red like fire.

"Don't do this!" A voice hung over the room. The girls recognized it. It was Mysteria.

"Oh, don't start again," Seville sighed and turned his attention away from the girls for a second. Then the voice stopped along with the echoing. He smirked at the girls again and Vic felt a pang of disgust at this—inhumane being!

"What did you do to her?" Amy asked, her face twisted in anger.

His grin only got bigger. "No need to worry about that now—you have something else to worry about at the moment."

He walked over to Vic. Reyna held her back with an arm against her. Vic wanted to escape. She was mad enough to run and fight him, but she held back.

"Vic, stay calm. Anger isn't going to get us anywhere."

Vic exhaled, and calmed herself down. Seville just chuckled. His was a cruel and evil laugh.

Suddenly, out of nowhere, Seville took the vial and spilled it in front of Vic.

"No!" Skyler screamed, but Vic was in too much shock to even process it. Seville backed away, tucking the empty vial away in his suit pocket as flames rose up around the girls.

"Why are you doing this? You heard Mysteria, didn't you? If you really loved her you wouldn't hurt us." Now, Skyler's anger started to pick up too. Vic thought she might have to hold Skyler back, the same way Reyna had done for her. But then she saw what Skyler's tactic was. She was making him feel bad for what he had done.

The flames crackled, and the girls tried to back away as far as they could, but they were slowly closing in on them. Seville tried to look cruel, but Vic could see how Skyler's words had affected him.

"And have you ever thought about why Griff hated you so much? I don't blame him," Vic retorted, with a blank face. Reyna gasped, surprised, but soon she understood the meaning behind it too.

"You've ruined so many lives. How can you even look at yourself? Oh wait, you never did!" Amy exclaimed, not keeping her anger back at all.

Regal Seville made a fist. "How——" But the girls weren't done.

"Take a look at what you've done," Reyna shook her head. The fire was rising higher and higher. "You were so selfish that you ruined so many lives and afterlives. You ruined Griff's. You ruined Hydrangea's life too. You said you would do anything for Mysteria, but what if you were in the place of someone who got separated from *their* equivalent to Mysteria? Look at what you've done!"

Seville screamed in fury, sadness—Vic didn't know what. The flames died down to ashes and the girls all gave a sigh of relief, but it was short lived. He brought out another vial. This one was bigger, meaning much more of a threat.

"You've made a grave mistake," Regal Seville snarled. He walked briskly towards them and the girls got their weapons ready. Regal Seville pulled out a gold blade and ran towards the girls, ready to fight.

Amy shouted, "You don't have to do this! You know Mysteria will be happier if you listen to her. She's always trusted you—do you?"

Regal Seville ran towards them and swung his sword. The girls dodged it with whatever strength they had. He pushed Vic so hard she rammed into the carved oak door. She winced and held her side. Reyna ran over and helped her up. Vic picked up her spear and flung it like a javelin, but unfortunately Seville's power was too much to handle. The spear flew back at her, but surprisingly, Vic caught the weapon. It was as if she had been using it for years.

The girls turned to see Brent's image again. They watched him wave his hands and then saw a blinding flash of green light, which threw Seville of balance. They saw Brent come out of the image and collapse as his real self. His appearance flashed between the basilisk and himself.

"Brent! Skyler shouted and ran towards his side.

"The only way to beat him is to make him accept that he has to die," Brent told her. Skyler looked confused.

"What?"

"The only way to beat him is to make him accept that he has to die!"

"What? How?" But before he could answer, he passed out.

Skyler processed what he had said. It took her a while to realize what he meant. "Don't do this Seville. I don't know how you'll ever live this down. Maybe it's time for you to pass. You've stayed in this world much longer than you ever deserved."

Vic stared at Skyler. She didn't think she would take it that far, but Vic joined in. "Go join your wife. I would be hoping that she would still accept you if I were you."

That seemed to have done it. Seville let out a guttural scream and collapsed on the ground, in pain from the sadness. And he uttered the most unexpected word: "I-I'm s-sorry! Take my life. I guess Mysteria and I will be happier dead and together than alive and apart. Kill me. I can't handle my bad reputation anymore."

"We don't mean to hurt your family. But we don't want you to hurt anyone else either," Reyna said softly.

"And just so you know, you didn't do much good to our lives here either. We're glad we can end this the right way, but just know that it wasn't easy for us to do it. For the past month, we've been risking our lives every day to stop you from hurting anyone else." Vic spoke clearly to him. For some reason, she wasn't scared of him anymore.

Then, Regal Seville took out a potion from his suit pocket and handed it to Vic. "Take this and pour it over me. It will kill me, once and for all. Once the potion does its work, I'll be gone for good. The curse will be lifted off of this mansion. All the captured servants and good ghosts will be released. You have my blessing to do this. But I assure you, there is more to be done. There are more mistakes of mine that you'll have to fix. More people you'll have to save. But that can wait. It's time you girls enjoy your childhood. The most I can promise you is that you will never turn into the bad person I did. Tell Griff—I'm sorry. I know he might not accept it, but he wasn't the disgrace I always told him he was. Apologize to all my good-willed servants. I regret destroying their lives to save mine for me. Just—remember that this mansion is named after my love, Mysteria. I'm telling you now, you'll never meet anyone else as kind and perfect as she was," he chuckled softly. He looked wistful, something Vic never imagined to be like. "Now kill me. I promise the world will be better without me."

Vic uncorked the vial. The potion was electric blue, like her eyes. She watched it change to red, green, and yellow, all the colors that represented the girls. She took a deep breath. Before she poured it on him she whispered, "You're a good person inside—I just know it." With that, she poured the liquid on him. The girls watched as he slowly disappeared like smoke, his remains floating up into the air before completely disappearing. Vic watched, almost sadly. She watched until the last wisp of smoke disappeared. She thought to herself about what had just happened. Something remarkable had happened this day. She knew that it would always stay in her heart, and that she would always remember the moment that she and her best friends had turned someone's heart from evil to good. She would always remember the moment that they really felt like they knew each other.

A thought lingered with her: *"More mistakes of mine that you'll have to fix. More people you'll have to save."* But as she looked at the other girls, she knew that this wasn't the time to think about the future.

Vic knew she needed to listen to what Regal said. They accomplished their quest after so much. After all the pain of the years before, they needed to enjoy the present they had now. After all, the future could wait.

Chapter 42

Amy

The girls pulled open the carved oak door and walked out of the room. Amy couldn't believe what she was seeing. There was a new glow to the library. Part of it was because dawn was breaking, but the other part—the other part was because it was almost as if a curse had been lifted. *Ironic right?*

Amy felt like crying. She never did, but it felt like she should have in that moment. She couldn't believe what they had accomplished. The curse was lifted! Their parents, Patricia, Nina and Aaron, all the servants, and the ghosts—all of them would be rid of the curse. They could finally see their parents again—at least she hoped they could.

Of course, Reyna was tearing up now. She smiled as she wiped her eyes. "I-I can't believe it! We did it you guys!"

Amy looked at the others, their faces smiling.

Amy laughed, "I know!"

Then they heard a voice behind them. "Yes, you did." They turned around, still in a state of alarm. There, behind them, was the Omega. It was the first time Amy got a good look at them. Amy was speechless. Their accomplishment seemed to be kicking in even more after seeing the Omega in front of them.

The old lady, Ūnus, looked frail but marched forward

with a look of pride on her face as she said, "Congratulations girls. We knew you would be able to complete your quest and lift the curse on Mystery Mansion."

Hearing the words Mystery Mansion made Amy remember Mysteria. *Where is she?*

"Mysteria—" Amy trailed off. "Where is she?"

Ūnus smiled. "Ah, Amy. Mysteria has gone with her husband. After all, she always loved him."

Skyler looked puzzled. "Where?"

A look of wonder came across Duo's face. "Not even us ghosts know what comes after we're gone." That got Amy thinking; was there a life after the afterlife? Amy's focus went back to Duo.

Trēs looked them in the eyes—after all, he seemed like the serious type. "Maybe we'll find out soon." He exhaled. "Girls, we have something for you."

Quinque twirled around and floated back down to the girls. In her arms was what looked like a wooden chest. It was a reddish color and had the carvings of the Omega symbol and intricate lines formed into the designs. Quinque handed it to Amy, who looked at the others. They nodded back at her.

Amy was hesitant; she knew whatever was in the box couldn't be bad, but the thought of seeing something mind breaking was definitely nerve racking. She flipped the lid open and saw twelve vials of a shimmery yellow liquid that had the consistency of maple syrup.

"*Another* potion? Again? Haven't we seen enough potions for a lifetime already?" Amy looked up to ask Quinque.

Quinque laughed back. "Not enough I guess. Oh, and just so you know, that's not *a* potion, that's *twelve* potions." She looked at the girls together. "Well actually, I think these are the last ones you'll be seeing in a while."

"Are all of these different? Do we have to figure out what

all of these potions do with another riddle or something?"
Reyna asked, almost as if she was annoyed. She reached over
to the box of vials and looked at them curiously.

"No dear. This time we'll tell you what they do. And also,
they're all the same." Quattor, Quinque's twin, looked at
Reyna. His eyes shimmered with—with excitement? "These
twelve potions are the key to what you never thought would
ever happen."

"With each one, you can revive one lost life. You should
have exactly one for each person you are destined to save."
Quinque looked at them and gave them a small smile.

"Y-you mean, anyone?" Skyler was stammering.

"But we have more than twelve lives to bring back." Vic
looked up at the five siblings sadly. "We have sixteen."

All the dead people that they loved in the mansion came
flooding back into Amy's mind. The siblings, Patricia, Griff,
and their parents.

"Wait, are our parents really in this mansion?" Amy asked
so suddenly it startled all nine of the people in the room.

"Yes! For once," Quattor beamed, "it feels so good to
finally give you good news."

Amy couldn't believe what she was hearing. Their parents.
They hadn't seen them for more than seven years! It was
almost as if they had grown out of having their parents in
their lives.

"We can't save everyone though. How are we supposed to
choose?" Vic's worry was starting to get to the others too.

"What do you mean? There are exactly eleven people
you need to save. Each one of your parents, which makes
eight, and three more: Patricia, Griff, and Brent." Quattor
looked confused.

"What about the five of you? We can't just leave you!"
Reyna looked up with them, the mood brought down again.

"Girls, we've lived for hundreds of years now, including

our time being ghosts. I think we've spent a fair share of time here." Ūnus spoke for her four younger siblings.

"But—" Skyler tried to speak

"There will be no 'buts', Skyler dear. I think it's time we carry on now. But first, let us help you bring back your friends and family." The girls reluctantly gave in. Amy felt like a piece of her had just died. After all that the Omega had done for them, how could they just let them die? But deep down inside, Amy knew that they had lived more than long enough.

"Okay girls, follow us." Quinque gestured for them to follow the five siblings into the center of the library. The sun was now shining brightly through the skylights.

Suddenly, Trēs waved his hand and the room darkened again. In the center of where they were standing, a mirrored table appeared.

"Every time you want to save one more person, you have to come up to this table, say their name, and pour the potion on top of the table. Once you're ready, the magic will work itself." Duo smiled at the girls and motioned for Vic to go first.

Vic slowly lifted one of the vials and walked to the table. She took a deep breath and said, "Griff Seville." She poured the potion on to the table. The potion sizzled and then rose up like steam before dying down and the mirror cleared itself.

Reyna was next. "Patricia Mister."

Skyler picked up the vial next. "Brent Mister."

Then it was Amy's turn. It was time for their parents. Amy grabbed two vials at the same time. It almost looked like she was going to reach for a third one. "Kathy Pierre." She poured one of the vials. "Mike Pierre."

Vic walked up again with two vials in her hand also. "Aaronia Harper." The potion steamed on the glass table. "Victor Harper."

Amy had never noticed before how alike the names in
Vic's family were. It was weird to her, recognizing that her
family's names were all different.

Reyna came next. "Lynda Aztec." She poured the eighth
vial. "Marco Aztec."

Skyler came last. She took a deep breath and grabbed
the last two vials—no, there was one more left. Skyler just
shrugged and walked slowly to the glass table. "Sofie Aeroluet.
Andre Aeroluet." The last potion they poured steamed up high.
The girls watched it die down slowly, expecting a reaction.
But for a minute or so, nothing happened. Then, Três waved
his arm again, the darkness caving in, slowly letting the light
shine back in. For a second, everything looked the same as it
had when they walked out of the room. Then, Amy noticed
it. Griff, Patricia and Brent were standing there, just as they
had always seen them, except, they weren't ghosts anymore.
Then Amy looked next to them and saw eight adults standing
there, smiling down at them. *Our parents. Mom. Dad.*

"Mom? Dad?" Amy whispered, her eyes watering. Amy
heard someone else say something similar to what she said.
Suddenly it was like a dramatic scene in a movie. The girls
bolted to their parents, running into their arms—they had
missed doing it for seven years.

"Mom; Dad!" Amy whispered.

"Shh, Amy. We're right here." Amy looked up into her
mother's eyes, which were filling up with tears.

It was the exact same caramel, hazel color she had remembered staring into when she was four years old. She looked
at her dad. He still had that same old smile that would
laugh and joke with Amy everyday a long time ago. Amy
turned and saw all the other family reunions happening
too. Nina and Aaron came into the library too, and were
also hugging their parents. Seeing Reyna and Nina, Vic and
Aaron, smiling and laughing, she sighed.

Amy's mom noticed and whispered to her, "It's okay Amy. We'll find him one day. I promise, we'll see him again, just like you saw us."

Amy gave into her parents' arms. *Tom.* Amy's long-lost brother. Seven years ago, when Amy was four years old, her older brother Tom who was eighteen at the time, was flying out to a different state for college. Unfortunately, he never returned. Amy still remembered the last words he had said to her: *"Hey—don't be sad. Remember—you're strong. And always remember I'll be there for you no matter what."* It was almost as if he had known that he wasn't coming back. Almost as if he could predict the future.

Amy knew the girls never knew him or even remembered him. That's why she had never mentioned him to any of the other girls. They didn't even know she had an older brother. It was a secret she kept for so long. It felt good to finally have her parents back and have someone else to talk about it with. Someone else who knew.

Of course Amy could have told them, but it had never felt like the right time. For seven whole years, she had never found a right time to tell them. Many days, right after Patricia had found them in the lake, she remembered crying herself to sleep, always thinking about Tom and her parents. Amy always knew that she would grow up to be like him: sporty, strong, and athletic. But she never knew she would lose him. But all she could do now was remember his last words to her, his last words when he had hugged her goodbye.

Chapter 43

Skyler

Skyler couldn't believe what had just happened. It was just a simple miracle. Her mom brushed away a tear from Skyler's cheek. *"Je t'aime."*

He dad smiled and hugged Skyler. "We've missed you *so* much, Skyler."

Skyler hugged then back. "I-I love you too."

It had been such a long time since she had heard anyone speak French to her. Well, except for the French teacher. But, her parents speaking the language—that brought tears to her eyes.

Suddenly, Ūnus spoke behind them. "It's so great to see so many families reunite again. I feel like it's time for an introduction." Ūnus smiled, almost mischievously. She led the huge group out of the library and into a common room of sorts. When Skyler stepped out of the library, she noticed that the mansion looked completely different. Instead of being dark, dull and musty, the ceiling high windows were letting in sunlight, lighting up the whole place with a new glow she never thought could exist in the mansion before.

Skyler looked around in amazement. Instead of the entrance of the library being the complicated steps up the walls and ceiling, it was just normal, like any other household, except that it was huge. It was grand beyond imagination. There were chandeliers in every hallway, huge windows, high ceilings with crystal chandeliers and satin couches, carved wood armoires and curios, armchairs and futons. There was too much for Skyler to wrap her mind around. It was just such a beautiful place that she knew was named after a beautiful person. It felt good to know that they were finally in a place that was ghost-free and safe for everyone to be. Deep inside, Skyler hope that everyone could stay and live in this mansion for the rest of their lives. It seemed ridiculous, but it was possible in such a big place. Skyler snapped out of her daze and came back to what was happening.

Soon, the families started talking. It felt weird to Skyler that after being separated for so long, they could talk normally!

Amy's parents walked over to Patricia and hugged her. "Thank you for taking care of the girls. How can we ever repay for what you've done?"

The other started saying their thank you's and hugging Patricia.

Patricia smiled and looked at the parents. "You girls have already repaid me. Just bringing me back to Brent was repayment for me. And how can I thank you for lifting this curse and for making us living again?"

Skyler's dad squeezed Skyler's shoulders and whispered in her ear, "Thanks to you too Skyler. We're so proud of you." Skyler's mom nodded and wiped away her tears.

Griff walked over to the girls. Now that they could see him in color, Skyler saw he looked exactly like they'd imag-ined: jet-black hair, a gray sweatshirt, black jeans, and black and white tennis shoes. His eyes were teal, just like Hydran-gea, his hair jet black like Vic's.

Skyler looked over at Patricia and saw she was wearing

a flowing purple dress with her dirty blond hair in a braid. Her eyes were brown and sparkled with joy.

"Well, I guess I owe you guys a thank you too. I don't know where I'd be now without what you guys did." Griff gave a small smile.

"Are you kidding? We couldn't have done what we did without you. As far as I'm concerned, we're even." Vic looked genuinely confused. Griff laughed back and turned around to see Brent.

"Don't forget my thank you too. I'd still be dead if it weren't for you," Brent said sincerely. "I hope you guys learned you can trust me." Brent also looked like Patricia, with the same dirty blond hair and round face.

Skyler rolled her eyes and looked at the other girls. "See, told you!"

The group laughed and Skyler looked over at the parents, Patricia, Nina, and Aaron. She smiled at the reunion. And then brought up a question again.

"Hey Vic," Skyler said, "so what is the language you speak?"

"Russian," Vic answered. "But to be honest, French probably sounds cooler."

"Uh, no way!" Skyler grinned. "Have you heard yourself speak?"

The group laughed and Skyler noticed Griff staring at his feet. A thought came back to her mind. *"Tell Griff—I'm sorry."* She knew it might not be what Griff wanted to hear but it was the only option.

"Griff." Griff looked up at Skyler. "He— he's sorry."

"What?" Griff asked.

"Y-you know, your dad?" Skyler was bracing herself for his reaction.

Vic stepped in. "I know you might not accept it," Vic tried to reassure him, "but—"

Griff smiled. "I know. And it's hard to accept an apology

from someone you hated but— I think it's better to try. I just wish that I knew whether he was sincere or not."

"Don't worry Griff, I think he was." Reyna smiled.

"Thanks," Griff nodded.

Another question popped into Skyler's mind. She sighed; she hated to ask this but—she also wanted to know. "Griff, the Legend of the Basilisk said something about your past. What—what happened?"

Griff sighed as if he knew this was coming. "It was in 1998, pretty far back from the year today, 2012. As you know, Hydrangea and I were thirteen at the time too. Brent was eight at the time—being a basilisk just slowed down his aging. The details are fuzzy, but what I remember is that Hydrangea *really* hated him." Griff took a breath. "I was unaware of what was going to happen. We took Brent and went into the forest—the same forest that had the portal to Mystery Mansion and the basilisk. That's when Hydrangea pulled out her weapon to kill Brent. I stepped in front of him, thinking that I could somehow prevent it. But—she had already pulled the trigger. The rest is history. Hydrangea killed herself after killing me, but because of her wrongdoing to Brent, she became an evil ghost."

"And Brent?" Skyler asked.

Griff nodded. "He ran away in time—but he ran off the cliff. The basilisk at the time didn't notice him and Brent went through the portal. So—my dad—Seville, killed the basilisk for letting someone through the portal without a fight and he turned Brent into the basilisk that you guys fought."

There was a moment of silence and then the girls hugged Griff. As they let go, Brent turned to face Griff, who looked puzzled. Brent shook his head and said, "Why? Why did you put yourself in danger just to save me? I can't help but thank you for it, but at the same time, I feel guilty. I feel guilty that you had to be in this whole mess. It would have been easier if—"

"No," Griff stopped him. "I know looking at everything that's happened here, and even just things going on in the world makes you feel like that's not how the world works. And—sometimes, it's not. But I did what had to be done, and I think if I hadn't done that, we would be looking at a whole different set of circumstances now."

Brent thanked him again, and so did the girls. Griff looked a little embarrassed, but he deserved the credit he was getting. *Everyone* did.

As they continued to chat, the Omega walked to the groups. Trēs cleared his throat. "Well, I think you guys are ready to see the outside of the mansion." Skyler was slightly confused as she looked at the other girls. They shrugged but decided to follow the Omega.

They walked for what seemed about five whole minutes to get to the front door. The front door was a giant door that was carved oak, like many others in the mansion. But this one had French doors with carved in glass inserts; it looked amazing.

The Omega pulled open the door gently and the whole group followed them outside. Right when they exited, in about fifteen feet, there was a huge fountain with Omega symbols carved along the side that was spraying water.

The Omega led them around the fountain and further back before finally letting them turn around. Skyler turned to see the mansion, tall with four floors, just like they had seen before. But this time, it was almost as if there were five different sections.

The one on the furthest left was like a typical mansion you would see in movies. It had dark brown wood and what looked like red velvet curtains on the inside. There was lighting on the porches that looked quite modern.

The one next to it was made of gray stone with black iron railing, stairs curving around that section. Inside, it looked like the main color was blue. It had balconies and terraces made out of the same gray stone, with carved pillars on the sides. It had lights glowing from the bottom, illuminating the section with a soft silver light.

The one in the center was the one they had just exited out of. For some weird reason, it looked like all of the sections combined.

The one next to it had vines growing on the side. It almost looked tropical, with its red cobblestone roof. The windows all had shutters that were white, matching the trim. The whole section itself was a soft yellow color.

The last one looked like the mansions Skyler had seen in France when she was little. It was made out of white stone with arches and pillars on the balcony, with lanterns hanging from underneath the roof. It had marble finishings and other designs on the balconies.

Skyler was in awe. *Whoa.* She looked at the other girls; they were in awe too.

Quattor looked pleased with their reaction. "I hope you all like it. Girls, this is your new home."

Skyler was shocked—no, *everyone* was. Even Patricia was, and she was the most calm person they knew.

Vic's mom, Aaronia, suddenly spoke out. "What did we do to deserve living here? I get that the girls did something extraordinary—but what did we do?"

"As long as the girls deserve living here, you do too," Ūnus said. "Now, the Pierre family, you're in the far left. Harpers, you're in the next one. The center will be where you all meet; a common place of sorts. Aztecs, you're the one on the right of the common room. Aeroluets, you're in the far right section."

"And the five of you?" Skyler's dad asked.

Duo looked wistful. "I think it's time now."

Quinque looked up at the sky. "Perfect timing." It started to rain.

"No," Amy shook her head. "There has to be another way!"

The Omega smiled. "We promise we'll see you again someday." And with that, they dissolved with the rain.

Reyna sighed. "I know it was their choice, but I'm still going to miss them after all they did for us."

Skyler felt her eyes sting with tears as she stared into the sky, rainwater mixing in with her tears. Maybe they were from the loss, all they'd been through, the happiness—she didn't know. But right now, all that mattered was being with the people around her, the people she'd come to consider as family and the people who'd always been there.

Skyler's parents wrapped an arm around her. Skyler looked over to the girls and they shared a knowing smile, their eyes watery. Reyna's face was streaked with tears as her mother brushed one away. Nina leaned on her mom's shoulder. For once, Reyna didn't try to hide her tears.

Vic had her arm around Amy, who was leaning against her, not trying to get out of the hug. Aaron stood by with Vic's parents who were hugging him, looking over with pride at Vic. Amy's parents stood along with Vic's, the same look in their eyes.

Brent and Patricia were sitting down on the stairs to the mansion, clearly having their own reunion.

Vic and Amy walked over to Skyler. A few seconds afterwards Reyna did too. No words were needed to express what everyone was thinking.

"Well," Griff said, appearing next to them. His face was blank but his eyes were filled with sadness and hope. "Things certainly have changed, haven't they?"

Vic let out a breath and looked around. She gave a small smile. "For the better?"

Griff nodded, "For the better." He finally let out a smile.

Patricia walked over to their group and hugged Griff.

Griff seemed surprised and awkwardly hovered his hands around Patricia. But soon his eyes started to water.

Patricia let go. "I'm sorry Griff. I—I wish I could have helped you. I always saw you in the mansion but—I couldn't do anything. So I want to be here for you now."

"I—" Griff started, but he couldn't seem to finish his sentence. "Thank you."

Patricia seemed to understand. She put her hand on Griff's shoulder and hugged the girls. "I'm so proud of all of you. I knew you could succeed at this quest!"

Reyna thanked Patricia, the others nodding in agreement. "Thank you for believing in us when at times we didn't believe in ourselves."

The group looked up again at the sky, as the rain started to pour harder. Their parents and family came closer and stood together.

A feeling of sadness mixed with happiness overcame Skyler.

Skyler couldn't believe this. This was finally the end—right?

Epilogue

A Couple Months Later...

While the lightning might have streaked over the mansion before, for once, it was *finally* a sunny day. Mystery Mansion laid still, now feeling like home. The servants continued to live near Mystery Mansion, but now finally having their own freedom to do whatever they wanted. Some still wanted to be servants for the mansion and the families let them, saying that they would always have the freedom to quit, or do whatever they wanted.

Lake San Cristobal rippled slowly as the four girls' families sat down talking near it. Though it was once the place that caused all their problems, it had become a place all of them enjoyed. The girls chatted with Nina and Aaron, sometimes retelling stories of the mansion. Life was finally returning to normal.

Mr. Mister had apologized to the girls already. He continued to be ashamed by his actions, even though they all suspected there was some evil magic behind what he had done. The girls knew it would be hard to forgive him, but they did, slowly. They would never fully forgive him, but it seemed to be enough for all of them.

After learning about Griff's situation, Patricia asked to adopt him. Brent and Mr. Mister agreed happily with the idea and Griff obliged. He usually tried to hide his emotions, but he was so overwhelmed with joy over his future, he couldn't stop smiling. Of course, how was Patricia supposed to show up in court when people thought she was dead? Well, what was the mansion magic for? Patricia now was recognized as being alive along with Brent and the girls' parents. The problem was Griff. Nobody knew he had existed, but with magic they were able to fix that. It took weeks, but soon Griff Seville was legally Griff Mister.

Brent and Griff became fast friends which was good since they would now be living together. Brent also became friends with the girls. The four families became close friends with Patricia's family and they met almost every day. The school year had already started and the group was attending Cristobal Academy together. Their life was finally happy.

Amy's birthday had come and gone, but she knew even that wouldn't make her feel happy. She was ecstatic that she finally had her parents back, but that made the pain of not having her brother with them worse. But, she still learned to be happy. Whatever happened, that was in the past. She needed to keep moving forward. After all of that, she told the other girls about her brother—Tom. They were silent, partially because of what Amy had been going through and because they were in shock. It surprised the girls that Amy had been holding something so close to her heart for so many years without telling anyone.

It felt good for the girls to know they had successfully completed a quest that had saved so many lives, but deep down they knew another adventure was just around the corner. So they'd be ready, Amy had kept a vial of potion capable of bringing back another ghost; but for now they were looking forward to some peace.

They would always be ready, their questing items laying still in a chest. After all, how fast could another quest arrive?

Acknowledgments

"All our dreams can come true, if we have the courage to pursue them." - Walt Disney

For as long as we can remember, writing this book has been a dream of ours. We've always had the courage to pursue this dream, but it was only made possible thanks to some special people. We've been writing our book for over five years, and we honestly couldn't have asked for a better five years of writing in our lives. After so many years of writing just the story, it feels like a dream to finally have a completed book! Because of this we have so many wonderful and important people to thank for making our story the way it is.

Thank you to our friends who have helped us: Arneet Bains, Arushi Singh, Jahnavi Tungtur, Joy Sha, Ruchira Prasad, Shriya Baradwaj, Tanisha Sinha, and Vedanti Shambhavi. You guys are the best! Thank you to those who have helped us out with our silly mistakes and who have stuck with us through the whole way. Out of these wonderful people, we give a special thanks to our friend Arushi Singh, who has been one of our dedicated readers since third grade, even after her move away. Thank you to our parents and siblings who have helped us keep persevering through this long journey. We can't thank them enough! Without them, the completion of our book wouldn't have been possible.

And last but definitely not least, a special thank you to our teachers who have helped us improve our story bit by bit. A special thanks to our Gifted and Talented teacher from third to fifth grade: Ruth Thom (Mrs. Thom). She was the one who inspired us to start writing this story in the first place, and actually, the one who embedded our love for writing in us. She had faith in us and for that, we can't thank her enough. Adding on, thank you to our sixth and seventh grade language arts teachers, who whether they know it or not, helped us take great measures in improving our writing skills even more. Thank you Mrs. Bernard, Ms. Hoch, Mrs. Parsons, and Mr. Holder. Again, we can't thank them enough for what they've all done to help us make this story as amazing as possible. Thank you to all who helped in influencing our editing steps to perfect all the little nuances of our book. Without all these people, our book wouldn't be what it is today, and even more, our lives wouldn't be what they are today. Inside, we truly feel that writing is one of the most important parts of us, and one of the most important things that holds our book and our friendship together. So here's a round of applause to you all!

Extras

Nina's Diary

Thursday, November 10, 2008

For some reason, It's almost as if my life was always like this. Almost like my life has always been just me and Aaron living in a huge mansion, saving captured servants from evil ghosts. Okay, I know this makes no sense, so let me start from the beginning:

I was twelve then, four years ago (I'm thirteen now, don't ask.) I had a younger sister, Reyna, who was four years old at the time. My family and I were going on a trip with three other families, all of them our close family friends. Each family had at least one child that was Reyna's age. I guess I was just unlucky. The three other girls were Vic, Amy, and Skyler. Vic had a younger brother, Aaron. I was used to Aaron. I babysat him more times than I could count.

So back to where I left off. We were all going on a family vacation to Colorado. We had rented a private jet and had big plans for our time there. If you're thinking that we all had a perfect vacation on a resort and happily went home afterwards, you're wrong. What basically happened was that a thunderstorm or tornado, or whatever, unexpectedly occurred. The small private jet wasn't able to handle the turbulence. We crashed. At the time we were over Lake San

Cristobal, near an area with private homes lining the bay. It must've been scary for the people living in those houses to watch us crash. But let me tell you, it was scarier to be dropped from the plane. Okay, you're probably thinking "you were dropped from the plane?" Well, yes, by our parents, so our lives might be saved. The jet was diving so fast that our parents panicked and put all the children into life vests and carefully dropped us into the water right before it crashed.

My sister and her three friends floated one way, and Aaron and I floated the other. I remember Reyna and Vic screaming for me and Aaron. I'm pretty sure I was doing the same. Suddenly, a fog filled the air, blocking us from seeing our siblings again. As the fog came in, it was almost as if we were being pulled onto the shore. Before we knew it, we were in the hands of a transparent person, floating so fast we didn't even have time to think about what was happening. If you haven't guessed by now, we were in the hands of a ghost, an evil ghost. Soon enough we were brought into a huge mansion, the one we're in right now. Aaron and I were left in what looked like a closet for a couple of days with no food, no water, nothing. I was worried seeing Aaron, a little one year old, cry continuously for days. All I could do was comfort him and think of what became of our siblings and parents.

Then one day, the ghost that had taken us from the shore let us out of the closet. I was grateful, but what I didn't know was that the ghost was evil. The ghost petrified me into stone. It was the weirdest experience I'd ever had. I could feel everything around me happening in almost time lapse, except I didn't feel any emotions, hunger, or anything. Four years went by, but to me, it seemed like a week. This day was one I remember so clearly. It feels like it happened yesterday.

I remember the feeling of a warm hand on my stone

shoulder. Suddenly, I was myself again. I wasn't stone. I turned around to see a ghost, a kind looking face. She had Aaron at her side, who was now four years old. I later learned that the ghost's name was Patricia. She had found Reyna and the other three girls. But she had died, and didn't know what became of them. When she came here, she found Aaron crying and raised him for four years. The weird thing was, he had grown to be four years old (almost five), and I was still thirteen. Patricia told us about her life and about how she found Reyna, Vic, Skyler, and Amy. Then Patricia told us about the curse on the mansion. She told us about Regal Seville, and how my sister and her friends were destined to beat him. Meanwhile, she told us one thing that would never change: the captured servants in the clutches of evil ghosts. I was confused why those people would always be captured. Patricia then explained how if the evil ghost died, the servants would die along with it. This left me thinking.

Patricia showed me and Aaron's room. There were six beds. We knew that all we had to do was wait for the girls to show up. At this point, we are giving up hope. This is when Aaron and I took matters into our own hands. The girls were destined to beat Regal Seville, but the servants would just die. Well, maybe not. We decided to figure out how to rescue them ourselves.

One day, we were walking through the hallways and saw a flash of darkness. Yeah, I know, that's weird. But anyway, we heard a scream, and ran after it. Suddenly the ghost fled, and there was a young woman sitting on the ground, breathing heavily. When she saw us coming to her she got frightened and inched back, whimpering. "Don't worry, we're not going to hurt you." Once we comforted her, we brought her to the kitchen. Patricia had showed us where it was a few days ago. Once we got there, I looked in the gigantic pantry and found almost no food. But out of oats, honey, and milk, I made what I could and gave it to her. After she was warm and more steady, we introduced ourselves. She told us her name was Eliza Buckingham. She was twenty-eight years old. She had been looking for work when she came across this mansion fifty-three years ago. Regal Seville hired her as a maid and waitress. For three years she worked, cleaning his and his wife's room, and delivering their breakfast every morning. She told us that for those three years, he had been a decent master.

But three years later, he turned vain and angry. No one knew why. Through his anger, he had placed the curse on this mansion. "Evil ghosts had flown in and captured us. I remember the feeling of being sucked into one's arms," she said. Then, I asked her how many more servants had been captured. According to her, there had been thirty-six others. Me and four year old Aaron looked at each other. We knew we had to save those other thirty-six servants.

The next day we saw Patricia. We asked her how we could get more food into the pantry. Aaron, Eliza, and I had been surviving with only those three ingredients for the past week. She told us she might be able to use her magic gradually to bring back the food that was there. So from then on, every day she would bring back two or three more food items.

After about a month, the pantry was fully restored. Then, Aaron and I continued our search for more servants. We hid Eliza in what seemed to be the old maid chambers. She told us she recognized it too. Surprisingly, that room, the kitchen, and our room, seemed to be some of the only places free of evil ghosts during the night. After a whole week, Aaron and I had found exactly two more servants, Rayla Flauter and Notra Raymond. Like our normal procedure after finding another servant, we gave them food and water and brought them to the maid chamber. It wasn't easy to find another servant. Many times, they were just as scared of us as they were of the evil ghosts. And also, every servant we found had something in common. Each one of them hadn't aged a day since fifty years ago when they were captured.

Apparently, since they were in the arms of the ghosts, they became painfully immortal, or at least that was according to Notra. It took me a while to understand that, but ever since, it just became more and more transparent to me. I realized how painful it would be to be in the arms of a ghost for fifty years, knowing that you were never going to escape or die unless the evil ghost died. Up till today, Aaron and I have saved thirteen servants, which leaves us with twenty-three more. It seems like a lot but even then, what else can we do here?

It has been one whole year since we started the search. I'm now thirteen and Aaron is now five. We have celebrated fifteen birthdays, including ours the past year. Even though ghosts don't age, we still like throw them birthday parties. They deserve to have as much happiness as they can. We can't wait for there to be thirty-nine birthdays to celebrate in one year. Actually, forty-three including Reyna, Vic, Skyler, and Amy. But as of now, Aaron and I have nearly given up hope of ever seeing our siblings again.

Bye for now.

-Nina

Wednesday, January 4th, 2009

Aaron and I celebrated New Year's three days ago with all the servants. It's almost as if we've found a new family. I still miss my sister though. I'm sure Aaron misses his too.. Since the last time I wrote, Aaron and I have only found two more servants. I hope we find more. It seems like it just gets harder and harder to find more servants. Meanwhile, I've kept a list of all the servants we've found in order:

1. Eliza Buckingham
2. Rayla Flauter
3. Notra Raymond
4. Marchione Lacter
5. Todd Simmons
6. Carola Guazer
7. Tella Wraw
8. Yin Zheng
9. Archi Zalton
10. Ursula Corner
11. Robert Rana
12. Greta Hazel
13. Bora Da'Len
14. Leslee Paige
15. Dawner Paige

It was heartwarming to see Leslee and Dawner reunited again. After years of being separated, they were ecstatic to see each other again. It made me miss my own sister a lot more, but it was still nice to see the touching moment. After a little bit, they told us they had a sister named Mayleen (they were triplets). We knew she had to be the sixteenth person we found.

Patricia came to see us regularly to give us lessons since there was no school. It was like we were getting home-schooled, honestly. Both Aaron and I caught on to lessons fast enough. In math, Aaron was already learning double-digit addition and subtraction while I was learning ninth grade math. Patricia was the best in math, not as good in the other subjects but still with the books she found, she taught us what we needed to know.

At night, Aaron and I decided to go and find the third triplet: Mayleen. We found a flashlight and began wandering the hallways. As soon as we got outside the room,

Aaron started shivering from the cold and nerves. I was getting increasingly nervous too as the brightest setting in the flashlight barely made a dent in the darkness.

It hasn't been even a minute when I felt something chill in my spine. I looked around and couldn't see anything, but I immediately grabbed Aaron's hand and ran back to our room. I locked the door and panted, happy that we were safe. I put my ear to the door and didn't hear anything so I opened it up a crack to see if it was nothing. Spoiler, it was something: Patricia.

She looked worried and came into our room. She asked us what we were doing out at night. I guess that was the end of our secret. We spilled everything. She then told us how we should have never done that and how much it had worried her. She hugged us and asked us to promise we would never leave our room at night. We obliged and Patricia carried the sleepy Aaron to his bed. Me? I was slightly confused and asked her why. She told me about how evil ghosts roam the halls, and they can be very dangerous to humans and good ghosts. I didn't ask any more questions and went to sleep. I could only imagine what would happen if I had continued on. I suppose it was just a mistake, but I decided to listen to everything Patricia said from then on.

-Nina

Monday, April 17th, 2009

Today was just another day for Aaron and I. We started our day by waking up, and getting dressed and ready, then we went to the kitchen to grab a quick breakfast for ourselves before heading to the servant chambers to wake the servants up. During our stay here, Aaron had figured out how to use little trinkets he found around the mansion to invent things. I don't know how a six year old can do things like that, but anyway back to the point. Aaron made a bell that hung from the ceiling of the chambers that we would pull every day to wake up the servants, who would then serve breakfast. So that's what we did this morning. Leslee came to me and asked if we had found Mayleen. I gave her the sad news, but promised we would find her. She hugged me and went back to working. After that, Aaron and I walked around the mansion on the lookout for any servants in the clutches of evil ghosts. Of course, we didn't find any. From what we had seen, the East wing (where we were looking), was clear of any evil ghosts, at least during the daytime anyway. We went back to the kitchen at about 10:00 to start cooking lunch. We usually serve lunch at about 12:00. Yeah, it takes us two hours to cook food for seventeen people, including us.

Here's the menu:

Tomato soup & garlic bread
Alfredo sauce spaghetti
Pineapple mango juice
Double chocolate layered cookies

Yeah I know, it's a lot, but what else do Aaron and I have to do in this mansion other than rescue servants, cook food for them, and do our missed school work? Okay, don't get me wrong, I don't mind my life being like this. It's just that I miss having friends, going to school, and all those things kids my age do. Instead, I'm stuck up in a gigantic mansion, castle, whatever, rescuing people from dead floaty thingies. I mean, what else can I do?

I guess this was a short entry. Anyway, I don't know when I'll be able to write again. Bye for now,

-Nina

Sunday, November 19th, 2009

Since I last wrote, we've found two more servants. I know, just two more. And the worst part, we haven't even found Mayleen yet. Anyway, the two we found were:

16. Cissy Melon
17. Amber Judi

I think Amber was by far the most scared when we saved her. It took us a lot of convincing, but even then I don't think she believed us, that is until she saw the others. I'm pretty sure she hugged everyone in the room at least four times, (Even me and Aaron). Aaron and I have no idea where Mayleen might be. But if I think about it, we probably haven't even seen even half of this mansion, and we've been here for five years! It's almost like this mansion never ends. Sometimes, I think it never does end.

Leslee and Dawner have lost hope of ever finding Mayleen again. It is heartbreaking not to be able to tell them any news about her at all. The good news is Cissy has become fast friends with Dawner and Leslee. The Mansion was so big, that Cissy had never seen the other two before, but they get along really well!

Today, Aaron and I just finished our night lesson with Patricia. Sometimes, it makes me feel proud that I could still learn even in the mansion. Today, Patricia ended up teaching me Algebra I, which is actually what people two grades above me learn. I guess I'm just a fast learner. Either that or I just have too much time on my hands for things like the quadratic equation. Anyway, I guess I've appreciated math much more than I used to. But really, it's almost as if Aaron and I will never get to be in the real world ever again. Never be able to grow up, get a job—you know what I mean. Maybe I'm just hallucinating or something here, but that's truly how I feel. I have to go now, I can't stay awake any longer.

  Bye for now,
  -Nina

Wednesday, November 21st, 2010

I can't believe it's been a whole year since I've written. So much has happened in the past year that I haven't been able to keep track of my time. As far as my studies, I'm still moving along two grades ahead. Instead of doing eighth grade work, I'm working at the sophomore level. I'm fourteen now, and Aaron is six.

Since I last wrote, We've found five more servants:

  18. Teresa Lionarka
  19. Marble Pronten
  20. London Pruitt
  21. Naya Garthen
  22. Margo Hansen

Sadly, we still haven't found Mayleen yet. To be honest, most of the days she's not a top priority on our list. Something bad has been happening lately. Apparently, Regal Seville is up to something that even Patricia doesn't know about. Today I found her crying in fear in the lounge. I tried to comfort her, but in the end, I just left her alone.

After I left, I started thinking about what it could be. I remember Patricia looking at a photo beside her. It was a photo of a small toddler boy with blond hair, and eyes exactly like hers. For a second, I thought it was her son, but then I remembered her telling me that she had no children, other than Reyna, Vic, Skyler, and Amy. And anyway, about them, they haven't come to the mansion yet. Patricia still has hope, but sometimes, it seems like she's almost hoping for someone dead to make it here. Aaron and I have given up hope, but inside, I know that would be a dream come true for me.

-Nina

Saturday, March 15, 2011

It has been a while since I last wrote. Since then we've found two more servants:

23. Pargomena Tewester
24. Darno Lueder

Aaron and I happened to one day find them in the clutches of an evil ghost in the West Wing. It was the first time Aaron and I have explored the West Wing. It was dark and gloomy— not to say the other parts weren't— but it was worse. We found them both in the hands of twin ghosts, which made it harder for us to save them from the ghosts. Other than this, it's not like anything exciting has been happening lately. I guess I'm just writing now to pass my time and document the people we've saved. This is probably going to be the shortest diary entry I'm ever going to write.

Bye for now,

-Nina

Monday, December 20, 2011

It's five days before Christmas, and let me tell you, I've never seen the servants more excited. It feels good to have a family once again to celebrate the holidays with. I miss having my family so much, it's hard to even put it into words. But I guess I've grown out of my misery, and thankfully, I've found a new family.

Since I last wrote, we've only found one more servant:

25. Tura Skyierre

Tura was probably the hardest one by far to save of them all. The ghost that she was captured by was the scariest one Aaron and I have faced. It was almost as if we were being sucked into a whirlwind. Honestly, I don't know how we survived. It was as if we were battling against the ocean or something.

Thankfully, Aaron and I made it out safely with Tura. Tura was also the one in the worst condition when we saved her. She was ill and coughing. But seriously though, who wouldn't be sick after living in a whirlpool for fifty years? Aaron and I cooked her a hot meal and then brought her into the room to rest. When she got there, she passed out. Aaron, Eliza, and I ran to get her water before she was completely unconscious. Thankfully, we saved her just in time.

Yesterday, Patricia came back from somewhere in a shocked state. We didn't know why, but she said we would find out sooner or later. I have no idea what it means, but to be honest, I'm not in a rush to know.

Mayleen still remains hidden within a ghost, or who knows where. I guess Dawner and Paige have just given up by now. As of right now, everyone in the servant chamber is celebrating the fifth night before Christmas. I better go tell them now it's past midnight and that the evil ghosts will be out any minute.

So I guess that bye for now!

-Nina

Wednesday, June 9, 2012

I can't believe that I finally have something amazing to write about today. Something that Aaron and I never imagined happening happened! You won't believe what happened. Reyna, Vic, Skyler, and Amy came to the mansion today! It was like a miracle that I had given up hope on years ago. Let me fill you in on how we found them. Patricia had left on a short errand. Aaron and I wished her goodbye and then started towards the south end.

Aaron and I had been there before, but a few days ago, Patricia had said there was a greenhouse. She said we could try to look for servants there, but she wasn't sure if they were there or not. Aaron and I decided to explore there anyway. Along the way, we stopped at a small closet to try to find any hidden ghosts. We spent about ten minutes there. After that, we continued around the corridor and into the greenhouse. Sadly, Aaron and I couldn't find anyone.

We then decided to head back to the kitchen to start dinner. And that's when it happened. That's when we found the girls. We were walking along when we came to a long hallway with a grandfather clock. But then, I saw four girls standing around it. That's when I recognized them. I called Reyna and she turned around, confused for a second. That's when Aaron noticed that Vic was there too. After that, everything was like time-lapse. We ran over to them, hugged them, rejoiced.

It was probably the best day of my life. At least so far. Then, we took them along with us to the kitchen. Apparently, they were on a hunt for clues and the next one was in the kitchen. For some reason, I expected their quest to be harder. From what I'd seen of the mansion in the past few years, there was no easy way out. But when I asked Patricia about this, she suddenly looked scared. She told me that was only the beginning of the quest, and there was much more. The bad part was that the girls didn't know yet. I guess this was probably one of the best days I've ever had in the mansion. It's so hard to really write how I felt when I saw Reyna, all grown up, having a life of her own. A life that I wished I could have been a part of too. But now that we've been reunited, who knows what adventures still await Aaron and I, and the girls.

Till I write again, bye for now.

-Nina Aztec

The Legend of the Basilisk

R egal Seville, keeper of Mystery Mansion, lays a curse on
the mansion, the curse coming with a guard. The guard
of the mansion was guard of the portal, the portal being the
guard of the mansion. Seville had his eyes on the guard of
the portal. If anyone passes through without an encounter,
punishment is a reward, the reward of death, the reward of
escaping the master's lock. But that punishment isn't enough
being for just the guard, but the one who passed without
encounter. The one who passes without encounter, falling
into the portal, falling into the clutches of the master, the
clutches of being the new guard. Once the transformation
happens, the cycle repeats again. For those who pass with an
encounter, pass with luck. Those who don't see the basilisk,
turn into one after only sight of luck.

But something comes of the master's curse, the something being another curse on himself. His ghost remains,
but lifeless, soulless, the soul that disappeared held in ashes.
The urn of Thanatos holds the master's remains, a cloud of
gray may be all that stays. To revive the soul and unite with
the ghost may be the one way, the only way, to break the
untied ends. But what comes with hope, comes with danger,

coming with danger is the fear held inside. The solution is held inside a solution, a solution of the potion, waiting to be created. A library is where the room of legend stays, the room of legends is where the room of potions stays. Under the ashes is what is above decision, for that may be the only way. The potion will revive an unwanted soul, but will prove necessary for those who've proved.

Now who is the basilisk you may ask, the answer is in between what you already know. Your promiser, your vower, your mother of sorts, holds lies she knows will be exposed very soon. She says you're her daughters, she says you're the only one. But soon you'll know what may be lies. Her son fell into the portal of doom, or more so *to* his doom.

Now back to Seville, why you may ask, but soon you will see what you never predicted before. Your close truster and his related evil spirit, if you are the hero, she is the villain. One trusted brother, one: the sister, the other neither, the last one both. The four traveled unwantedly here, to defeat the evil Seville and to meet two more. Brother and sister, son and daughter of who you seek but who you don't, son and daughter of the soul before you...

Now let's tie the two stories to create this legend—the Legend of the Basilisk. Brother and sister in charge of son of vower, one with care, one with hatred. Hatred threatens the life and soul of Brent—Brent Mister. But instead of him, her brother was gone. With fury of her mistake she too becomes a ghost. Now the fate of Brent you already know. Now he is the one you battled to get here—the one you battled to save his life.

Now you know what to do, revive a life, a soul, a curse of sorts. But the curse and life must be destroyed once more, but by the hands of those who've been promised by else's behalf. Now it continues to—

SIGMA'S BOOKSHELF

Sigma's Bookshelf (www.SigmasBookshelf.com) is an independent book publishing company that exclusively publishes the work of teenage authors, who are between the ages of 13 and 19. The company was founded in 2016 by Minnesota teenager Justin M. Anderson, whose first book, *Saving Stripes: A Kitty's Story*, was published when he was 14, and has since sold hundreds of copies.

"I know there are a lot of other teenagers out there who are good writers and deserve to have their work published, but don't have access to the kinds of resources I do. I wanted to help them," he said.

Sigma's Bookshelf is a sponsored project of Springboard for the Arts, a nonprofit arts service organization. Contributions on behalf of Sigma's Bookshelf may be made payable to Springboard for the Arts and are tax deductible to the extent permitted by law. Donations can be made online at www.SigmasBookshelf.com/donate.

CPSIA information can be obtained
at www.ICGtesting.com
Printed in the USA
LVHW030528230920
666816LV00003B/213